Connie spotted the ring box as soon as she entered the darkened kitchen.

It was hard to miss, given that it sat beside a lit tea candle on the island. Her chest tightened and wild panic surged through her.

"No. Don't you dare."

She raced down the stairs and flung open the front door. Barefoot in subzero temperatures and with no coat, she ran to the curb. Ben and his truck were nowhere in sight. Of course.

Giving her space. Uh-huh. She tiptoed up the snow-packed walk and then up the frozen steps back into the house, the sudden warmth making her toes tingle. Her defrosting feet left damp footprints on the plywood subfloor.

Maybe the box had just been a figment of her Valentine's Day–stressed imagination. She crept into the kitchen. Nope. Still there, with its pale blue velvet and gold lettering.

Maybe it wasn't what she thought it was.

But what if it was?

Dear Reader,

Welcome to the second installment in the A True North Hero series. You might've met Connie in the first book, *A Roof Over Their Heads*, where her troubled story is hinted at. Here it is, laid out for you. After twenty years of hard living, Connie decides to make a list of people she's wronged and then sets out to do right by them.

As with most of life's ambitions, it's easier said than done. Particularly when her childhood friend and one of the names on her list, Ben Carruthers, still wants to put his ring on her finger.

I dug deep into Connie's heart. She has the toughest time loving herself, and wrestles with feelings of unworthiness—the kinds of struggles we've all had and probably still contend with daily. I know I do.

But Connie has Ben to help find her way, even though he is dogged by the shadow of abandonment and loneliness. Loneliness can do strange things to a heart, can make the need to love stronger than love itself. What happens when he needs to love a woman who doesn't want his love? How does a woman learn to accept the love she feels she doesn't deserve?

Into this mix walks Ariel, an orphaned teenager who forces Ben and Connie to become good parents and better people. The three of them hammer together a family.

Let me know how their story touched you. I can be reached at mkstelmackauthor.com or on Facebook under M. K. Stelmack.

Happy reading!

M. K. Stelmack

HEARTWARMING

Building a Family

M. K. Stelmack

ISBN-13: 978-1-335-63365-1

Building a Family

This edition published by arrangement with Harlequin Books S.A.

For questions and comments about the quality of this book, please contact us at CustomerService@Harlequin.com.

Printed in U.S.A.

M. K. Stelmack writes contemporary romances set in Spirit Lake, which is closely based on the small town in Alberta, Canada, where she lives with pets who outnumber the humans two to one, and with dust bunnies the size of rodents—because that's what happens when everyone in the household prefers to live in their imagination or outdoors—but she can also be found on social media, where you can share your comments on her stories or her breathless one-sentence bio on Facebook or at mkstelmackauthor.com.

Books by M. K. Stelmack

Harlequin Heartwarming

A True North Hero

A Roof Over Their Heads

Visit the Author Profile page
at Harlequin.com for more titles.

To Carol, who builds family, friends,
food and fun times.

CHAPTER ONE

ON VALENTINE'S DAY NIGHT, the most romantic event of the year, Connie Greene watched the love of her life walk out on her. Well, okay, he left Smooth Sailing, where she was waitressing, so it wasn't as if they were on a date. They weren't even dating, anyway, so leaving her workplace hardly constituted walking out on her. And he didn't say that he wasn't returning at the end of her shift to pick her up as he always did.

That was the problem. Ben Carruthers left without a word to her, which was not like him at all. He didn't even stay for his dinner. She was holding it, warm and heavy, when he swept past her and out the door.

Connie brought the full plates over to the table, where his regular dinner companion was seated. "Marlene, what did you say to Ben?"

Marlene dragged her gaze from the three built-in screens where she was tracking hockey, poker and skiing to the plate of food Connie put in front of her—a full rack of ribs with a double order of fries. Marlene sat back in her booth, but her waist, covered with a Toronto Maple Leafs hockey jersey, still grazed the table's edge. The last thing Marlene needed was the heaping plate Connie set in front of her. Connie also understood that it was the *only* thing her friend felt she needed.

Connie held on to Ben's order—a heaping plate of nachos just the way he liked them. Marlene reached for the bottle of ketchup still there from her earlier order of fries.

"Did you hear me?" Connie asked.

Instead of answering, Marlene squeezed a nearly empty plastic bottle until it wheezed and splattered a meager amount of ketchup onto a single fry. "Could we call this one done? Or do we cut it open and I wipe it clean with my fries?"

Connie snatched up the bottle. "That's rich coming from the woman whose idea of a tip is to pass off discontinued pennies. The bottle was half full when I brought it here. Quit wasting it."

"Quit bad-mouthing the customers."

"Quit harassing the staff."

"Who wants me to tell her something I know and she doesn't?"

Marlene had her there.

"So, he is coming back?"

She shrugged.

"What did he say?"

Marlene finally came to the point. "Nothing, and I said nothing to him. He guzzled a couple of beers, went to the washroom and you saw the rest. I dunno, maybe the appies didn't agree with him. He was a little heavy on the hot sauce."

"Hot sauce doesn't affect him," Connie said. Ben was twelve when he'd swallowed a whole teaspoon of Tabasco sauce and hadn't coughed once. Seth, her brother, hadn't made it past six drops. Her eyes had teared up just from smelling the sauce, but then again, she had been only eight.

Connie gestured to Ben's plate. "What am I supposed to do with his food?"

"Here, I'll eat it," said an all-too-familiar voice behind her.

"Mel." She watched her half brother, her senior by nearly eighteen years, slide into Ben's spot. He pulled the plate toward him and lifted off a nacho strung with a long tail of melted cheese. "I'm going to need more of those wipes. Hey, Marlene."

Marlene raised a sauce-covered finger in greeting, her eyes once again glued to the screen.

Mel was another regular. Never on a particular day, like Ben with Wednesdays, but often enough.

"Saw Ben." Mel dipped a nacho into the sour cream she'd specially peppered for Ben. "He said he had to run, but that I could have his dinner. You're looking really nice."

"Thanks," Marlene said absently, and then groaned when the hockey team playing the Leafs scored.

Mel winked at Connie, all three of them knowing perfectly well he'd been talking to Connie. "You're welcome," he said nonetheless.

Connie hoped she did look prettier than usual, considering how much time she'd spent getting her entire outfit of red, pink and silver coordinated, accessorized, applied, spritzed, curled or strapped on. Of course, she always got dolled up on special holidays. It made the nights more fun, that's all. "Did Ben say where he was going?"

Mel lowered the loaded nacho he was about

to ingest wholesale and gazed soberly at Connie. "On this of all days, don't expect a man to say where he's going unless he tells you himself."

"Good policy for all days," Marlene said pointedly to Connie. She pushed her empty beer mug toward Connie. "Another one of these. Wait!" She looked at Mel. "Since Ben's wandered off, you want to be my date? Then I drink half-price."

Mel rubbed his chin, leaving a streak of sour cream that Connie swiped off with a napkin. "How about we take turns being each other's date? That way, I'll get every other beer half-price, too."

"The deal is only for females," Connie clarified.

Mel continued with the chin-rubbing. Connie glanced impatiently at her next table. Lindsay, the town's event coordinator, was seated with her husband and another couple. They'd finished their dessert, and Connie wanted to speak to Lindsay before they left. She was turning back to Mel when she caught sight of what was happening underneath Lindsay's table. The wife of the other couple had her foot hooked around the ankle of Lindsay's husband.

Well, now.

"I got it," Mel said. "How about after Marlene's drink I pretend to be a female?"

"Works for me, Melissa," Marlene said, her gaze lifting again to the screen. "I should have reached my nightly quota by then, anyway."

Connie was not going to fight it, not when she needed to get to Lindsay. "Billing you two is going to be a nightmare. Better make my tip worth it."

Marlene nudged her empty mug at Connie and said, "Don't forget about the ketchup, neither."

"Yeah, yeah, yeah." Connie took Marlene's mug and walked over to Lindsay's table. "How are we doing here?" She turned to Lindsay. "Didn't I tell you that was the best cheesecake you'd ever taste?"

Lindsay's eyelids grew heavy and her face softened—it was the same look she saw on all the other customers who ate Dizzy's chocolate and one-other-secret-ingredient dessert. "Yes, yes, yes, yes!" Lindsay reached for her husband's hand. "Thanks, Derek," she said. "I needed a night out."

To which the hypocrite answered by squeezing her hand and saying, "You deserve it."

Wow. Derek held his wife's hand while playing footsie with the wife of another man—whom Connie knew to be his best friend. Then he made it even weirder by asking Luke, "So we still on for the game Saturday?"

"Let me guess," Connie cut in, and stared down Derek. "Poker? Isn't it? From the way you can keep a straight face?"

"Are you kidding?" Luke said. "The guy's an open book. There's nothing he can hide from me."

Oh, my… "Lindsay," she said, "we should meet to talk venues. For the Lakers-on-the-Go summer events. Can I come by? Maybe tomorrow morning?"

Lindsay reached for her phone. "Let me see…" She scrolled through her day timer. "That should work. Eleven, say?"

"Perfect," said Connie, her eye on Derek. "Looking forward to sharing my thoughts."

Derek straightened in his seat, and pulled his straying foot back into place. Luke's wife, Shari, played with the diamond pendant on her necklace, nicely displayed in her low-cut dress. "I believe it's our turn to pay," she said.

"No way," Lindsay said. "Derek, get out your card."

So began that friendly back-and-forth contest between prosperous couples about who had the longer credit card. Connie took the opportunity to slip away. She brought Marlene's beer and the card reader for the foursome, but they were still at it.

"Here." Connie handed the reader to Derek. "I've decided you owe your buddy. It's the least you can do. Don't you think?" She flashed him her brightest smile. He took it and handed it back with a hundred-dollar tip.

She almost felt sorry for him. Guilt was a terrible thing. An acid that burned into every thought, stripped away any peace of mind.

Still, a hundred extra dollars would help her deal a little with her own guilt issues. She tore off the receipt and offered it to him with her friendliest grin. "Thanks for spending your special evening with Smooth Sailing. Come again."

By closing time, Connie was ready to bust out of her skintight outfit and kick her high-heeled ankle boots to the corner. She was cranky, made crankier by the fact that she had no business feeling that way. Her tips had been less than usual, yes, but she couldn't blame the men for not spending on the busty waitress when they were on dates with girlfriends or wives. Or, in the case of Derek, with both. Nor was it anyone's fault that some of the couples had lingered so long, staring all lovey-dovey at each other, that it cut into another sitting. And it most certainly didn't matter that Ben hadn't returned, hadn't texted, nothing. Nor that she couldn't text him because Mel had a point about men's destinations on Valentine's Day.

She attacked the bar counter with her cleaning cloth. Fifteen minutes to closing, that was usually when—

The outside doors opened and she heard the familiar wiping of boots on the mat, and then the inside doors opened.

"Where have you been?" she blurted.

Ben gave her a slow, satisfied smile as if he'd eaten a big meal. Somewhere else. "You don't know?"

"I wouldn't be asking if I did."

He settled on a bar stool across from her. "It's good to hear that I'm still a mystery to you after all this time."

He had this way of making it seem as if they were in a relationship. They weren't. They absolutely weren't. "Just so you know, Mel paid for your meal."

"Not my meal if he ate it."

"And paid the tip."

"Which wasn't as good as mine." Ben's smile grew even wider. Honestly, what had he been up to? He zipped open his jacket to reveal his shirt underneath.

"You changed your shirt."

"I did."

Nothing more. No explanation. No point asking why, either, because it was none of her business. Then again, if his absence had nothing to do with her, why couldn't he tell her?

He broke into her thoughts. "You need to do cleanup?"

Connie glanced over at Dizzy, who was coming over with money that she slapped down in front of Connie. "Your cut."

Connie could tell by the size of the stack that she'd been right about the tips. She'd have enough to clear her phone bill and buy apples. She tucked the money down between her girls. Dizzy shook her head. "You'll need to crowbar them out of there, you know."

"You say the nicest things," she said. "We've all got assets. You, too."

"So I keep hearing," Dizzy said, and gave her own behind a friendly smack.

"Who said it? You got a special someone?"

Dizzy smiled and strutted off. “Have fun, you two.”

Once again there was the implication that she and Ben were in a relationship. Everyone assumed that nowadays.

It had begun back in the fall, when Matt, her step-nephew-to-be, had crawled up onto the roof of her house and quite literally shouted from the rooftop that Seth was his new dad.

The stunt had attracted quite a crowd, including local media. Ben had taken advantage of all the people there, and when the cameras had switched to her, Ben had staked a claim at her side. Thankfully, the media hadn’t made the connection between this Connie Greene and the one who’d appeared in court a few times a decade ago.

From then on, Ben had insinuated himself into her daily life.

She left the bar with Ben and automatically headed for his truck, parked in its usual spot, all part of the too-tempting routine she’d fallen into with him.

Inside his truck—his warm but not-too-warm truck with its optimally heated seats—she buckled herself in and directed her gaze straight ahead.

She would get through the five-minute ride home and go straight to bed. No studying tonight.

"What's wrong, Connie?" Ben said as he swung onto her quiet street.

"Nothing." It sounded petulant even to her ears. She needed to fill the air with something. "It sucked seeing Marlene all by herself on Valentine's Day, drinking too much and watching her favorite team lose again."

Ben shrugged. "You get used to that when you cheer for the Leafs."

"Still, she had to realize she was all alone in a booth meant for four, surrounded by couples."

In the light from the dashboard, she could see a smile slink across Ben's handsome face. "You didn't like me leaving you, right?"

"That's not it," she lied. "Don't be so dramatic." He kept right on smiling. She rattled on. "Hey, you were there when Derek and Luke came in, right?" The two men played rec hockey with Ben. "I caught Derek playing footsie with Luke's wife, Shari."

Ben's smile disappeared. "That'll hurt when it comes out."

"What makes you so sure it will come out? It could go on this way for years."

Ben drove over the train tracks, and the vibration hummed through Connie despite the cushy seats.

"Connie," he said quietly, "these things always come out." He crawled to a stop in front of her house. Her big, broken house.

"I'll have to tell her," Connie said.

Ben shifted in his seat. "Why?"

He of all people should know the answer to that. "Because she deserves the truth."

"Not sure you're the one to deliver it."

"If not me, then who?"

Ben looked past her to the dark house. She hadn't even bothered to leave the porch light on. "I don't know, but I'm sure you don't want to cause anyone pain."

Connie sucked in her breath. She had a history of inflicting it, anyway.

"I hope—" Ben stopped, and his voice dipped. "I hope they find their way back to each other."

He was talking about them. Pain—and something ridiculously like hope that she had absolutely no right to feel—fluttered inside her. They weren't a couple. But they had been. Before she could muster up an answer, he carried on. "You're beat. Have a good sleep and I'll see you tomorrow, okay?"

"What, no patrol?" Usually he came inside with her and switched on lights, checked the doors and scanned the backyard. But tonight, he clearly wasn't concerned about her safety.

"Thought I would give you some space. Unless, of course, you want me to come in. Do you, Connie?"

She grabbed her purse. "No."

"See? I do know what you need," he said, a smile still threaded through his words.

She hopped from the truck. "Then there'd better be some of Dizzy's cheesecake in the fridge."

CONNIE SPOTTED THE ring box as soon as she entered the darkened kitchen. It was hard to miss, given that it sat beside a lit tea candle on the island.

Her chest tightened and wild panic surged through her. "No. Don't you dare."

She raced down the stairs and flung open the front door. Barefoot in subzero temperatures and with no coat, she ran to the curb. Ben and his truck were nowhere in sight. Figured.

Giving her space. Uh-huh. She tiptoed up the snow-packed walk and then navigated the frozen steps back into the house, the sudden warmth making her toes tingle. Her defrosting feet left damp footprints on the plywood subfloor.

Maybe the box had just been a figment of her Valentine's Day–stressed imagination. She crept into the kitchen. Nope. Still there, with its pale blue velvet and gold lettering.

Maybe it wasn't what she thought it was.

But what if it was? To verify her assumption, she'd have to open the box. And she knew—like she knew every line on Ben's face—that above all else, she must resist the temptation. For she was quite sure that if it turned out to be the ring Ben intended to bind her to him with, she would put it on and never take it off.

She loved him but she didn't deserve to love him. The one good thing she'd done in their relationship was end it. Cruelly and quickly, but effectively.

Until now. Why now, after three Valentine's Days had passed, did he give her an engagement ring? How, when they'd not gone out on a single date, not kissed, not even held hands, when she'd not given the slightest encouragement—driving her home most nights absolutely did not count since she barely showed the decency to thank him—how in his right mind could he have possibly concluded she would marry him?

She reached for her cell phone. He'd be awake. She called, and it went straight to voice mail.

"Oh, no, you don't, Ben Carruthers. You will pick up your phone. Right. Now."

Five more times it went to voice mail before Connie admitted defeat. She didn't leave another message. The world could rightly accuse her of a lot, but she did possess the decency not to reject a marriage proposal via voice mail.

She set her elbows on the island, lowered her chin into her hands and contemplated the box in the flickering shadows of the tea light. She didn't recognize the jeweler's name, and searched it on her phone. A custom jeweler from Calgary. She scanned through the creations, each a glittering marvel. Connie stretched out a finger and touched the velvet top of the box. Smooth and a little rough. Like Ben's jaw before his morning shave.

Connie pushed herself straight. "Why, Ben? Why could you not keep it simple between us?"

A sudden thought struck her and she flung open the fridge door. Sure enough, there in the middle of the fridge on a plate fringed with red rose petals was a wide wedge of Dizzy's cheesecake.

"No," Connie said, reaching for it, anyway. "No, no, no."

CHAPTER TWO

CONNIE HUDDLED ON the cement floor of her basement before the coffeemaker her mother had drunk her last cup of coffee from. She had called it My Maker, and as she'd grown sicker, her humor had grown blacker than the coffee that now slowly dripped and burbled into Connie's largest mug.

Normally, she made her morning coffee in the kitchen, but with the ring box calling to her there, she had swept up the coffee machine and paraphernalia and fled to the farthest basement corner.

She eyed the boxes and tubs of her mother's stuff banked high and long against the wall. Stuff untouched in the one year and one month since Seth and Mel had packed it down here after their mother's funeral.

Connie was supposed to have dealt with it all—fair exchange for her inheriting the house.

Connie knew full well why her mother had

left her the house. Her whole adult life could be summed up as: Connie leaves home to do something big and important with her life, fails and moves back into her mother's house.

After high school, Connie had lived with her BFF, Miranda, to help the too-young mother with her baby. That had ended badly, and she'd moved back in with her mother. She'd then gotten a job as a grocery clerk and rented her own place, but she'd been rude to one too many customers and come home again. She'd cleaned up her act, and started dating Ben. Two years later, she'd found herself in this house again.

When her mom died, she'd been renting a duplex with her then-boyfriend, Trevor McCready. She'd intended to renovate the house, flip it and make a bit of cash. But Trevor had gambled away all her money at a Las Vegas blackjack table, and she'd realized that her plan of reforming him was never going to work. She'd dumped him and moved back in seven months ago, the renovations half done and her mother's boxes still stacked in the basement.

Refocusing on the coffeemaker, Connie snuggled deeper into the flannel shirt she'd taken from Ben three years ago when they'd broken up. It had been outright theft, but she'd needed something of him.

The shirt was all thready and the dark green of moldy wood, the armpits hanging four inches below her own. It was the ugliest thing she possessed, and it had to be a record-hot summer morning for her not to wear it when she woke.

She switched the now-full cup with the pot, and leaned against a cardboard box. It cracked and folded under her weight and her backbone bumped against something ribby and flexible. A book? Hmm…well, this was one box she could safely open…

Inside were her dad's old steno pads. Dozens of pocket-size, coil-on-top ones in blue, green and red.

Every August during the back-to-school sales, Connie had bought twelve pads for her father. She'd print out the months, color and tape them on, apply appropriate stickers, date the pages and note special events such as holidays and birthdays. Then she'd stuff all twelve into her dad's Christmas stocking. Mel and Seth had complained that there was no room for their gifts. Connie had said they should buy their mother more because she'd taken care of their dad.

Her mother must've saved the pads all these years. Who knew why she'd bothered.

Elastic bands held together five bundles, but one pad was loose. The one marked "June," the month her dad had died suddenly, horribly, twenty-one years ago when he'd fallen from a roof.

She flipped through the pages, rippled from the press of her dad's pencil and her own.

Her dad had entertained all her schemes. A class party at the house, Thanksgiving meals at the pet shelter, a one-girl show at the beach with proceeds going to her newly formed theatrical company. She'd pitch her idea to him, and no matter how wild, he'd accept it and say, "Better write it down." And then it would happen. Her dad had taught her the importance of a simple list.

The little red pad suddenly felt to Connie like a wisdom book that revealed her life since her father died.

She'd lost him and her lists. No one to listen to her crazy ideas and put it on a list. And reminded her to stick to it until she got what she wanted.

Her brothers had repurposed their lives. Mel and Seth worked harder with the roofing business, and her mother had tried to become both parents. Even Ben had helped with the roofing, still did for that matter.

Only Connie had been given the luxury of carrying on as if nothing had happened. She went to school, hung out with friends, earned money to spend on herself.

Connie slowly flipped the small pages, and it was like reading her past in clear order. The more everyone else sacrificed for her, the more undeserving she felt until she'd gradually become the despicable person she believed herself to be.

For the last twenty years she'd unleashed her misery on her mother, her brother, her friend Miranda…and Ben.

Connie crushed the red pad in her hand. She didn't deserve happiness again, and yet there it was, upstairs, sparkling, in a box. Hers to grab hold of.

Except first, she wanted to be the kind of person who believed she deserved a ring. And the only way to do that was to right twenty years of wrongs. Then she would be the kind of person who made lists and dreams come true.

Except…she could be that kind of person right now.

She pressed the little book between her palms to smooth the crushed pages, flipped it open to the first empty page and slid out the short HB pencil still tucked into the coils. She crossed out June 18 and put February 15, and updated the year.

She jotted down five names in no particular order. Her list.

Trevor McCready: for wanting you to be hurt after you took my money. And then getting my wish.

Miranda Sloane and her daughter, Ariel: Ariel, for how I slept through your crying when you were a baby. And for choosing Ben over you both.

Connie crossed out the last bit.

Miranda: for not stopping you from making me choose Ben over you.

That still wasn't it, was it?

For letting you think I couldn't love all three of you.

Seth Greene: for letting you take the fall for the police charges against me.

Finally, Ben. She crossed out and erased until she arrived at her best attempt at truth.

Ben Carruthers: for not loving you right.

She poured herself another cup of black, bitter coffee. Now, to make these wrongs right.

First: Trevor. She hadn't seen him since the summer, when she'd followed him and her money down to a blackjack table in Las Vegas. And Google didn't track the whereabouts of people that biker gangs had contracts out on. She put a question mark beside his name.

Next up: Miranda.

If only she could go straight back to her teenage years, to when she'd met Miranda in high school. Miranda had been fifteen to Connie's fourteen, and that year had made Miranda something of a hero to Connie. She'd made it all glamorous—the partying, the alcohol, the drugs. When Miranda had become a mother at eighteen, they'd moved in together, though the wildness continued.

They'd lived together on and off until five years ago, when she'd started dating Ben.

Miranda had freaked when she heard the news, told Connie that it was either him or her, said that she and Ben hated each other too much for them to share her. Connie had believed that was the only option, and wanting a new start, she'd dumped Miranda and her then eleven-year-old daughter. They'd left town shortly after. Hard to make it up to them when she had no idea where they were.

So maybe she'd start with Ben. The solution there was straightforward: return the ring box unopened and immediately.

With him, she'd have stability, love, someone who didn't steal, lie or cheat. But what would he get? Her poor credit rating and a bad girl who meant well. True, she hadn't had a drink since last spring and her credit card balance hadn't increased in the last three months. But those sad facts didn't make her wife material.

He deserved better, even if he couldn't see it for himself. Someone had to save him from his own stupidity.

CONNIE DIDN'T EVEN bother knocking on Ben's door, but rounded his house to the backyard, where his workshop dominated.

She pushed open the workshop door and, sure enough, there he was. He sat on a sawhorse, in front of a huge sheet of wood leaning against a wall. She inhaled the smell of newly cut wood and the chemical tang of varnish. When they had been together, she'd breathed in the same smells on his neck.

"I haven't been here in years and it still stinks to high heaven," she declared.

Other than turning his head to her, he didn't move. Connie checked for the box in her front jacket pocket for the thousandth time. "You didn't return my calls."

Ben shrugged. "I didn't know that I was supposed to."

"After six calls, it should be obvious."

He went back to studying the sheet of wood. He was going to make her spit it out. Fair enough. The ball—or the ring—was in her court.

"I found the Valentine's Day gift you left in the kitchen." A part of her still hoped it wasn't him, though who else?

He didn't lift his eyes from the absolutely riveting wood. "Did you like it?"

"I never opened it."

Ben's shoulders curved in a kind of cringe. She'd hurt him. Well, let the bleeding begin. She pulled the box from her pocket and set it beside him on the narrow wedge of the sawhorse. "Here. You can have it back."

He maintained his focus on the wood. “I’m not taking it.”

“You have to. That’s one gift you have to accept if the recipient declines.”

“No, I don’t. You can keep it.”

“What would I do with an engagement ring if I’m not going to marry the man who gave it to me?”

“I suppose you could give it away. Or sell it. It’s yours to do whatever you want with.”

“Don’t be a jerk. You know that I don’t have the willpower to sell it or give it away. You also know that it’s taking every last bit of my self-control not to flip open that box, jam on the ring and make you marry me. I am really that shallow.”

Finally, he dragged his attention away and looked at her with his strange brown eyes flecked with yellow. Polished and stained circles of natural mahogany. “Connie,” he said, “I don’t know that at all.”

She glanced away. Had to, if she was going to get through this, if writing his name down not a freaking hour ago was to have any meaning. “Well, it’s true,” she muttered to the cement floor. It had a crack in it. She marked its path across the cement to where it forked underneath the sawhorse, the two paths fading away underneath the sheet of wood.

"Just to be clear," he said. "You wouldn't be making me marry you. The fact that I gave you the ring indicates a certain amount of free will on my part."

"Ben. But—" how to say this without sounding mean? "—you were always a bit dumb when it came to me."

He traced his finger along a curving grain in the wood. "I'm aware of that," he said softly.

"Ben, listen to yourself. You sound like someone on a suicide mission. Are you out of your mind?"

"Yes," he said, "I am." He picked up the box. "I'm so far gone that I bet I will go ahead and open the box, show the ring to you and you will cave and put it on." His fingers settled on the lid.

She lunged and stripped it from him. "Don't you dare."

He returned to contemplating his big screen of wood. "I guess you'll be keeping it."

She chucked the box into her purse. "How long have you been keeping it? You didn't have the time to drive the two hours to Calgary and back again last night."

He didn't answer and she was about to repeat herself, when he quietly said, "Since a week before we broke up."

That was three years ago. When she was a drunk, unemployed and…hateful. How could he have even considered marrying her? "Why?"

"Connie, I get it. You've given me every reason not to love you. But last night you slipped up."

"I slipped up? What are you talking about?"

"I saw you. I was coming out of the washroom. I spotted you over at the bar. You were picking olives out of my nachos."

Her stomach flip-flopped. "The cook messed up. You hate olives. I didn't want to hear you gripe about the mini rubber tires."

He turned and raised his index finger, a detective about to break the case. "The reason I have always ordered nachos is because I thought your kitchen made them without olives. I assumed other people ordered them as an extra. But they didn't. You've just always made sure that mine came without rubber tires." His smug smile widened and softened into one that made her insides all squishy. "You've always known what I wanted."

Panic ran circles around inside her. *Remember the list, remember the list.* "You're nuts. I have no idea how you draw a line from me making sure you don't get olives to proposing marriage. I mean, if the criteria's remembering what people like or don't like, I'd be getting marriage proposals every other day."

He shook his head, again in that slow way of his. "Not buying it, Connie."

What would it take for him to understand? "Ben. I broke up with you. I cheated on you with another guy. Another guy that I didn't care to date again, that I can't even remember the name of, because he'd served his purpose of making you see that I didn't want you then, and I don't want you now."

There, she couldn't be blunter. Some of that wasn't entirely true, but it was all for his own good.

Ben didn't even blink. "Don't tell me what you believe I need to hear, Connie. I love you, you love me—" she squawked in protest but he sailed on "—what's holding you back?"

Your name on my list. I can't do or be anything with anyone until I can strike off each and every name. Until then I can't look you in the eye. And looking someone in the eye when you promise your life to them is kinda important.

She could say none of that, because he'd tell her that he forgave her—giving her a ring proved that. He'd push her to move on, even while she still felt like the same destructive cheat who'd wrecked so many lives.

The best she could do was stay silent. Let her heart tie her tongue.

SHE LEFT. As Ben expected. He would've been more surprised if she'd burst into his workshop and jumped into his arms, his ring on her finger. He stared at the wood. The answer was there, he swore. He could sense the form begin to surface and then it would blur and sink back down.

Like his hopes.

Which was exactly what they did when the workshop door handle turned again. Soared at the thought it was Connie, and then nose-dived when in walked her brother. Seth was the male version of Connie. The easiest way to rile either one of them was to mention how much alike they were.

"Ben, you got to help me out here," Seth said. He pushed aside Ben's cans of stains and paints and slapped down a pink folder and a pencil. "It's these vows. They're the next thing on the checklist."

"You're not going with the traditional 'for better or worse, in sickness and in health' ones?"

"No, Alexi said them with her first husband, so she wants to do something new with me."

"Sure, glad to help. It's not as if I've got anything better to do."

Seth cut him a look. "Sarcasm's *my* thing. What's with you?"

There was no good answer. If he said he'd proposed to Connie, Seth would blow a gasket and tell him how stupid he was. If he then said she'd refused, he'd blow another gasket for how stupid *she* was.

"I'm just jealous," Ben said, because that was true. "Not that I want Alexi for mine," he added quickly. "Just the idea, I guess."

Seth said what he'd been saying every few months for the past three years. "I could set you up with somebody."

Ben repeated his standard reply. "I'm not looking right now. So," he added quickly, to get Seth back on track, "what have you got so far?"

Seth flipped open the folder. "According to

Amy, I should say, 'I will love you forever. I want to spend the rest of my life with you. Thank you for marrying me.'"

"Are you sure Alexi's seven-year-old said that? Sounds more like you," Ben said. He opened his phone. "Let's see if Pinterest can do better."

"You're kidding, right? You are the first male I've ever heard of who's on Pinterest."

"For my woodworking." Which wasn't entirely a lie but there was no way he was telling Seth that he had pins on wedding lists. Ben tilted the phone away from Seth as he scrolled to a site with his red pin.

He'd pinned it when he had high hopes.

When the ring had sat on the highest shelf in his workshop in the wooden box he'd made for Connie during his grade ten industrial arts class.

He'd never given her the box because it had been too weird for a sixteen-year-old to give anything to his best friend's sister who was twelve. Even if he'd meant it as a small way to cheer her up after losing her dad. When they'd become a couple fifteen or so years later, it hadn't seemed necessary.

"How about this one?" He began reading one of the several examples on the site. Seth listened, head bent, butt to the bench. When Ben finished, Seth seesawed his head. "Not bad. Any others?"

Ben wasn't halfway through the next one before Seth nixed it. Two more got the same treatment and the third one didn't go beyond "Insert name, you were the only one who could rev my engines…" before Seth groaned. "Isn't there one there that says it like it is?"

There was—the one he'd chosen for himself. Ben must've spent too long staring at the phone because Seth prompted him. "Well? What is it?"

"It's not the entire thing," Ben said. "Just some, uh, lines."

"Anything at this point," Seth said, and waited for Ben to deliver.

Ben didn't want to. It felt like a betrayal to his fantasy of love everlasting with Connie, an admission of surrender. He swiped the screen away from the leaf-embroidered words and began to make stuff up. "You are my one and only, my alpha and my omega, my world without—"

"Stop, stop. No man talks like that. You're on this site with *woodworkers*, you say?"

Ben really didn't want his Pinterest addiction investigated. "More to see what's trending. Look, why don't you ask Alexi's maid of honor for ideas? She probably knows Alexi's vows, and then you can coordinate yours with hers."

Seth rolled up the folder, drummed it quickly on a can of stain. "Thing is, she doesn't have a maid of honor. She feels she's not close enough to anyone in town to ask them." He paused. "And before you ask, she's not asking Connie."

"Because you said so or she said so?"

"Neither of us. It's unspoken. We both have issues with her."

An image of Connie's defiant eyes this morning came to mind. "Who doesn't?"

Her brother immediately went on high alert. "Why? What's she done now?"

"Nothing." The truth and the problem.

Seth's green eyes—Connie's eyes—narrowed, and Ben dug deep for something to redirect Seth. "You should reconsider. Alexi needs someone, and Connie is your sister."

Seth rerolled the folder so tight it took on the dimensions of a plastic straw. "You think I haven't considered her? Connie would make an awesome maid of honor. She could fix up Alexi, decorate the venue, organize all the parties, everything. What'll happen, though, is that something'll come up, she'll chase it and we'll be stuck with the mess. Don't think I'm right? Two words—*Mom's house*. Our wedding will end up looking like the house. Trashed with no idea when it'll get done."

Seth's frustration and bitterness were unmistakable—and justified. Three years ago, he'd taken the rap for Connie on police charges. He'd expected Connie to take advantage of the break he'd given her, and he'd never forgiven her for running it into the ground instead.

"All I'm saying is that you and Alexi should think about it. I'm sure Connie would like to help out."

"She babysits every Thursday night. That's enough."

"And the kids call her Auntie Connie. Isn't that reason to involve her in the wedding?"

"Look, when Connie shows up for something, she's all in. *When*. I can deal with her skipping a Thursday if she decides she's got better things to do. I can't have her skipping my wedding."

"A maid of honor isn't required for a wedding to take place. You and Alexi will still get married, even if she doesn't show."

"Better none than one who can't be trusted."

Stubbornness, that was the other thing the two siblings had in common.

"Give her a chance," Ben said.

"We have. You more than me. I've learned my lesson. Have you?"

Ben didn't answer, looking back at the wood. Images rose up through the grain of what he could carve. A vine, probably inspired by the tattoo that twined up her leg. A wheel from when they'd met as kids. More. Ben reached for his pencil, flicking in marks here and across there, following the lines that finally, finally matched what was in his head.

When the design was captured, he stepped back and reality drifted down like sawdust.

He whipped around. "Seth! Sorry, I—"

Seth was gone. Probably a good thing, too, because if he'd seen all Ben had drawn, he would know the answer to his question.

"WHAT'S YOUR PLAN if it rains?"

Connie snapped her attention away from the wedding photo on Lindsay's desk, and focused on the town's special events coordinator. Right, they were talking about the upcoming Lakers-on-the-Go Summer Launch event she was organizing for the community.

"What are my options?" Connie asked. She

knew the answer, but it bought her a few seconds to figure out how to tell Lindsay about Derek and Shari. It had seemed like the right and good thing to do—right up until she'd sat across from Lindsay and seen the photos of her and Derek at their wedding and of them with their two kids. Suddenly, it was impossible to form the simple statement: *Derek is cheating on you.* Five words that would destroy those photos as surely as if she had torn them from the frame and ripped them to shreds.

Ben's advice to stay quiet might be the wisest course. Maybe things would work out on their own.

Snatches of Lindsay's answer drifted into Connie's brain. Move to the civic center. Same activities. Cancel the bonfire.

Connie jerked. "We can't cancel the bonfire. What kid above twelve comes to a school-end party just to get their face painted? Remember the event is aimed at middle school and high school."

Lindsay interlaced her fingers and rested her elbows on the desk. The pose of a patient adult dealing with a poorly informed human. "Then maybe consider expanding on activities to attract the higher grades in case of bad weather. That way all your bases are covered."

Connie didn't want to compromise. Lakers-on-the-Go was her brainchild, a social club for the people of Spirit Lake to do ordinary and extraordinary things together. She'd conceived it less than four years ago when they were all sitting in the kitchen—her, Mel, Seth, Ben and her mother. She remembered the growing excitement in the faces of her mother and Mel as the ideas had tumbled loose from her imagination. Even Seth went so far as to say that it might be a good thing.

And Ben... Ben had watched her with his knee-buckling, private look.

Not two months later, she'd ruined everything, particularly with Seth. A drug boss had come up from Calgary, looking for Miranda. He convinced Connie to make it right between him and Miranda by making a single delivery of cocaine and meth for him. Seth had insisted on coming along to protect her.

But it was a setup. Cops walked right in.

Seth had taken the fall for Connie. She had a string of minor charges from her wild days, and he hadn't wanted a fresh one to derail her attempts to get into nursing. With his clean record, he'd argued, his sentence would be easy.

He was right; he'd gotten off with community service. She'd done nothing to stop him. Loathing herself, she'd fallen straight back into her bad habits. She took to drinking again, partying all night. She withdrew her application for the nursing program. She lost one job after another. She drove Seth and Ben away. Ben had taken longer to shake, but faking an affair had done the trick. And in the nick of time, too. She wouldn't have resisted the temptation of a ring back then.

Seth had worked off his community service with Lakers-on-the-Go, but now he was too busy, so she'd made it her responsibility again. This time, she wasn't going to screw it up.

"The point of the event is to celebrate a change, right?" Connie said. "Moving on. Moving up. Freedom. New challenges. All that."

Lindsay bobbed her head, encouraging Connie to keep brainstorming.

"New friendships. New connections. New… new memories." Her eyes strayed to the wedding photo. Luke and Shari would've been at the wedding—he'd been Derek's best friend for years. Had Derek been happy with Lindsay then? Or had he been faking it right from the start?

Focus.

"We could launch balloons with messages inside, or write one in permanent marker on the outside and then let them go."

"In the rain?"

Good point. "Look, if it's too miserable, I'll just cancel the event. It's supposed to be a happy day, not something where no one shows up and those that do wish they were playing a video game in their basement." In the wedding photo, Lindsay was smiling up at Derek while he smiled at the camera. Had that been a planned or spontaneous shot?

"You're going to hope for good weather?" Lindsay prodded.

"Just hoping it all turns out for the best."

Lindsay huffed. "I have to say it, Connie. As special events coordinator, the way I keep it special is to imagine every scenario and plan for it."

And what is your plan if you find out your husband is cheating on you? "Let's just say, Linds, that I'm an optimist."

"Okay." Lindsay drew out the single word of agreement in a long, slow way to indicate she wasn't at all okay with Connie. "I'll send you links with the forms we need completed." She turned to the computer, tapped and clicked, clicked and tapped. In the forced quiet, Connie set up a silent chant: *Do as Ben says, do as Ben says.*

Given that her record with relationships was as abysmal as a Hollywood star's, his advice was probably sound. Besides, it wasn't as if she and Lindsay were BFFs. Who'd believe a waitress?

Lindsay sat back and laughed. "This is all your fault, Connie."

She'd heard that said plenty in her life, but this was the first time from Lindsay.

"You showed us too much of a good time last night. I can't find the forms—my brain is so blitzed.

"I'd forgotten how good it is to be with others and have fun. Don't get me wrong, but my whole job is to create fun for others—and that's work. As you know. And I love my kids more than life itself, but it was nice to have someone wait on me. So…thanks."

Lindsay had headed into personal territory. Yikes. Connie opened the calendar app on her phone. "Glad to be of help. The forms. When's the deadline on them?"

Lindsay ran a finger along the keyboard,

releasing a low staccato purr. "It was nice having Derek to myself," she added softly. "It's been a while."

Stop talking, Lindsay. Get back to work. Please.

"Of course, I had to share him with Luke and Shari. But they've been part of our lives for so long I can't imagine Derek and me without them."

Connie hunted for something neutral to say. "Luke and Derek have been best buds since elementary."

"So I hear. I grew up in Calgary. But yeah, I guess they're the same as Ben and Seth."

An image of Ben cheating on Seth with Alexi rose in Connie's mind. Seth would be devastated, their friendship over. There was no coming back from that kind of betrayal. As for her and Ben, well, she had no claim on him so it wouldn't be as if she had a right to feel hurt.

Still, for what he'd done to Seth, she would burn him alive.

"They are close," Connie affirmed. "No getting between those two."

Except she had and still did. She was the constant burr, thorn, fly, poison, wrench in their friendship. She was forever grateful that when she broke up with Ben, Seth had sided with him. If anything, it had made them closer.

Lindsay would have heard the story of her betrayal from Luke and Derek. Not the heart of it—only she knew that—but the bare fact that Connie had dumped Ben for another man. They would have judged her, and rightly so.

Lindsay had resumed her job at the keyboard. Tap, tap, tap. She stopped. "It's why I try so hard with Shari," Lindsay said in a rush. "I don't want our husbands to feel any kind of…I dunno, divided loyalties. Do you know what I mean?"

Connie raised her head to look at Lindsay. It was like lifting a ten-pin bowling ball. "Yes. I know what you mean."

Lindsay's eyes rounded. "I'm sorry. I forgot what happened with you and Ben. I'm sorry. It wasn't directed at you. Honest."

Connie felt a wave of sympathetic embarrassment for them both. "Listen, it's fine. I hear you. I'm glad you and Shari get along." *Unless the proverbial poop hits the marriage fan.*

"Nine years," Lindsay said to the ceiling, and then looked at Connie. "Shari and I see each other every week, two at the most. We have kids the same age. Our youngest are a month apart. But I still feel we have no connection. We're just two people whose husbands are best friends. That doesn't seem right, does it?"

Connie had no idea. Would she and Alexi have the same stilted friendship nine years from now? She had to make a relationship with Alexi work, or she could never erase Seth's name. "I don't think anyone expects you two to be best friends just because your husbands are."

Lindsay leaned across her desk and whispered, "But I don't know that we are friends *of any kind.* You and I have talked maybe a dozen times in the past ten years, yet I feel closer to you than to Shari." She frowned. "You get what I mean?"

Yes. They worked well together when organizing events, shared the same political views, enjoyed the same veggie dip, detested the same breed of dog. Except that if she was really Lindsay's friend, she'd tell her that her husband was cheating on her.

Connie dug deep for some kind of truth. "I want to be your friend. Only, let's face it, I have a lousy track record." There, that was the best she could do—an invitation and a warning.

Lindsay clapped her hands, as if Connie had informed her of an excellent deal on venues. "You saying that means you'll be an awesome friend." She swiveled her chair to the computer screen. "Now, where were we?"

Sitting here, launching a friendship already weighed down with secrets and half-truths, with no chance of taking off.

"The forms," Connie said. "When is my deadline?"

A WEEK LATER, Trevor McCready walked into Smooth Sailing ten minutes before the last drinks were served.

Now, as he swung himself up onto the bar stool, he was finally making an appearance in her life again, and from the state of his face, what an appearance it was.

"Looks like you got rocks thrown in your face," she said.

From his one good eye, Trevor shot her a murderous glare. Nervousness shivered through her. She glanced about to check her options.

The bar was the island kind, square in the middle of the establishment. Tables skirted two walls with windows along the front. Regulars sat around the restaurant. Dizzy, always on the go, would be in and out, too. Plenty of witnesses.

"Hey. Get me a beer."

Trevor's order swung Connie's attention back to him. "Show me the money first."

He tried his one-eyed glare on her again, and despite her tumbling insides, she stood her ground. He slapped down a ten-dollar bill. "I want the change."

"Of course, hon, to the penny."

"You can't. The country's phased out pennies. You work at a bar and you don't know that?"

He was actually sneering at her, not realizing how stupid he sounded. "It's an expression, Trevie."

Trevor hated that nickname. Sure enough, his torn-up face reddened. "I know that. I'm just saying that the words don't apply."

"Thanks for the advice." Connie resisted adding more and got him his beer and change.

"This isn't what I wanted," he said when she set it in front of him.

What game was he playing now? "This is the only beer you ever drink."

"You thought wrong. You didn't take my order. You need to take my order."

"Very well. What is your order?"

He named a specialty beer he'd likely spit out.

"Sorry. We don't serve that here."

He named another.

"Sorry. Not that, either."

He glared. She smiled.

"What do you serve then?"

She pointed to the beer between them. "That."

He told her what he thought of *that*.

"Language," she warned. "And may I remind you that this business reserves the right not to serve customers." From the corner of her eye, she noticed Ben slip in and take up a spot at the bar kitty-corner to them.

She left Trevor to figure out his comeback and poured a Coke, no ice, from the fountain.

"Everything okay?" His lips barely moved as he indicated Trevor.

"Oh, yeah. I worked him over but he's back in line now."

"You say the funniest things." He wasn't smiling.

"Hey," Trevor called, "get me another beer."

In the brief time her back was turned, he'd downed his glass.

"And before you ask, I got the money." He slapped down another ten-dollar bill.

"I'll be back," Connie said to Ben.

This time when she set the beer bottle in front of Trevor, he grabbed her wrist. "You didn't ask how I got these." He pointed to his face.

From Ben's direction, Connie heard the chair being scraped back. Perfect, the last thing she needed was gentle Ben in a bar fight. He was tall and well-built, but he had no idea how to throw a punch. Then again, his opponent didn't appear to know how to dodge them.

"Let go of me," she said, "and I'm all ears."

He released her and clutched his wet beer bottle. "They think I should work for free." Trevor had this habit of talking as if she should understand what was going on in his head. The scary part was she usually did.

Trevor painted bikes for gang members across the country, though he wasn't a member of any. He was so good that even rival gangs used him, and he had the nickname Michelangelo. Very lucrative and very dangerous money. Connie had preferred that "career" to his other job of selling drugs for support groups of the gang Trevor's older brother belonged to.

"You tried to rip the club off again?" she whispered. Hadn't he learned his lesson in the summer when he'd tried to double-cross the bikers?

Trevor carried on at his regular, voice-carrying level. "I wasn't ripping them off. I didn't get any money from them, so how could I have ripped them off, eh?" Trevor drew a finger through the condensation on his defrosting mug. "All's I did was delay delivery."

Connie groaned. Typical Trevor McCready. "That's called theft."

He took a pull on his beer. "Only in their world."

"That," she said, "is the only world that matters."

"I just want fair compensation for the work I do. I got bills to pay."

Trevor never cared if the rent or utilities were paid. Or even if there was food in the fridge. He only attended to one set of bills.

"Keep your voice down. You used from the supply again and tried to short them, didn't you?"

"I can handle it."

"Right, I can see how well you are handling it." Every day for the past week she'd written his name down on her list with a question mark behind it. How to help someone who refused to help themselves? "Have you seen your brother? Maybe he can talk to them."

Trevor's hold on his bottle tightened. "No. I can handle it. Don't you go blabbing to him again, okay? That other stuff back in the summer was supposed to be just between you and me, but no, you had to go blabbing."

"I didn't tell anyone—"

But Trevor was on a roll, his voice rising. "Mouthing off to him, mouthing off to everyone about how you were better than me, you weren't going to have anything to do with me. If you'd left me alone I could have found a way out, but you sicced them on me. You—"

"Hey!" It was Ben. Connie had never heard him shout before, and his voice only lowered a fraction when he added, "Stop before I make you leave."

Trevor's black and puffy eyes drifted over to Ben. "You're her old boyfriend? Or her new one?"

"Not new," Connie cut in. Trevor was goading him, and Ben was naive enough to fall for it. "He's a customer trying to enjoy his drink."

Trevor snorted. "Yeah, right. Drinking a Coke." Trevor shook his head as if he'd just been hit again. "Hey, I know you. You always come here. You're the guy always looking at her. Even when we were together." He turned to Connie. "He's stalking you."

"No, he is not," Connie enunciated in a low hiss. She glanced around. No one else was paying attention. "He's an old friend."

"Actually," Ben said, his voice closer. Connie glanced around to see him rounding the corner of the bar to come up alongside Trevor. Within striking distance. Connie's insides clenched. "Actually, I am her boyfriend. We're just not making a big production out of it."

"We're not—" Connie snapped her mouth shut. Denial would just prove his point. She bugged her eyes at Ben, trying to convey her displeasure. He grinned.

"Some advice, my friend," Trevor said. "Quit while you're ahead."

"Thanks," Ben said. "It's a little too late for that, but I appreciate your words of wisdom. I bet you're glad I got her off your hands."

Trevor smiled, or at least he tried to. "I feel

for you, man. You just got yourself a whole world of grief."

"Yep," Ben said, his eyes on her. "Don't I know it?"

Trevor rose from his stool. "I don't have anything against you, but she crossed a line with me and now there's a penalty to pay."

Ben straightened to tower above the other man. That was the thing with Ben. He always worked to be at the same height as others, then when he forgot himself, everyone became small.

"I hear you, Trevor. I'm a line that she's crossed, too, and she'll just have to get used to the fact like everyone else that whoever messes with her messes with me."

It sounded like lines from a junior high play. She couldn't wait to get Ben alone, so she could cross a few lines with him herself.

Trevor shrugged. "Whatever. Your grave." He sauntered off, but Connie knew from the way he rolled his shoulders inside his fleece-lined denim jacket that he wasn't happy.

And if Trevor wasn't happy, he made sure everyone around him wasn't, either.

CHAPTER THREE

BEN DIDN'T LET Connie take control of the conversation for their short drive to her house, as he usually did. Instead, he switched the heat controls to Connie's preferred toasty levels and let the truck idle at the curb.

"How much trouble is Trevor McCready?"

"Trouble? He isn't trouble."

He didn't take his gaze off her to nudge her into a better answer, and also because he loved her face. For sure, she could transform herself into a magazine model with a little makeup, but it was her expressions that did it for him. When she squinted her left eye a titch or widened them into a glare, or the several hundred ways she shaped her mouth depending on the message she was delivering. Right now, in the shadowed cab, it was a careful neutral line.

He switched on the interior light. She blinked at the sudden brightness, then quickly shifted back into her constructed poker face.

"Liar."

Out came the widened eyes. "What? You don't know anything about the situation. And I'm not explaining it, either, because it's none of your business." She slipped her hands under her thighs against the heated seats. "Let's go. I'm freezing."

"The truck is warm," Ben said. "We can talk here."

"No, we can't," she said, "because there is nothing to talk about. Other than the fact that you are not my boyfriend."

"Yeah, it kind of doesn't work when you get to be our age," he said, allowing her this distraction because he wanted the issue hashed out, too.

"What do you mean, it doesn't work? I'm only thirty-three and you're thirty-seven."

"All right," he agreed. "Let's be boyfriend/girlfriend."

Out came her squinty eye. "That's not what I meant and you know it. We are not together. And Trevor is the worst guy you could've said that to."

"Why?"

"Because—because he's not worth the trouble."

"Just like me." The words tumbled from him before he could stop them.

"Yes, you're worth the trouble. But not my trouble. And not his trouble. You're worth the trouble that a single woman with a decent job and no debts and a brother who's not ashamed of her and…and a vehicle, her own vehicle, can bring."

The closest to a declaration of love in three years. "You don't want me to get hurt."

She pulled her hands out from underneath her and shaped them into rigid claws. She shook them, as if his neck was in her grasp. "Of course I don't want you to get hurt. You're a friend. An old friend. I haven't told anyone about what happened with Trevor because, trust me, the less said, the better."

He was more than an "old friend," but to get her to admit that was like sawing through a knot in wood—slow-going as all get-out. "I don't like the fact that he threatened you."

"He didn't threaten me."

"Correct me if I'm wrong but 'now there's a penalty to pay' sounds like a threat to me. It took all I had not to add more color to his face."

"I *am* correcting you. Promise me you

won't get involved with Trevor in any way, shape or form, okay?"

Her voice was shaky from emotion. Question was, what kind of emotion? "Motivate me," he said. "Give me a reason."

She growled in frustration and raked her hair behind her ears. "Because the people who left his face like that will have no trouble sorting you out the same way if you cross them."

"Tell me what Trevor did so I don't do the same."

She did a bit more growling and raking of hair, and then spilled. "Last summer, he thought he knew better than his client how to paint the bike. Maybe he did, but the point is, the customer is always right, especially with this bunch. Trevor threw a fit and painted the bike with a pink-and-purple unicorn."

Ben was pretty sure he wouldn't do the same. "You got caught in the cross fire?"

Connie twisted her beautiful mouth into all kinds of shapes. "Well," she said, drawing out the single word, "you could say I played a more active role."

He waited.

"Trevor drained my account and skipped town. I found out he went to Las Vegas—in

July, no less—so I followed him to get my money. I was too late, so I maxed out my card to fly back. So yeah, when the club came knocking on my door the day I got home, steamed and broke and cheated, I was more than happy to share his location."

"Cheated?"

"He took all my money."

Oh, yeah. *Cheating* had more than one meaning.

Connie cleared her throat. "Anyway, long story short, Trevor was hauled home and forced to make amends, believe you me. I'm not thrilled about my role in that, but from the state of his face tonight, he hasn't learned his lesson."

Annoyance bit through her every word, and if Connie was annoyed with someone it also meant she cared. She was funny with her love that way.

"Do you still love him?"

"What?" The single word shot from her mouth and she let fly with a stinging spray of words. "You have got to be kidding me. You can't think I'm that stupid. No one can love Trevor better than he loves himself, and I never tried to compete."

He believed her. At least, that she wasn't

in love with him. "Then why did you hook up with him in the first place?"

He expected her to tell him that it wasn't any of his business, and she'd be right. But the question had eaten away at him for a year now.

Instead, she looked out her passenger-side window. "Mom was dying," she said. "I didn't have the...energy to end it, even though I didn't love him. It was...easier to be with him. I'd come home and he'd be there and... and I wasn't alone."

He'd been alone. Ben gazed out his own side window, where an ownerless dog trotted by.

He'd been alone in his workshop thinking of her, then alone at Smooth Sailing eating the food she served him. Alone everywhere... wanting her.

"I feel bad about it," she said. "I used him."

Ben wished she'd used him the same way. "Is that why you care that he's in trouble now?"

She pressed her head with its bright hair against the headrest. "He's deaf in his left ear because they beat him so bad. It should've healed but it never did. I think some bones inside his ear were damaged."

Ben could guess where she was heading with this, so he cut her off. “Not your fault, Connie.”

“Yes, it is. I knew he was going to get beaten, and I was so angry I didn’t care.”

“He broke the rules,” he said softly. “He understood the risk.”

“I didn’t have to tell them where he was. I had a choice.”

Placing herself in danger to save others had always been Connie’s weak point—the stunt to save Miranda that ended up with Seth in jail was a case in point. “If you cared to live, I don’t think you did.”

She shook her head, her hair rustling against the leather headrest. “I was…under protection. From somebody who owed me a favor, okay?” She closed her eyes. “Please. Can you take me home now?”

Somebody. Another man. Another one she’d gone to for help instead of him. “Are you seeing someone, Connie?”

You would’ve thought he was pulling her intestines out through her nose from the way she squirmed. “No. I’m not. Satisfied?”

“Considering I proposed marriage to you, yes. Yes, I am.”

“I wish I was dating someone. Then you

wouldn't have proposed and things between us wouldn't be so…confusing."

Things between them had always been confusing, at least for him. Giving her the ring had been more like taking a board he'd spent all his adult life moving around and finally cutting into it, giving it shape and purpose. He wasn't about to argue the point, not now, anyway. Not until the matter of Trevor was sorted. "But I did and they are. You have the right to refuse to marry me, but you also said I'm an old friend. That means I won't sit on a bar stool and watch you get threatened. And as a friend, I have a certain right to ask questions. Can we agree to that?"

Her chin came up. "Then you have to respect my concern for you, too. You can't worry a friend. You have to stay away from Trevor."

"Sure," he said. "I'll leave Trevor alone if he leaves you alone. If he comes anywhere close to you, if he crosses the boundaries we set with him tonight, then I have the right to make him step back. Agreed?"

A full minute ticked by on the digital time display before she finally said, "Okay."

He'd take it. He didn't like his relegation to "friend" status, but for the first time since they'd broken up and after forty-seven rides home—yes, he was counting—she'd acknowledged that he had some kind of place in her life.

"AND NOW FOR our last brave entrant in this year's Polar Dip. Connie Greene, representing the community activity group Lakers-on-the-Go," the host announced.

Good-hearted applause crackled through the circle of watchers as a figure emerged from the huge white participants' tent. The tent was set up on the other side of the snow-covered lake surface from where Ben stood with Seth, Mel, Alexi and her four kids by the ice hole. Ice *square*, really. The square was about five by five feet, with four rescue divers at the corners.

"What's Con done now?"

Ben had no answer for Seth. To entertain and thank the crowd for their pledges to the various causes, many of the entrants in the Polar Dip dressed up. Connie wore the costume of the mascot for Lakers-on-the-Go. A merperson, she'd described to Ben. A gender neutral, nautical character.

But he felt far from neutral seeing her in this particular getup. Her blue-green bikini top glinted in the sharp winter sun, and her lower half was encased in a matching fish costume, skintight and narrow at her feet. It became immediately clear that the outfit was so tight she could only shuffle forward a few inches at a time. In flip-flops. In minus-fourteen-degree Celsius temperatures. With a middle bare except for the tattoo of a single green leaf.

She shuffled along, her wide, curved tail plowing up snow behind her like an upside-down shovel. Ben could tell from her bent head, her long blond hair blocking her face from view, that Connie was as embarrassed as all get-out. What had possessed her to wear that outfit? He was torn between wanting her to turn tail quite literally and call it off, or to keep going and finish now that she'd committed herself.

"Never seen her in that before," Mel said.

"Neither have I," said Alexi. She made stuffed animals for a living and knew her way around a sewing machine. She might've helped Connie. If Connie had asked.

Shuffle, shuffle, scrape, scrape.

The crowd gradually fell silent and settled in for the long wait.

"Ice will have melted under our feet by the time she gets over here," a man remarked.

"Not if she doesn't freeze solid first," a woman farther along added.

The divers in the square of open water began chatting among themselves, killing time.

Connie was about a third of the way there when the plowed-up snow caught in her tail brought her to a full stop. She reversed to loosen the tail's load but her foot twisted and she fell flat on her back onto the snow.

The crowd gasped. Beside Ben, Seth moved to swing over the rope.

Ben grabbed his arm. "Let her be."

Seth frowned at him, as if he were cruel or insane. It killed Ben to see Connie down, but it would kill her to have her big brother come to her rescue.

The same thought must've leaped to her mind because she thrust her arms straight up and extended her palms outward, a signal to the approaching volunteers to hold off.

They halted and waited.

"Get up," Seth muttered. Ben's thoughts exactly.

"Come on," Mel said from Ben's other side. Firemen tilted their heads together, probably consulting about what to do with her.

"Why is Auntie Connie just lying there?" said Amy, Alexi's seven-year-old daughter.

"Just…resting," Alexi said. Ben supposed there was some truth to that.

Connie flipped her palms upward and bounced her hands. When she still couldn't get up, she flapped her arms, like an overturned bird.

"Oh, I get it!" Amy exclaimed, and began clapping. "Come on, Auntie Connie! You can do it!" she shouted. "You're the best, Auntie!" Connie flipped to her belly and pushed up to a kneeling position. Stopped. All of Alexi's four kids shouted to her this time, and a smattering of applause broke out elsewhere. In a single gymnast move, Connie shifted from knees to flip-flops. Stopped. By now the entire crowd had caught on and played along, clapping out and encouraging her.

She broke into a little dance, her arms moving like a hula dancer.

Mel, beside Ben, cheered the loudest. Even Seth clapped along with the kids, while Alexi filmed it on her phone. Ben joined the clapping, now that everyone was doing it.

Here was the woman he loved, dancing along, reversing and zigging to the side now and again to off-load snow from her tail. By the time she'd hopped onto the mat laid beside the square of water, the crowd was wild with its hoots and whistles and clapping.

Connie gestured to the crowd with fluttery, downward waves to quiet, and they did. She listened to instructions from the guys in the water, then her arms came up like an Olympic diver and in a final set of fast and furious penguin hops she flung herself forward. The slap of her body against the water was like a gunshot in Ben's ear.

The divers immediately scooped her out and deposited her on the ice, where attendants bundled her in towels and blankets and lifted her to her feet. She turned to Alexi's kids and blew them kisses. She waved in the general direction of Seth and Mel, and then to the cheering crowd.

She didn't seem to notice Ben at all.

He didn't care. It was enough that Connie had shown the town—and her brother—that she could go from flat on her back to bringing on wild cheers all by herself.

If only she could convince herself.

A QUARTER OF an hour later, Connie's teeth were still clacking together, despite having shimmied out of the stupid, stupid costume and jumped into her fleece suit, and then into outdoor gear. She shoved the mermaid costume already hardening with frost into a reusable grocery bag and stepped out from the tent.

Seth was right there, pulling on thick winter gloves. She'd seen his expression of disbelief when she'd emerged from the tent, which only deepened just before she jumped in. Him coming specifically over to tell her the obvious seemed over the top.

"Before you say anything, I know I looked stupid, okay? I assumed the tailor understood I needed to walk in the outfit. I didn't check because Dizzy was giving me a ride and I was already making her late. The first time I tried it on was in the tent and…you know the rest. So, save your breath, okay?"

Seth tugged on the cuffs of his gloves, even though they were already on. "Crowd seemed to like it well enough."

They had. When she'd fallen over, she'd stared up at the blinding blue of the winter sky, her bare back freezing to the snow, and figured she'd rather be laughed at than pitied. "Everyone appreciates a good joke."

Another pull on the gloves. "Do you want a ride home?"

The lake water must've frozen the nerves in her ear, because she was pretty sure she was hearing Seth being nice to her. Alexi must've put him up to it. Ben would give her a ride home.

"No, thanks, I—" She shouldn't assume Ben would drive her. It was one thing to catch a ride with him when he specifically came to pick her up from work, but expecting him to do it because he was nearby was a little much. "Thanks, that'll be great."

"Come on, then. Alexi and the kids are hanging out here for the games and stuff. I'll drop you off in the meantime."

He took off, no doubt expecting her to trot behind him like she had when they were kids. She sighed, about to do just that, when she heard her name.

It was Mel, Ben beside him. "Me and Ben thought you were the best one out there." Mel always complimented her, even when it was a blatant lie.

"Waiting," Seth commented.

Something must've happened for Seth to want her away from the others. Had Ben said or done something to make her brother worry they were a couple again? She didn't dare look at Ben in case it added more fuel to Seth's fire.

"I also noticed," Ben said loud enough for Seth to hear, "the dollar signs in her green eyes."

The perfect deflect. Make her seem greedy in Ben's eyes, which, given her chronic impoverished state, was pretty accurate. "Speaking of which—" she made a "gimme, gimme" hand gesture "—time to pay up, boys."

Mel and Ben dutifully pulled out their wallets. Off to the side, Seth spoke. "You didn't ask me."

Because she loathed to ask him for a stick of gum, even if it would benefit Lakers-on-the-Go. He'd already given too much. "It's okay. I made plenty."

Ben and Mel silently handed over their cash, both men well aware that Seth was übersensitive about family finances with the wedding coming up.

She could feel Seth watching as she checked off the other men's names on her long pledge sheet, so she wasn't surprised at his question: "How much did you make?"

"Three thousand, four hundred and fifty-seven dollars." She tucked Ben's and Mel's money into her jacket pocket and zippered it shut. “If everyone pays.”

Mel gave a low whistle. “Way to go.”

She risked a glance at Ben. The quiet pride in his eyes melted the last of her lake-water chill.

Her phone hummed with a new message. Alexi’s video of her jump. She waggled her phone at the guys. “Perfect timing. Alexi handed me all the evidence I need.”

Seth squinted at the screen. “Alexi sent you that?”

Connie was a little surprised herself. The two women only spoke on Thursdays, and strictly about the kids. “Without me asking. Which I appreciate,” she added so Seth wouldn’t think her rude.

“Do you mind forwarding me the video?” Ben asked, leaning back on his heels, as if his request was perfectly ordinary. “I’ll add it to my collection.”

Connie paused in her text of thanks to Alexi. Had he any idea what he’d admitted to? To them having each other’s number, to keeping in regular contact, to soliciting a video of her to his collection, which he didn’t even have, to suggesting that they had a very recent history. And then he added the clincher, "You ready?"

For what? A bomb?

He must've read her confusion. "A ride home. As per usual."

Seth tensed. If he was a hawk, he'd have let out a loud piercing cry right about now. This was not happening. The last thing she wanted was to push them apart. Again. She was not another Shari.

She picked up her grocery bag and pulled away from them. "Seth offered to take me home, but I just remembered I should collect my money first. If I need a ride," she said to none of them in particular, "I'll be sure to text."

She'd be sure to text Mel.

CHAPTER FOUR

THURSDAY NIGHTS WERE Connie's favorite nights of the week because she got to spend them with Alexi's four kids while Alexi and Seth had a date night. Connie would arrive at five thirty for a supper of all-beef hot dogs and chili, and then the real fun started. She'd play Twister, or braid hair or bracelets, or build sky stations in a video game, or stage stupid stuff like walking with two-liter pop bottles between their thighs and tossing popcorn into each other's mouth. When there was no school the next day, the kids could stay up one hour past their bedtime. One more hour of cuddling four-year-old Callie, playing thumb wars with the boys and styling Amy's long, black hair.

She'd had to earn her way into the weekly gig. Mel had been their usual babysitter, but he hadn't been able to come one night because of a bad cold. Seth had already bought tickets for the theater, so Mel asked Connie to cover. He must've done an incredible sales job on Seth and Alexi because they'd agreed.

Alexi had scheduled everything out to the freaking quarter hour, and Connie would've followed it to the T, except that the internet went down, and she'd had to improvise some games. She'd lost track of time, and the kids were still up at 10:45 when Seth and Alexi returned. Actually, Callie had passed out on the couch in Connie's spiked-heel boots, and Amy was headed for bed as soon as she found her prosthetic leg. It was mostly the boys, Bryn and Matt, who were still flying high from the drink-induced sugar high.

Seth had driven her home in silence.

Except the next Tuesday, he'd called her. The kids wanted her back, which didn't surprise her. What surprised her was that Alexi wanted her back, too. "It meant something to her that you got in there with the kids and made them happy," Seth had explained. "Between suppers and helping out here, Mel is with the kids nearly every day, anyway."

With that backhanded endorsement, Connie booked off Thursdays at Smooth Sailing and typed Kids! into her phone calendar. It was perfect. She enjoyed laughter and hugs and stories, and Seth got a little one-on-one time with the woman he loved.

But this Thursday, things were…off. Seth was even more tight-lipped with her than usual on the drive to the farm, which she put down to the thing with Ben at the Polar Dip. But when they arrived at the house, the kids had already started their hot dogs in the living room without her. Seth disappeared outside to check his cows and told her that Alexi was waiting to speak to her alone in the bedroom off the dining room. Which explained why the kids were out of earshot.

This couldn't be good. How had she screwed up? Had she fed Bryn with his food sensitivities something he wasn't supposed to eat? Had she upset Callie? She couldn't remember swearing or shouting in front of the girl, and she'd only nixed snacks because Alexi herself didn't want the kids to eat right before bed.

It didn't look any better when she knocked and entered. Alexi was perched on the edge of a chair in her one decent outfit—a plain blue dress with a V-neck, dangly earrings and her hair pulled into a tight twist. She'd look better with a few strands tugged free from the twist, but she and Alexi didn't have the kind of relationship where they could be honest with each other. They didn't have much of a relationship at all, really. Less than three months from now, she would get a sister in name only.

Seth's silence, Alexi's formality, the kids' change in routine. Connie didn't need any more evidence to know that she was about to be fired from her favorite job.

"Connie, I was wondering if we might talk a bit." Alexi gestured to the bed but Connie pretended not to see. She'd take the news standing, thank you very much.

"It seems that Ben and Seth were talking."

The Polar Dip. Or had Ben talked about Trevor? No, he wouldn't, would he?

"And apparently the issue of the wedding came up."

Connie had no idea what to say. She went with "Okay."

"As you know, I don't have a maid of honor."

Connie didn't know, deliberately staying out of the wedding preparations, which was easy because she wasn't included. She wasn't even sure if she was invited. Was Alexi looking for suggestions? "Okay."

Alexi licked her lips. "I was wondering if you would consider being my maid of honor."

Connie wished she'd sat down. "You can't think of anyone else?"

If possible, Alexi's back straightened even more. "No. I never had…girlfriends. I came here in July, and I realize it's almost March and I've met people but no one…close."

Connie could've kicked herself for being so blind. If she wasn't getting a sister, then neither was Alexi. And neither of them would admit that it mattered, so Connie wasn't surprised when Alexi added, "You'd be doing Seth a favor. He said he'd not have Ben as best man if I couldn't find anyone, so things would look…balanced, but I know he wants Ben. They've been best friends forever."

"Since the day they met at age twelve to be exact," Connie said. If she said no to Alexi, she'd be complicating things for Seth and Ben. She wouldn't do that to them.

But if she said yes, the chances of her screwing up somehow were excellent. Then she'd disappoint Seth, Ben *and* Alexi in one fell swoop. Not to mention the kids, who'd likely feel the consequences, too.

Then again, if she got it right, she'd be a little closer to crossing out Seth's name on the list.

"Fine, I'll do it," Connie said. "But you're

not sticking me in some hideous dress just so you can be prettier than me."

It was the right thing to say because Alexi rolled her eyes, and they were back to being two people who loved the same man for different reasons. "You and I both know," she said, standing, "that your dress would have to be made of newspaper and duct tape before I'd be prettier than you."

True, but only because Connie knew her way around clothes and makeup. Her beauty was a gimmick only, one she'd show Alexi given time. "As maid of honor, it would only reflect badly on me if you went down the aisle looking anything less than as if you walked off the cover of a bridal magazine."

Alexi reached for the door handle. "Well, as long as we recognize that my special day is all about making *you* look good."

Connie made a show of sweeping out the door Alexi opened, tossing over her shoulder, "Glad we've come to an understanding."

THE NEXT MORNING, browsing through her laptop for maid-of-honor dresses while her nursing textbook lay open and untouched, she forced herself to call Seth. He answered with "What? What?"

She drew a breath. "Most people say 'hello,' you know. Am I special, or do you answer that way with everybody?"

"Just you. I'm busy. Get to the point."

Connie drew another breath. Everything with Seth required deep breaths. She'd had easier interrogations with the police. "So, what are you busy with?"

"Watching a cow calf and figuring out my vows. I tried Ben but he was as helpful as an old dog."

"It's not his job to write your vows."

"What's the point of a best man if not to get you through the wedding?"

"I'm sure Alexi wouldn't be impressed if she heard you were just trying to 'get through the wedding.'"

"You don't need to be telling her."

Connie had no intention of telling Alexi anything, but Seth didn't have to know that. "As her maid of honor, I feel she ought to be aware that you are finding it difficult to hold up your end of the bargain when it comes to the vows."

"I didn't say I wouldn't write them. I just said that it's hard."

"Do you want help?"

"Didn't I just get through saying that?"

"You didn't. You complained about Ben. You didn't ask for my advice."

"I didn't say I wanted your advice. For the record, you're the one calling me. What do you want, by the way?"

"I—I was just going through Mom's stuff today—" mostly true, though that had been yesterday "—and there were some pictures here I thought you should have."

"Whatever you decide."

More than a year had gone by and his hurt over the house being deeded to her was still tender and raw. How to tell him that their mom hadn't left him without money or a house because she didn't love him, but because she believed in him and not in Connie's ability to provide for herself?

She couldn't. "There's a wedding photo of Mom and Dad. You remember the one that sat on the mantel? You should take that for your place. It'll look nice with the one you and Alexi will have."

"Maybe. Anything else?"

"You mean photos, or things I have to tell you?"

"Whichever."

Connie breathed in and out.

"I can hear you breathing, Connie. Am I really that hard to deal with?"

Yes. "No."

"Then what?"

"I—I…could help you with the vows."

Seth hesitated, then said, "I can ask Mel."

She pressed on. "Really? Let's face it, Mel has a bigger heart than both of ours put together, but which one of us knows what a woman wants to hear on her wedding day?"

A longer silence. "You're not going to feed me a bunch of lines and embarrass Alexi on her wedding day, are you? Because I swear—"

"Seth," she said. "I promise I won't. I promise that you will only say what you want Alexi to hear, and I swear that Alexi will want to hear it."

"You've broken your promises before."

Connie pulled the phone away so she could draw a steadying breath and he'd not think it had anything to do with him, then returned it to her ear. "No, Seth. I've never broken a single promise in my life. It's just that I don't make them. But today, I am making you one. I promise to do everything in my power to make your wedding day one you and Alexi can cherish for the rest of your lives."

Silence. “Okay.” He added, “Not that I’ll hold you to it.”

“Because you don’t think I will make good on this promise.”

“Because,” he said tiredly, “I don’t think you can.”

He was probably right. Still if he was willing to give her a shot, then she would try. “I’ll bring out the photos when I’m there next Thursday, and I’ll text you some suggestions for the vows later today.”

AT THE EXACT moment Connie was about to purchase online her maid-of-honor dress, she realized her shift at Smooth Sailing had begun thirty minutes ago. She launched off her bed and raced for the bathroom.

How was she going to explain this to Dizzy? Showing up a half hour late was such a regular occurrence that it had almost become her new shift. She made it up to Dizzy by staying late and raking in the tips. But today, another half hour would pass before she’d get there, even if she dressed down and even if Ben for once broke the speed limit. Speaking of which, where was he? His presence usually got her fast-forwarding through her routine.

Where was her phone?

A bun. She'd twist her hair in a bun.

Right, her phone was charging in the kitchen.

She made it to her bedroom door before she turned back to the bathroom. Better plug in her hair straightener first. She raced to the kitchen to find the charger plug-in had separated from the phone. She swore she'd plugged it in. Okay, no phone. And she didn't have a landline. No way to contact Dizzy or Ben. Or a taxi. She'd have to walk, which would take twenty minutes if she hoofed it.

She'd plug the phone in now and maybe she'd get enough charge to make one call by the time she was ready to go. She hurried back to her bedroom.

Pants tonight, otherwise she'd freeze. Her black stretch pants. No, her galaxy-print leggings! With her black boots. And didn't she have that oversize shirt with black stars somewhere? A sort of starry-night theme. She shed her pajamas and yanked open her underwear drawer.

The doorbell rang. Ben. Yay! She snatched up a pair of panties. No, a thong because of the leggings.

The doorbell rang again. Ben knew the door was always open. What was his problem?

"Come in!" she screamed like a banshee, hoping against hope that he'd hear. She heard the door open as she wriggled into panties and rummaged for a black cami. No wait, it was in her closet. Maybe.

"Sorry I'm late," she called. "I was searching for a dress for the wedding for hours, and then I checked the time, and yeah, Dizzy is going to kill me. I might not even have a job for you to drive me to."

There was a pause and then a very girlish, very non-Ben "Hello?"

What? Connie thumb-snapped the built-in bra of her cami into place and slipped on Ben's flannel shirt before peeking out the door. At the far end of the hallway was—no, it couldn't be.

"Miranda?"

The girl shook her head. "She's dead. I'm her daughter. Ariel. Remember?"

Connie gripped the door frame, trying to process. Miranda, dead. Ariel, nearly grown, very much alive and ten feet away.

"Of course. Ariel." Connie choked on the ridiculous name. She had spent Miranda's final trimester trying to talk her out of the name of the Disney mermaid. As usual, Miranda hadn't taken her advice.

Connie's point was proven now. Never was there a name more unsuitable for the girl before her. No fish tail, yeah, but no singing, sweet-faced young woman, either. The human Ariel was full Goth. Black lipstick, black eyeliner, black hair shaved to within an inch on the left side and hanging in daggerlike sections on the other. She wore black jeans, a black T-shirt, a black jacket—real leather—and the traditional Goth black boots. Black on black with accents of black. Chunks of silver hung from her ears, neck and fingers.

Connie blurted, "What are you doing here?"

Ariel's painted face was a mask. "Nice to see you, too." She took in the stripped floors and half-painted walls. "You live here now?"

"Yes."

She drifted into the kitchen and opened the one excellent piece in the entire house—a stainless-steel fridge with an ice maker and a drawer freezer. All the parts worked. Connie had bought it before her breakup with Trevor on a credit card she now battled each month to make the minimum payment on. Ariel popped open a can of Coke. "Okay."

Okay? Okay to what?

"I'm staying here now, too." She crossed to the kitchen island, where there was a bulging backpack. She picked it up and looked down the hallway. "Which one is my room?"

Connie blinked. "Uh, don't you have somewhere else to go?"

Ariel's mouth twisted. She reached into her backpack and took out a bright yellow file folder. Yellow was Ariel's favorite color. At least, it had been five years ago. She flipped the folder open and handed over a couple of stapled sheets to Connie.

"It's Mom's will. She says you're to be my guardian."

Connie scanned the pages. It read nothing like the tidy will that her mother had prepared at a lawyer's office. This was typed with weird fonts and riddled with spelling mistakes. It looked like something that a kid would pretend was official. Connie was ready to hand it back, except on the last page was Miranda's signature and one line: "Your turn now, C."

This couldn't be. It wouldn't hold up in court. Would it?

Okay, she needed to sit down for maybe a year. She eased herself onto the couch, the fabric rough against the back of her bare thighs. She patted the seat beside her in invitation but Ariel didn't move. "So what happened?"

"The long or short version?"

"Whichever you want to tell."

"The short version is that she died last month from hepatitis because she used a dirty needle."

Connie's chest felt as if it were in a vise. Crap. Miranda had become a druggie. "I'm so sorry, Ariel."

The front door opened. "Hello? Sorry I'm late. Big accident on the highway. I tried texting."

Ben, picking her up for work, which she was now—she glanced at her phone—fifty-seven minutes late for. Dizzy was going to grind her into cheesecake. She shot to the top of the stairs. He stood in a toque and snowmobile boots, the only man other than maybe her brother who could pull off the rough, outdoorsman look. The fact that he was not smiling, his focus clear on Ariel, added to the effect.

"Ben! Something came up..." Ariel slurped her can of Coke beside Connie. "Uh, this is Ariel. Miranda's daughter. Remember Miranda?"

Ben, with his elephantine memory, nodded. "How is she doing?" he asked Ariel before Connie could signal anything.

"Dead." Ariel turned to Connie. "My room?"

That was twice the grieving daughter had announced her mother's death as if her own flesh and blood was no more than roadkill. It was on the tip of Connie's tongue to give Ariel real grief but she resisted. A tough front hid a hurt heart. "I don't really have another room set up, Ariel. There is the couch."

Ariel looked at the lumpy love seat as if it were a garbage heap. She regarded Ben with equal disgust. "Do you live here, too?"

"No," said Connie. "He's giving me a ride to work, which I am really late for. I'm going to have to call Dizzy but my phone is dead." She mentally kicked herself for her poor choice of words.

"Don't," said Ben. "I'll call Dizzy."

"What are you going to tell her?"

"The truth."

"No, don't. That will not work. Anything but the truth." Great, she was making Ben into a liar. "Let me call her."

"That'll take time you don't have. Go get ready." He paused. "Even though I like seeing you in my shirt."

Oh, no. "This old thing? I keep forgetting to give it back." She tugged on a thread to prove her point.

Ben gave her a look she'd only ever seen

aimed at her. The kind that made her squirmy and warm all over. "No point after all these years," he said. "I'd wondered where it went." A slow smile curved his mouth. "I should have guessed."

Connie scratched her neck, the spot between her breasts, her upper arm. She caught Ariel's expression. It was cold and…resentful.

Of course. When Ariel had left five years ago, Connie and Ben had been together. No doubt Miranda had told Ariel that Connie had chosen Ben over them, and now they were no longer together. It must seem all rather pointless to Ariel.

"Ariel. I—" Connie glanced at Ben. His special look had hardened until it matched Ariel's. What was that all about? She focused on Ariel. "I have to go to work. Will you be all right on your own?"

The motherless Goth pivoted on her boots back to the kitchen. "Been all right for five years now. Nothing'll change."

The implication was clear. It wouldn't change unless Connie did something about it.

CONNIE THUNKED MARLENE'S favorite beer in front of her. "It's on me."

Marlene didn't look away from the hockey

game. "Go, go, go, c'mon, c'mon! Shoot! For crying out loud, don't just skate around! Shoot!" Customers at the other tables joined her coaching with similar calls followed seconds later by collective groans as once again the professionals failed to take their advice.

Marlene started on her free beer, her attention still on the game.

"You're welcome," Connie said.

"Thought I'd soothe my throat before you fire questions at me."

While Marlene was absolutely right, Connie was curious. "What makes you think I'm going to do that?"

Marlene lowered the level of her pint a good inch before answering. "Because you always do. Remember the kid upstairs when you lived in that apartment? You wanted to know if your testimony would be admissible in court. Or the other kid you thought was homeless and you wanted to bring inside like he was a stray cat? Or the kid who came by in January with a Halloween bag looking for candy or packs of crackers and cheese? Each time, a beer. So, go ahead. Tell me something I come to a bar to get away from."

Said that way, maybe she did lean on Marlene's position at child protection services, but always for a good cause. Like today.

"This teenager—the kid of someone I knew from years ago—turned up on my doorstep not three hours ago, just before my shift started."

"So that was why you were so late. Dizzy was foaming at the mouth when she took my order. Surprised you're still working here."

Connie was, too. When she'd skidded into the kitchen, Dizzy was working the fryer and only had time to deliver Connie a thin-lipped glare. Connie had beetled back out to the front and got busy, and she'd made sure she'd stayed that way ever since. "I've got a job for a few more hours. Anyway. This kid, she plans to move in with me, and as you know, I'm not exactly equipped for the job. I don't want to throw her out, either, because she's going through a rough time."

She glanced over at the customers moving into the booth across from Marlene. Derek and Luke. She tossed them a smile and a quick "I'll be right with you."

Marlene dragged fries through the slough of ketchup on her plate. "Have you called her parents?"

"The mom is—" How had Ariel stated it

as if it was a newspaper headline? "The mom passed. A month ago. She was a high school buddy." Buddy. It hardly covered how the two of them had once been joined at the hip. "The dad was never in the picture."

"Who's taking care of her now?"

"I don't know. She literally showed up as I was getting ready for work."

Marlene gave Connie a quick head-to-toe scan. "You are a little underdone." She pointed at Connie's pink, flouncy top. "That doesn't go with the leggings."

Connie waved at Marlene's hockey jersey and unlaced snow boots. "You're one to talk. Look, could you just tell me what my options are? With the girl?"

"You're dealing with a minor, right? How old is she?"

Connie did some fast math. Her last contact with Miranda and Ariel had been five years ago, when she'd started dating Ben. Ariel had turned eleven that April.

"She'll be sixteen in April."

"Sixteen? That means—"

"Hey, Connie." It was Derek. "Do you mind getting us a couple of drinks here?"

She did mind, but she pasted on her best

tip-raking smile and strolled over. "The usual, then?"

Derek nodded but Luke didn't even glance up, his shoulders hunched. Uh-oh. Connie had worked long enough in a bar to know the look of woman-trouble. "How are you doing?"

"Been better," Luke said. "The wife wants a divorce."

Connie glared at Derek. He was shredding the napkin.

"I'll get your beer," she told Luke, and because she knew he'd need something to sop up the inevitable pitchers of drink, she added, "And bread sticks."

Connie placed the order with the kitchen and was waylaid at three other tables before she could get back to Marlene, who had downed the beer and was coaching the Leafs through a power play. Connie prayed the Leafs would put one in the net so Marlene would be happy and talkative.

When Marlene erupted in cheers, Connie came back to her with a second beer. As she passed Derek, she saw his phone light up with an incoming message. S, she read. Shari. What a jerk, texting with the woman whose husband he was buying condolence beer for.

She set down Marlene's beer so hard it sloshed over the top. "I'm not paying for spilled beer," Marlene said.

Connie mopped up the puddle. "Never mind. I'll pay for this one, too." Before one more thing could interrupt her, she rushed on. "The girl shows up with this bogus will that says I'm her guardian but it has the mother's signature. Does that make it legal?"

"Am I a lawyer? No, I'm just someone who's trying to drink in peace." Marlene swung her beer to her mouth and took a long pull.

Connie dug her fists into her sides. "You never drink in peace. You are always shouting or talking or slapping the table or punching or something. Could you just answer my question?"

"I did! I have no idea." She gestured for Connie to come closer. "I think Luke is crying," she muttered. "Do something."

"First tell me what I do with Ariel."

Marlene blinked.

Oh, for the love of— "The kid. Do I have to keep her?"

"You don't have to do anything. You of all people should know that. But that doesn't mean there won't be consequences, either.

Another thing you know about." Marlene locked on the screen. "I'm okay for now." She chin-pointed at Luke.

Connie picked up the bread sticks from the kitchen and walked to Luke's table. She squeezed in beside him and rubbed his back between his shoulder blades. He was on the verge of tears. Derek looked as if he was sitting on nails, which Connie wished he was. "I'm sorry, Luke. She tell you why?"

Luke blew out a shaky breath. "She said she's tired of going through the motions. Found someone else. I didn't even know. How could I not know? She's my wife."

Connie'd completely blindsided Ben, too. Of course, he had had no reason to be suspicious. The only time he'd had reason to believe she'd been with another man was the night he'd "discovered" them together. A scene she'd engineered to drive Ben away. Which had worked better than any of the previous arguments she'd tried to make. "Because you love her and you trust her and because she is your wife. Nothing wrong there, Luke."

"Nothing wrong there," Derek parroted.

Luke picked up a bread stick, then set it back down. Chugged his beer. "The thing is,"

Luke said, after coming up for air, "the thing is, at some point, I should've noticed what was happening. You can't be that close to someone and miss all the signals. Can you?"

Ben would've wondered the same thing. Not that he'd told her that. Since their friendship had restarted, they'd not said a single word about what had broken them up. In fact, Ben seemed determined to bury the whole incident, which wasn't what Connie wanted. She needed him not to forgive her or else she might drag him down again.

Just like Shari was doing to Luke. He drained the rest of his beer and Connie pushed the bread sticks in front of him. Instead of taking one, Luke answered his own question. "'Cause if I had known, I could've done something about it." His wet, glazed eyes settled on Derek. "At least I got you. At least you're here for me."

To his credit, Derek actually looked a little guilty. "No worries, Luke. Glad to…to help out."

"Maybe I should tell her that? Tell her I want the chance to fix things."

Derek glanced at his phone, picked up his beer, set it down.

Connie thought of Ariel. Her second chance to make it right with Miranda, maybe her only chance now. In her heart, Connie had sensed that when she chose Ben, it meant nothing good for both Miranda and Ariel. She'd done it for her own happiness. A purely selfish act. Now it was payback time.

"I think," she said to Luke while looking at Derek, "if you're given a second chance, you should grab hold of it with both hands."

"LETTUCE? TOMATO? PEPPERS?"

Ben waited for Ariel to answer the questions of the Subway sandwich maker, but she was too busy scrolling through her playlist. He got in her space. "Ariel. What do you want?"

"I thought you were ordering."

"No. I'm paying."

"Whatever. Everything except no olives, no jalapeños. Mustard, mayo, salt, pepper."

"Tell him that."

Ariel did an eye roll, the third since he'd picked her up, and repeated the information in the general direction of the sandwich guy.

At the pay counter, she informed the cashier she wanted the order combo'd, without clearing it with Ben first. Not that he would've refused her, but could she not have shown common courtesy and asked first?

Then again, what did he expect from someone raised by Miranda? Connie's old BFF had defined the word *selfish*.

Back in his truck, Ariel ate her foot-long sub in great tearing gulps. Into his mind leaped a sudden memory of Ariel's mother eating pizza in his kitchen the same starved way. In the low light of the late afternoon, he started the engine and rolled down the street. "You're welcome," he said pointedly.

Her cheek popped out with stored food, she said, "You're only doing this because Auntie Connie told you to."

"Auntie Connie doesn't tell me to do anything." Except not marry her. "She said you were probably hungry and I said I'd take care of it. I'm doing it so she doesn't worry. That doesn't mean I have to accept rudeness."

"Whatever." Ariel ripped off another huge chunk. Bits of lettuce dropped down onto his floor to be ground into the carpet. No use telling her that. She'd deliberately shake some more loose, just to rile him.

The last time he'd been this annoyed with anyone was years ago with Miranda. The very mention of her had been enough to make him want to kick walls. The Miranda Effect, Connie had called it. Connie had been immune to it, but Seth, Mrs. Greene and Ben had all been on its receiving end until the day she moved away.

Connie had always seen the best in people, totally blind to their faults. Ben could *only* see Miranda's faults because she'd been the one to introduce Connie to partying, alcohol and drugs.

Now the Miranda Effect was back, her daughter as the carrier. He'd caught Ariel's ugly look at Connie, who had curled in on herself as if she deserved it. Connie owed nothing—nothing—to Miranda's kid. It was Miranda, not Connie, who had left with Ariel five years ago.

Ariel gave a sudden cry and cupped her jaw. Good, she'd bit her tongue.

No. No. He gripped the wheel. He needed to get his nasty thoughts under control. Sins of the mother didn't extend to the daughter. "You okay?"

He expected a "Whatever," but she whimpered, "My tooth. Sometimes it hurts."

A cavity. A dental bill Connie would have to pay. She had no insurance, either. "Can't you get dental work covered through the government?"

"No."

"Have you checked?"

"No."

"Then—"

Her pale hand squeezed hard on her sub, the veggie innards plopping onto the paper wrap. "I'm not a foster kid."

"That's not what I meant. I just thought there might be a few programs out there for minors, those on low income. I don't know."

"You're right. You don't know."

Ben chose silence over a retort for the last few blocks to the house. Ariel clutched her destroyed sub to her chest and grabbed for the chips and bottle of water. Hands full, she couldn't unbuckle her seat belt. To get her out of the truck, Ben released the belt and it zipped up into Ariel's food, catching the wrapper and flipping her entire sub onto the truck floor.

Miranda, too, had complicated the simplest things.

"Why didn't you marry Auntie Connie?" Ariel's pale fingers clenched on the empty wrapper. "You made Auntie Connie choose between you and us. She chose you, so why didn't you keep her?"

She made no sense whatsoever.

"Don't act as if you don't know what I'm talking about. You always hated me and my mom, even though we did nothing to you. Nothing. Fine, hate me all you want." She pushed open the door, ran out and slammed it shut.

Ben watched Ariel stalk up the driveway and enter the house. He sat there as questions crackled and popped into his brain.

"Connie," he whispered. "What did you do?"

THE INSTANT CONNIE slid into Ben's truck, she was hit with the smell of mustard and bread. She squished stuff under her boot. She looked between her knees.

"Uh, Ben," she said as he took the driver's seat. "There's a whole salad down here."

"That was Ariel."

Connie tensed at the sharpness in his voice. "Are we about to have another conversation in which you advise me against consorting with certain people?"

"You mean a conversation in which you confess to more feelings for me than you say you have?"

The temperature in the cab was suddenly unbelievably warm. The heat from her seat alone was enough to make her squirm. "I said we were friends, which—"

"Ariel told me I made you choose between Miranda and me. We both know that I did no such thing. What is the truth?"

Shame drew her insides into a tight ball. "I thought I couldn't have you both," she whispered, her head bent toward her fisted gloves. "You two didn't get along."

"For good reason! She dragged you into her illegal schemes. You were charged with crimes she instigated, remember."

"I know that, Ben. But—but she was still a friend, and it was hard for her, too. She gave me an ultimatum. Her or you. And I chose you."

She closed her eyes and saw Miranda's stricken expression. Then she'd drawn herself up to say, "Have a nice life, Cons." She had called to Ariel, who was working on her turns at the skateboard park. Miranda had walked away and Ariel had had to run to catch up to her, giving Connie a quick wave goodbye. She never saw Ariel again, until today.

She felt her hair being smoothed away from her face, felt the gentle swipe of Ben's finger across her cheek. His signature gesture of affection. Years ago, the gesture would have been accompanied by soft, teasing words of love. Today, he said, "I wish I'd known. It would've made a difference. Later."

"Later? You mean when you discovered that I was a lying cheater? No, I think you got that right." Actually, he still had it wrong.

Ben gave her a sad, little smile. "Yeah, but I wouldn't have concluded that you never cared."

Connie was never hotter. Her throat was sandpaper, her jacket a boiling wrap, the air from the heater a blast from the desert. She fumbled with the heat controls. "That's stupid, Ben. You know I've always cared."

He leaned against the headrest, and in his profile was the sad downturn of his mouth. "No, Connie. I've always believed that you started dating me because I was there. You didn't choose me. You ended up with me. The one time I'd seen you choose…it wasn't me."

She pressed on the passenger-side window button and in swept cold air. Lifesaving. She drew in a cool, cleansing breath.

"But now I know," Ben continued in his slow, soft way. "You keep showing me how much I mattered to you, Connie. How much I still matter."

There it was. His deep, to-the-marrow tenderness that was strong enough to crack her wide-open. She couldn't let him in. Not when she had so many messes left to clean up. Especially when a mess like Trevor could draw Ben into a whole world of hurt. She sucked in another cold breath. "I have a list. Five names are on it. These five names represent the people that I have hurt so badly that I can't move on until I've set things right with them."

A second cleansing breath. "You are on that list, Ben. But so is Miranda and Ariel. I'm not turning Ariel over to foster care. She's my one chance to do right by my friend."

"Connie—"

"I know she's dead. But I didn't know that when I put her name on it, so it stays."

"Connie—"

"I bet you can guess the other two. Seth. Trevor."

"Connie—"

She couldn't bear the soft persistence in his voice. "Ben. Don't you dare say that you've forgiven me. That all you want is for me to marry you and be with you for the rest of our lives. Don't you dare take what I did to you and sweep it away, as if it didn't matter. Because it should. It should. Forgive me if you must, but don't take up with me again. What does it matter if I care for you, if that won't stop me from hurting you? Don't you get it?"

Silence settled in the cab. She stole a look at him. He was smiling at her. Smiling! "How, then, Connie, do you intend to make it up to me if you won't marry me?"

"I have no idea," she admitted, "but I'll figure it out."

"Do you want a clue?"

"All right."

"You chose me once. Choose me again."

Connie closed her eyes. How she wanted to. But if she chose him now—really chose him above all else—she'd be turning her back on the others she'd hurt. And her guilt over not finishing her list would eat away at their marriage.

She shook her head. "No, Ben. Not now. Maybe never."

She risked looking at him again. His smile had faded but had not disappeared. "I'm proud of you," he said.

How to get through to him? Before she could answer, he added, "You take care of that list. Leave me to last." He gently swept her cheek again. "I'll be waiting."

CHAPTER FIVE

BEN HAD HIS own mental list with its one name: Connie. Which meant that in addition to keeping a watch out for Trevor McCready, he also needed to manage Ariel. If Ariel was going to be a part of Connie's life, then she'd be a part of his, as well.

How to make that happen? Under the mid-morning light, he worked his chisel along a faint line for the first spoke in his wheel. It was a wheel that had brought him and Connie together.

People assumed that Ben and Seth had become friends and Connie had tagged along behind, but the truth was Connie had found him first.

He'd been twelve and biking around town alone. Biking was something normal for a kid to do in the summer. It wasn't normal to be alone in a house. Houses weren't made for one, especially one kid. He would've biked straight past Connie's house—a long, white, split-level bungalow, except this girl in pink shorts with lace edging, a sparkly pink top and a high ponytail was in his way on the street, drawing with chalk.

He stopped to look at her sketch of a giant yellow flower, which spread a good yard or two on either side of the street's yellow line. In the center of the petals was a chalked blue face with pink heart-shaped sunglasses and a thick pink smile. A human, a much smaller version of the face, lit on him when he stopped.

"Hi!"

How to talk to a happy girl in pink. "Why are you drawing in the middle of the street?"

"So the most people possible see it." She looked over his shoulder. "Car coming."

She scooped up her bucket of chalk and stepped against a parked truck. He followed, walking his bike. The girl waved at the passing car. The old man behind the wheel honked back. The girl jumped out onto the street and waved more vigorously at the car's rear window.

"Here," she said. "I need to get the letters done. You watch for traffic. Both ways, okay?"

He did, because he had nothing better to do. He later admitted he would have, anyway, even if he'd been promised a million dollars to keep going. He and Connie had talked—or, to be exact, she'd asked questions and he'd answered them. Between cars and honking and chalk breakages and washings for misspellings, she'd gotten Ben to drop the whole story. About how his mom had left for a family visit to Ontario four years ago and never came back. How his dad worked oil and gas out west and would often be gone until late at night. How he could cook anything out of a box or can.

He'd been in the middle of telling her that he was thinking of a getting a newspaper route so he could buy a power drill when a boy about his age had popped out from between the parked vehicles.

"Connie! What are you doing in the middle of the road? Serves you right if you get run over." He frowned at Ben. "Who are you?"

Connie stood from where she'd been squatting over the *O* in *AWESOME*. "This is Ben. He's my spotter. So I *won't* get run over. So there."

The boy's frown deepened and he said to Ben, "You don't have to listen to her."

"When Dad comes home," Connie said, squatting again at her *O*, "he's barbecuing hot dogs and hamburgers and then we're having watermelon and Neapolitan ice cream for dessert. Do you want to stay, Ben?"

Ben had been pretty sure he should say no. His dad had warned him about not going into strangers' houses. But supper was soup from a can because his dad's shift didn't end until after ten.

"Car's coming," Ben and the boy he figured to be Connie's brother said at the same time. They shrugged and smiled at each other.

"You can stay if you want," Connie's brother said.

Ben's dad usually gave him ten dollars to buy something to eat from Mac's. He'd bought corn dogs and ice-cream bars for a while, until he'd grown tired of people looking at him strange because he stood outside and ate by himself. Eating at home alone worried him because what happened if he choked? There'd be no one to perform the Heimlich maneuver. His dad said if that was his only problem, he didn't have problems.

"Sure," Ben said to the boy, answering Connie's invitation, "if that's okay with your mom and dad."

It was, because they'd assumed Seth had invited Ben and Seth rarely had anyone over.

Connie, he learned later, invited anyone—cat, dog, girl, man on motorized chair, kid on skateboard. On that first night, after a supper of meat and sweetness, he played with Seth and Connie in the backyard. That night, for the first time ever, he got home after his dad, who had been happy to hear where he'd been. He handed Ben twenty dollars to buy his new friends treats at Mac's.

Ben did, and from then on he was over at the Greenes' nearly every day for years. He was one of Connie's lost kids who had worked out. Other kids hadn't, and her parents had cut off those friendships fast. After their dad died, the screening system had weakened and Miranda had sneaked in. Well, this time he would be the one doing the screening.

He laid down the hammer and went over to his computer. A quick Google search called up Miranda's obit. It wasn't long, but it looked accurate enough, especially the mention of their town—Spirit Lake, Alberta. It said she'd passed away after a brief illness. Ariel's name was stated as the surviving family member. Nobody else was listed. She'd been cremated. Obits cost money. So did cremations. How had Ariel afforded it? Had the government paid?

He called Seth. "How are the vows going?"

"Good. I got Connie helping me."

"Connie? Helping you?"

Seth gusted out his breath. "Word for word, that's exactly what Alexi said."

"Can you blame us?"

"I can, when you are the two always telling me and Connie to get along. You two act like it's a miracle."

It very nearly was. It would be unbelievably good if Seth and Connie reconciled. Well, as reconciled as those two ever could be. "Careful she doesn't slip in something about how you vow to obey your wife's sister-in-law."

"She tried. She's treating these vows like a contract. I might as well be reading a legal document. She's acting as if being maid of honor makes her Alexi's legal representative. Did you know she asked me about a prenuptial agreement?"

Ben had only half heard the last part. "Whoa, wait. She's Alexi's maid of honor?"

"Yeah, she didn't tell you?"

"No."

"Typical Connie."

"What do you mean by that?" Ben couldn't help himself. He always got defensive about Connie with Seth.

"Okay, I take it back. Otherwise I'll get into trouble with both you and Alexi. She and Connie seem to be getting along, mostly because Alexi has the patience of a saint. Not that Connie is misbehaving," he added quickly. "Anyway, what can I do for you?"

Well, now that Connie had been the warm-up event, he was going to have to lead with her, too. "It's Connie."

Seth groaned. "What now?"

"It's actually not her," Ben began, and filled Seth in on the details of Ariel's arrival.

"Doesn't she have anyone she can go to besides Connie?" Seth said.

"The obit was pretty short."

"She's not Connie's problem."

"I tried to tell your sister that."

"She's finally taking responsibility, and it's with the wrong person and for the wrong reasons."

Seth obviously had no idea about Connie's list. Ben doubted Seth knew that Connie had started studying toward her nursing certificate again. He was also pretty sure that she hadn't told him that Trevor McCready had resurfaced. Connie was taking responsibility for plenty of people.

"Not to her way of thinking," Ben said.

"She feels guilty about what happened to Miranda and wants to make up for it with Ariel."

"You want me to talk to her?" Seth said.

That wouldn't work. Seth and Connie were now on talking terms, but he bet the language was loud, fast and frustrated. "No. I just wanted to keep you in the loop, especially with Alexi and the kids."

Which was to say that Ariel might be a bad influence around the kids, so heads-up. Seth caught on. "Do you think the kid's using?"

"Her mother was, but I'm not sure about Ariel," he admitted. "Truth is, I don't know much about her. I don't have any reason to distrust her, or trust her." Ben stabbed the sawhorse with the chisel. "I get that her mom's just died. I get that she's alone in the world. Believe me, I understand that. But she's been rude to both me and Connie, and Connie doesn't deserve it."

Seth made a disgusted noise. He did that regularly whenever the conversation turned to his sister. "You think the kid's got to go?"

Leave it to Seth to be blunt. "Connie's bound and determined to keep Ariel. I have an idea how to help them both."

"No way," Seth said. "You don't want me

to get involved, fine. By the same token, you need to stay out of it, too."

"You should've told me that when I was twelve."

"You wouldn't have listened then, either. Ben, when will you learn?"

Ben had to laugh. "Believe it or not, Connie asked me the same thing."

"Then take her advice."

He was. He was going to do what Connie had asked of him twenty-five years ago. Keep a lookout at all times, in all directions, so she stayed safe.

THE WITCHY SHRIEK of the coffee bean grinder woke Connie. She flung herself into the hallway, the bare boards cold and barbarous on her toes. She stumbled like a drunk in an earthquake to the kitchen and grasped a kitchen counter.

Ariel, dressed in yesterday's clothes and, from her crossed arms, in yesterday's attitude, stood over the appliance. Its shrieks had deepened to a guttural howl as semiground coffee and untouched beans rattled around and around and around.

"It doesn't work," Connie croaked out. She cleared her throat and repeated it louder.

"It works. It hasn't finished."

"No. It'll just—" Forget it, she was not competing with a coffee grinder at—she read the microwave clock and adjusted for the time change she'd not accounted for when it happened back in November—8:07. She threw herself across the island and killed the grinder's power switch. The howls receded to whimpers, to the ricocheting of a single bean, to silence.

Ariel took up her own aggravated howl. "It wasn't finished." She switched on the grinder but Connie yanked out the plug and held on to it.

"It *is* finished. Trust me. It starts off fine but the ground coffee gets under the blades, then they stick and half the beans never get done."

"Put in less."

"It can only handle enough beans for one cup of coffee. It takes forever to make a pot. I use that." She pointed to My Maker, then opened the freezer drawer and took out the only thing in it, an economy-sized Tim Horton's tin can of ground coffee. "And this."

Connie slid it across the island at Ariel. "I'm going back to bed." She took two steps when her flickering consciousness registered the coffee table in the living room. She spun back to Ariel.

"The box on the coffee table. The ring box. You moved it."

Ariel had the coffee can in a headlock and was prying open the frozen lid with her chewed nails. She kept her head bent to the task as she answered. "There was no do-not-disturb sign on it, so yeah, I saw it."

"*Saw* it? You opened the box? You saw the ring?"

The plastic lid gave away, releasing the sweet smell of coffee. Ariel eyed the coffee-maker. "How does this work?"

"You need to—never mind." Connie got to work on My Maker. Her mother had often made coffee while arguing with Connie, frantic as she now was for a cup of patience. "You looked at the ring?"

With no coffee grinder to glare at, Ariel targeted Connie. "Yes, I looked at the ring, okay? What's the big deal?"

"Did you touch it?" Connie was struck by a horrible thought, and she crumpled the coffee filter. "Did you put it on?"

Ariel seemed equally horrified. "No! That would make me engaged to Ben. That's sick."

Relieved, Connie tapped the filter into

place. "Don't think it quite works that way. How do you know it's Ben's?"

"Who else? Are you dating two guys?"

Connie lifted the coffee can out of Ariel's arms. "No. I'm not even dating Ben."

"But it's his ring?" Confusion outweighed belligerence in Ariel's voice.

Connie mouthed the count of teaspoons as she scooped in the ground coffee, digging out an extra heaping one just because.

She could tell Ariel the box was none of her business, except it was the proverbial white elephant in the house, and Connie detested white elephants.

"Look," she said, gushing water from the kitchen tap into the pot. "Ben gave it to me on Valentine's Day. I told him I wasn't going to accept it, but he refuses to take it back and I refuse to marry him, so there it sits."

"Why won't you marry him?"

Because of the list. Shoot, the list! Connie halted the water and muttered the five names under her breath. "Timing's not right," she said, resuming the flow from the tap.

"It's been five years! What kind of perfect timing are you looking for?"

Connie poured the water into My Maker,

and flipped on the switch. It gurgled and sighed. "Now we wait."

"Hopefully not as long as Ben with the ring."

Connie had never felt more awake at this hour of the morning. "It's not my fault he won't accept the ring back."

"Then sell it. You could get, like, thousands for it."

My Maker released a single brown drop into the mostly clean pot. Connie rattled through the dirty dishes in the sink for two mostly clean mugs. "Why do you say that?" she said, aiming for casual as she rinsed off one black and one pink cup.

"Have you seen it?" Ariel asked. Her back to Ariel, Connie shook her head, realizing too late that Ariel's question had been rhetorical, that she assumed Connie had opened the box.

Ariel headed into the living room. "You have got to see it. It will change your life."

"No!" Connie ran after her. "No, leave it alone. Ariel. Leave it alone." But Ariel had snatched up the box and was opening it, whipping to face Connie as she did. Connie clamped her hands over her eyes. "No, close the box. Do you hear me? I'm not opening my eyes until you close the box."

"Because you know that if you see the ring, you will put it on, right? Right?"

Connie's fingers were pressed so hard against her eyeballs pricks of light moved like roving constellations inside her eyelids. "Yes, yes! Okay? Just put it down!"

"Look at it, just once."

"No. Put it down."

"Once. That's all I ask."

"No. It's mine. Put it down."

"Once."

"No."

Back and forth they went, coffee burping into the pot.

"Okay, fine, then," Ariel said. "I will put it down."

"You did?" Connie eased the pressure off her eyes and then squeezed them again when she realized what Ariel had failed to mention. "Did you close the lid?"

"No."

Connie heard Ariel's boots stride across the living room and back into the kitchen. "Ariel? Wait." Connie shuffled after her, still self-blinded because she couldn't be sure that the little sneak didn't have the ring, ready to flash it the second Connie opened her eyes.

"Let's make a deal. You close the box up

and I'll—" *think, think* "—I'll let you have a birthday party next month. A sweet sixteen one."

"I don't want a party. I don't know anybody."

"You know me and Ben and Seth, and I could introduce you to his fiancée and their kids."

"That would be so dumb, and not fun."

"All right, then," Connie said. "Close the box or else I will throw you a party *tomorrow.*"

She heard Ariel's boots return to the living room and then the sound of the box snapping shut. Connie removed her hands just as Ariel reappeared in the kitchen, box free. She proceeded to pour herself, and only herself, coffee into the black mug.

Ariel extracted her phone from her back pocket. "For the record," she said. "You should put on the ring." She tucked in her earbuds. "You're not getting any younger." She waved a hand at the general state of the place as she left for her room. "Or richer."

BEN CRACKED OPEN Connie's front door late that afternoon to hear her and Ariel going at it in the kitchen.

"I'm not going to school."

"You're going to school."

Ben shook off his jacket, hung it on the coat rack and then sat on the bottom step to take off his boots.

"Besides, I'm not in grade ten."

"You're nearly sixteen, aren't you?"

"Yeah, but I missed a bunch of school, so I'm taking grade nine courses—but I'm not sitting in a grade nine class so they can all stare at me."

"You're not giving up on school, so you can end up working a dead-end job and trying to upgrade in between shifts. School's important. You're smart, so you're going. That's final, and that's the law."

Laces loosened on one boot, Ben started on the other.

"Anyway, what else are you going to do? Lie on the couch with those things stuck in your ears all day?"

"I'll get a job. So I can have cream in my coffee."

"I can afford cream. I just need to go to the store and get some."

"How? You don't have a car. You don't have a car, floors, cream—"

"Enough," Ben said, loud enough for both

females to hear. He pulled off his boots and set them by the door.

Connie appeared at the top of the stairs. "Ben. I didn't hear you come in." She looked… frayed. Her hair was long and wild with bobby pins jutting out like landed stick insects. As he climbed the stairs, her eyes tracked him, her pupils dilated black pools. The reason for her stress appeared behind Connie at the kitchen entrance, dressed in black and scowling.

"Your auntie Connie is right," Ben said. "You're going to school."

"You can't make me."

It was the same line Connie had used on her mother. Her mother and Seth had argued with her amid slamming doors and shaking fixtures. Connie hadn't dropped out because he'd asked her not to, but she had downgraded her subjects so that she could pass with no effort.

He tossed aside Ariel's quilt on the love seat and sat square in the middle, setting his socked feet on the coffee table. He tried to ignore the pale blue ring box in the corner.

"You're right," he said. "I can't make you go. Instead, I'll give you a free lesson from the school of reality."

Ariel leaned against the wall that backed

the kitchen. "Yeah, yeah, school of hard knocks. Been there. Still there."

Ben didn't doubt that, but he went in a different direction. "Yesterday you insisted that Connie take care of you. If you want that, then you can't get your back up if she actually tries."

"She's got bigger problems than worrying about me and school."

"You mean money?"

"I don't—" Connie began.

"Yes," Ariel said.

This was his moment. Ben's hands reflexively tightened on the soft back of the love seat. He'd hoped to do this without Ariel present, but it might work out better this way. "I have a solution to the money problem."

Both females waited with deeply suspicious expressions. "I propose to buy the house. Immediately. At market price."

"No!" from Connie.

"Good idea," said Ariel.

"It's not for sale," Connie objected.

"I thought your first question would be 'Why?'"

"I don't need to know that since I'm not selling."

"You're planning on flipping the place, anyway."

"Not to you. It's going to be part of the terms of sale. I will insist on knowing the seller's name."

"Take the money," Ariel said. "Your problems will be solved."

"My problems, not his." Connie jabbed a finger at Ben.

Ben folded his hands behind his head to make it appear as if the outcome didn't matter to him. "I can fix the place up and recover my investment and profit. You can stay through the renovations. You can even pay rent if you want. We both win." He fully intended to have that ring on her finger by the time he finished and a new house for her wedding gift.

"This house is my mess. I want to fix it myself."

Typical Connie. As big a hole as she'd ever dug for herself, she'd never called upon anyone to fill it for her. When Seth had taken the fall for her, it had nearly destroyed her. It had destroyed their relationship, that was for sure.

Connie swept her arm about the place. "I mean, look at this house. I get a house—a house!—and I wreck it."

"You're not wrecking it. You're renovating it."

"No, I wrecked it because I couldn't afford to renovate it."

"Then let me do it. Tell me, if anyone else made you this deal, would you take it?"

She gave him that consternated look, like an ornery cat. "Yes. Unless it was Seth. But he hates renovating, so he never would offer."

"So you admit you owe me something, yet once again refuse to give it."

Her frown deepened. "That's because you don't know what's good for you."

"And the one who self-destructs knows better?"

Ariel was still leaning against the wall, her booted ankles crossed, eyes and ears tracking the conversation. He must be holding his own if she wasn't interfering.

Connie glared. "I don't want you taking on something that has blown up in my face. Why would it be any different for you?"

There was no beating around the bush on this, so out he came with it. "Because I've got the cash."

Her face paled, her shoulders sagged and she hung there, as if suspended by a thin thread.

"Connie—"

She flipped up her hand. "No. You're right." She cranked her head to Ariel. "I'm being selfish." And to Ben. "Fine. I'll sell to you."

He aimed for lightness to shake her from her slump. "Good, because I've just put my house up for sale. I might need a place to crash."

His words had the exact opposite effect. Connie's eyes widened in horror. "You've lived there practically all your life. Your workshop is there. Your dad gave that house to you. It's paid off. It's your home."

She was right, except for the last part. "This—" he pointed to the stripped floor, then at her "—with you, is my home. Has been for the past quarter century."

She looked ready to bolt—or faint dead away.

Ben didn't want to leave it there, but he didn't want Ariel part of a conversation that had become personal. Leaving Connie time to recover, he focused on Ariel. "You just saw the roof over your head being sold out from under you. You want to keep it over you, then you'll do what Auntie Connie and I tell you to do. I make the rules, you choose if you wish to live with them or leave them. Understood?"

A look of triumph flashed across Ariel's face. Not at all what he'd expected. Had she manipulated Connie and him into giving her what she wanted? She pushed herself off the wall and pulled out her phone. "I guess I'll call the school counselor." She disappeared into the kitchen.

Connie's shoulders were still slumped, her head bent so her uncombed hair hid her face.

"Connie—"

"It's all right," she said. "I understand. I guess I got my lesson in reality, too."

She'd read the situation wrong, except had she? She had bungled the house, yes, and she didn't have the resources for Ariel. But a cold hard fact was that he would fix those problems.

What he couldn't fix, as he watched her retreat down the hallway to her room, was her conviction that she was a hopeless loser.

CHAPTER SIX

THREE WEEKS LATER, no money had changed hands, no papers had been signed, which suited Connie just fine. She'd told Ben nothing would happen with *her* house until *his* house sold. She didn't want him leveraging his house on top of juggling renovation costs. Lack of true ownership hadn't stopped him from turning the house into a construction zone, however.

He'd moved in his saws and sawhorses, grinders and power drills, working with an electrician one day and a plumber the next. Dust from the drywall and floor sanding hung in the air, so she kept her bedroom door shut at all times, a towel blocking the crack at the bottom. Ariel had relocated downstairs to a couch bed borrowed from Dizzy. Ben had thrown up plastic sheeting stapled to studs around Ariel's bed to form a kind of bedroom. Ariel said it was a cage; Connie was reminded of a fish bowl; Ben called it good enough.

She didn't know where he got his energy from. He still picked her up at 2:00 a.m., and was at the house by nine thirty. He worked there until late afternoon when he drove her to work. She suspected that he had an evening nap. Knowing for sure would mean asking him, and she tried to avoid talking to him. It was too easy, too fun, too confusing, too… too much.

Avoidance was why she was at the town library now, studying for her nursing certificate. Actually, she was avoiding studying. Everything distracted her—the comings and goings of patrons, the chatter of the librarians, the flashing screens of the computer users, the nearby vending machine. She'd tried all sorts of mind games, from timings to short walks to reading breaks. Nothing worked.

Worse, she had the sneaking suspicion that in her heart of hearts she didn't want it to work.

Five years ago, when she'd first wanted to turn her life around with Ben, nursing was something she thought she might like to do. Everyone agreed, and she'd started upgrading her courses. Then, when Seth had taken the fall for her, it had become something she had to do, but she hadn't been able continue… until now, after she had added Seth to her list.

But if she dropped out of nursing now, what was her backup plan? What would she tell Seth? *Yes, bro, once again I'm giving up and I've no plan of action. Don't worry, I've written your name down on my redemption list every day now for nearly a month, so I'm sure I'll make it right by you.*

Yeah, right. Planning his wedding wouldn't make up for his criminal record. She checked the time on her phone—1:02 p.m. Still too early to head to the house to change for work, and no way was she going home early, not with Ben in residence.

She could discuss with the high school vice principal the promotion for the Lakers-on-the-Go Summer Launch. Might as well shoot him a text to set up a meeting. She got an immediate reply to say he was available in forty minutes.

Great! I'll be there.

She resisted adding a smiley face. Too unprofessional.

Try not to be late as usual.

What? She checked his name and groaned. He was her old math teacher.

I'll try. Still working on the time unit.

She was shoving the last book into her backpack when he sent a reply. A smiley face.

She took the trail to the school that cut through the trees—the same hard scramble she'd used twenty years ago because it shaved four minutes off her morning sprint to class.

Connie was about to clear the trees when she heard voices from The Ditch off to her right. It was a natural hollow where a stream surfaced and then ran along before going underground on its downward path to the lake. The Ditch couldn't be seen from the school, creating a safe haven for illegal doings.

She might've carried on, except that she recognized a voice. Low, male, adult. *Trevor.*

"I can give you more next time but start with this. I don't know you, you don't know me. We need to build a relationship here."

Anger blazed through Connie. She could guess exactly what kind of exploitive relationship Trevor had in mind. She gained the edge of The Ditch to catch him in the act.

Sure enough, he was there. But who he was with doused her anger with a cold wash of fear. Ariel. There in her leather jacket, with her hood up and her hands shoved into the front pockets. Connie was fairly certain that more than her hands were taking up space in there.

Ariel's eyes widened at seeing Connie and she dipped her head so Connie could only see bits of her black hair sticking out from the gray hood.

"Ariel, hand it back to him. Now."

"What are you talking about? What are you doing here, anyway?"

As if Connie had no right to be there. Huh. There was only one bad guy in this situation, and he stood there with a weaselly smile.

Yes, he was on her list, but today it was all about Ariel. Every bit of Connie ached to drag her home. But Ariel would fight her long and hard, and in the end hate and resent her, just as Connie had with her own mother. Better to let Ariel figure it out on her own.

With a little help from her auntie.

"I'm here to get my stuff." Connie slipped through the snow down the embankment to them and fixed her eyes on Trevor. "You didn't give her mine, did you, Trevor?"

"Wait," Ariel said. "You sell?"

Connie rolled her eyes. "I'm not here for the fresh air."

Ariel took in Connie's rubber boots, pale blue with mauve flowers, and her windbreaker meant for running. "You don't look the type."

"Yeah, that's the point. No one suspects me. You'd do well to think about that if you want to stay in this business."

"She's lying," Trevor finally got in. "She doesn't sell. She doesn't need to. She has her own house and everything."

"Wait," Ariel said again. "You know her?"

"We dated," Connie cut in, "then we broke up. Now we're just in business together."

"No, we're not," Trevor said. "She betrayed me. And all she's going to ever get from me is what she deserves."

He meant it, his voice laced with pure venom. This was his idea of revenge. By taking it out on Ariel.

The girl gave Trevor the stink eye. Ariel might not trust Connie, but neither did she seem wholly convinced by Trevor.

Connie countered with her own version of

the truth. "Believe what you want, Ariel. The fact of the matter is that Trevor McCready is not to be trusted. The only reason I deal at all with him is that his bosses know me. With me, they're assured that if anything goes sideways, they can come to me and get a straight answer. With him, you'll never know."

Connie could see Ariel's right hand move around inside her pocket, holding on to the drugs. Was it fentanyl? She had no experience with the poison beyond news footage, but what she'd heard of the drug was enough to chill her blood. Way more addictive than heroin, and far, far easier to die from.

Connie kept driving home her point. "Trevor," she said. "prove it. If you haven't given away my portion, then hand it over. And let her get back to school before she has a whole lot of explaining to do to her teachers."

As she hoped, Trevor fell into the trap. "I don't have it because I don't work with you."

Connie made a noise of disgust. "You and I work for the same people. Why do you think I'm here? Right now? Because this is where we meet. Why else would I be here in the middle of the afternoon on a Wednesday? In a bush behind a school I left long ago?"

Neither Ariel nor Trevor jumped to the obvious answer—as Ariel's guardian, Connie could be visiting her teachers at school. Neither one of them had any experience with responsible parents, and Connie was counting on that to win Ariel over.

She went for the kill. "The thing is, Ariel, if he can stand there and rip me off, knowing the kind of people who back me, then what will he do to you?"

Connie didn't wait for an answer. Ariel had to feel that she was in charge—which sadly she was—and that meant granting her the space to make the right choice.

Instead, Connie gave Trevor one last scathing look, which she didn't fake, and walked away to keep her appointment, making as much noise as she wanted, as if she had nothing to hide.

CONNIE SAT CROSS-LEGGED on Alexi's bed, helping her future sister-in-law with the table arrangements for the wedding reception and wondering how to tease tips 'n' tricks from the mother of four about handling Ariel without revealing details.

Alexi frowned at an invitation and tossed it onto a paper circle marked with a "5." Connie spotted the names and pulled it out. "Bad idea. He's having an affair with the wife of him, and now the wife wants a divorce from the husband."

Alexi took the card, read the names and groaned. "Great. I have to look over at two marriages disintegrating on my wedding day. I don't even know these people. They're Seth's friends. Why are they even coming, if they're getting a divorce?"

Connie repeated what Luke had told her on her last shift. "They are going to work on their marriage for the next three months and then reassess. But we might want to avoid putting the wife in the way of temptation, if you know what I mean."

Alexi dropped the card into the highest stack marked "1." "I can't have everyone sitting with Mel. I'm already expecting him to put out quite a few fires."

Connie riffled through the stack. "If anyone can do it, it's Mel."

"I wish he could have his own wedding," Alexi said.

Connie felt a sudden upwelling of love for her sister-in-law. It was exactly what she'd always thought herself about her bighearted oaf of a brother. At fifty, Mel had yet to find his bride.

"Here. Let's put Derek and his wife with Marlene. She'll keep him in line."

Alexi pinched her nose bridge. "I swear I'm this close to calling the whole thing off and eloping."

"Funny, Seth said the same thing when we were working on the vows."

"I told him that after all the time and effort I'm putting in I would kill him if he cheated me out of the wedding."

"Is that what you're telling me, too?"

Connie checked another invitation. Paul, a police officer. She tossed him and his wife in with other Lakers-on-the-Go. "Yep."

"So we're doing this wedding for you?"

At this point, when the plans seemed all about taking care of others and none of it about them, neither Seth nor Alexi could see they were also doing it for themselves. They just needed to get over this hump, and if that meant directing some hostility at her, she could take it. "Yep."

Alexi pushed her pile across the bed to Connie. "Then you deal with this. I'm checking to see if Bryn has finished his math homework yet."

Alexi hadn't answered her questions about Ariel yet. "Wait!"

Alexi froze, one long leg still in midswing. "What?"

"Um...how do you get a kid to do something that they have no intention whatsoever of doing?"

"Ariel giving you trouble?"

So much for subtlety. Connie read an invitation and then studied the circle. "If I told you, you'd feel honor-bound to report to Seth, and I don't want to put you in that situation."

"I also know that Seth wouldn't want to see his best friend hurt. Or his sister, either."

Ben could take care of himself. If he got wind that Ariel was involved in any way with drugs and/or Trevor, he would come down hard on the girl. Maybe even work to push her out of the house. Connie had no idea if Ariel had returned the drugs because the second she'd come home from school, she'd headed downstairs to her fish bowl. Connie didn't pursue her because she was late for work, as usual. More to the point, Ben had been laying the floor in the living room and he would've heard every last single word.

"I could tell you what I do with Bryn," Alexi offered.

"Sure."

"Bryn never has to do the right thing, he

never has to do what I tell him to do. But I make sure he understands what the consequences will be if he doesn't. If he slacks off on his homework one night, he will have to do it the next day at school when the other kids are at recess. For every choice, there is a consequence."

And wasn't her life a screaming example of that? Then again, she hadn't made Miranda's choices. Yet despite witnessing the consequences of her mother's bad choices, Ariel was following in her footsteps. Shoot. She shouldn't have left Ariel this afternoon with Trevor. Getting involved with Trevor proved Ariel didn't have the strength to make the right choice.

"When Amy or Callie are teenage girls," Connie said carefully, "do you think that strategy will work with them?"

"I would say," Alexi said, "that the message is the same but they would have to trust the source."

Connie sighed. "In that case, I'm screwed."

"I'd say," Alexi answered, "that you are the most qualified person I've met."

"You haven't met that many people," Connie said bluntly. "I mean, you don't even know the people coming to your own wedding."

"I know a social worker, a cop, a business owner, a school principal and a bunch of mothers. That is enough to be sure of your qualifications."

"Ariel wants me to be her guardian, but only because she hasn't got anyone else and she doesn't trust the foster system," Connie said. "I'm not naive enough to think it has anything to do with my awesome parenting skills. I can't see her taking well to a lecture from me about making good choices. I mean—she already has this erroneous impression that I sell drugs."

Alexi cut her the same look that drew immediate confessions from the kids. She'd even given it to Seth and he'd coughed up the location of their honeymoon. Connie dipped her head to avoid direct eye contact.

"Now why," Alexi said, "would she have that impression?"

Connie examined the next invitation and studied all the circles. All the while her mind raced to come up with a good story. She was sixteen again, talking to her mother. "She saw me with a drug dealer. Trevor. My former boyfriend."

"Oh?" Alexi said. That single syllable was universal among mothers. It was part interrogation, part invitation. Her own mother had used it, too. Connie was pretty sure that when babies were born, there was a synapse fired in the mother's brain that activated the sound. Even if Alexi had adopted all four of her children, she was still a mother. The synapse had probably fired for her at puberty.

"Yeah, he came over with my—my old cosmetic bag. As if I needed old eyeliner and a tube of lipstick. Anyway, I think he was there to get inside and check out the place. I didn't let him in but he did see Ariel and Ariel saw him. She asked me about him afterward."

"Oh?"

"I told her that he was my old boyfriend, that he was a drug dealer and that I had no business with him anymore."

Alexi's mouth started to form another "oh" but before she got anything out, Connie hurried on. "Except I'm standing there with a cosmetic bag and you know what that means."

Alexi blinked. "Actually, I haven't a clue."

Connie had no idea, either, but in a burst of brilliance, she said, "A cosmetic bag is the perfect place to carry drugs, and what kind of ex would return a cosmetic bag? Ariel's not dumb. She grew up on the streets. Her conclusion, while erroneous, is reasonable."

"So...he really was returning eyeliner and lipstick?"

"Actually—actually, it was a bracelet. Sapphire and diamonds."

"In a cosmetic bag?"

"I thought it strange, too."

Alexi nodded. "I see. So you figure because of this, she won't believe anything you say?"

"Yep," Connie said, "exactly."

"Just like I don't believe a word of it," Alexi said softly.

Connie took Alexi's wrist, sinewy and bony but with soft spots. "Listen, Alexi. Yes, Ariel has got herself mixed up in bad business. I am trying to get her out of it. If you tell Seth, he will get himself mixed up in it, too, and none of you need that. And Ben doesn't need it, either. Ariel is none of his business. Please don't say anything."

Alexi looked at Connie's hold on her wrist. Right, they weren't that close. Connie released it. "I won't make you promise not to say anything, Alexi. I have no right to ask that. I honestly think it would make matters worse, is all."

Alexi placed her finger on the rectangle for the head table right where Ben was going to sit. “Seth is worried that you and Ben are getting close again.”

Seth was right, and he didn’t even know about the ring. “I’ve told Ben that isn’t happening, but he won’t take no for an answer.”

“That was Seth’s take on it, too.”

“Wait, he knows that I don’t want to ma—I mean, make up with Ben?”

“He understands that you’re trying to get your life back together.”

No way. They couldn’t be talking about the same man.

“To get into nursing school,” Alexi said. “That you don’t want to repeat mistakes.”

“Yeah.”

“You know Seth. He scares easily.”

Connie shook her head. “What? Seth? No way.”

Alexi stood. “Yes way. When it comes to those we love, we all do.”

Seth. Alexi. The kids. Marlene.

Ben.

Ariel.

Alexi was right. Even when she’d been a dropout and a criminal, she’d never been more scared than she was now.

BEN FOUND PEACE in working with his hands, always had, always would. His brain and his hands and the tool he held, whatever it was, were a kind of trinity, building anew. Even if all it required was that he sand an old chair smooth, or apply paint, or lay the floor in the living room of the house, he intended to live out the rest of his days with the woman he loved.

With Connie and, down the road, their children. Not with the scowling teenager forced by a weak Wi-Fi connection from her basement bedroom to the kitchen island.

He'd made better time on the flooring than he'd hoped, the trinity in full sync. He was about to text Connie the good news when he decided to set the room to rights and surprise her.

He bent to lift the coffee table and take it from the kitchen back into the living room when he noticed the missing box. Ariel was the only other person in the house. There she sat, acting all innocent with her earbuds in and images of the parliament buildings on the laptop screen.

"Where's the ring?"

Ariel pulled out an earbud. "What?"

He pointed to the coffee table. "The box. Where is it?"

"Not you, too. I don't know where it is,

okay? You're the one moving everything around. Maybe it's fallen under something. Look for it."

She reinserted her earbud and fastened her attention onto the screen. Three strides and a slap of the laptop later, he had her attention again.

"Hey, the laptop needs to be closed properly or else—"

"Bring me the ring."

Ariel stood, her stool shooting back to hit the new counter drawers.

"Fine. I'll find it." She walked to the coffee table, scanned the surface, dropped to her knees and checked underneath. She lifted a magazine that had fallen there to reveal the box, upside down and closed.

She handed it to Ben. "There's your precious, Gollum."

Ben flipped open the lid and found the ring, unharmed.

Ariel dragged the stool back to her screen. "No need for an apology. You'd choke on it, anyway."

He set the box on the table and carried it all into the living room. He applied new felt pads to the feet of the couch and set it in the exact spot Connie liked it. He did the same with the end table and floor lamp. Later, when she wore his ring, they'd shop together for new furniture.

Ben entered the dark kitchen and stood at the island, where Ariel sat in the glow of the screen, her pale face taking on an alien glow. He coughed. Ariel didn't look up. He coughed and coughed. Still her gaze stuck to the screen, even though there was no way she wasn't aware of him. In the middle of another spate of coughing, he choked out, "I'm sorry."

He turned to leave.

"She's not what you think she is."

Connie, of course. Even when she was not here, she was. "And what do you think I think she is?"

"Perfect."

The word came out with a puff of contempt. Ben hadn't ever believed Connie to be perfect; a perfect person wouldn't need him.

"Clearly you have a juicy bit of gossip about her you want to share."

She took out both earbuds and tapped off her music on her phone. "It's not gossip. I saw it with my own eyes."

She waited and so did he. She caved first. "She sells drugs."

Ben kept his face still. "There was a time she might've done that. Not now."

"If by 'not now' you mean in the last two days, then sure, you go on believing that."

The Goth was lying, trying to drive him away, so she could have Connie for herself just as Miranda had tried. Both would fail.

"You know The Ditch?" Ariel said. "Yeah, I was there for a smoke instead of—a smoke between classes—and she's there with some guy named Trevor." Ben jerked, and Ariel gave a little smirk. "Heard his name before?"

No, Connie. Don't do this to me. "Did you see her take anything from him?" Ben gritted out.

"As if they'd do anything in front of me."

"Then how do you know that he deals drugs?"

"Because I've been at school for nearly a month, that's why. It doesn't take long to figure out how this stuff works."

"It's a little suspicious that you showed up in the exact spot where nothing good ever happens."

Ariel shrugged. "Smoking isn't condoned, but it isn't illegal."

"Consumption of tobacco products is illegal for minors," Ben clarified. He didn't care if she sucked on the cancer stick or not, but her attitude annoyed him no end.

She shrugged again. "Anyway, it's not as bad as what Auntie Connie is doing."

Ben told her what he knew. "Connie said she went to the school to speak to the vice principal about a Lakers-on-the-Go event."

"Yeah, so?"

"So maybe she was on her way to do that when she came upon you in The Ditch with Trevor. She *condone* you being there?"

Ariel's eyes shifted, which meant that she wasn't so sure of herself. But—and Ben felt a punch to the gut at the realization—it did mean that she wasn't lying about the incident itself. "For your information, I know about Trevor, okay? Connie and I don't keep secrets. At the end of the day, it's your word against hers."

Her alien-lit face suddenly hardened.

"And what do you think she's going to say? She'll blink her pretty green eyes at you and swing her pretty blond hair and tell you that she would never do such a thing. And you'll believe it because you want to believe it." She pointed to the wall and the living room behind it. "But, deep in your heart, you'll always wonder if I'm right. You'll always wonder if you paid too much for that ring."

She swept up her phone and Connie's laptop and exited to her downstairs room. Ben made it to the couch, sat and stared at the box and wondered.

CHAPTER SEVEN

CONNIE KNEW SHE was in deep trouble when Ben didn't come into Smooth Sailing as per usual but texted her to say that he was waiting outside. Once inside his truck cab, he'd told her that they were going to his place first. When she'd asked him why, he'd cut her a look and said, "Later."

He took her to his workshop, which had changed in the six weeks since she'd last been in it. It was emptier and seemed unused. Stuff was missing—the sawhorses, tools, stacks of wood. Wait. It was all over at her house—or his. The boundaries were getting fuzzy.

Ben leaned against his bench and unzipped his jacket. Connie left hers fully zipped because they had differing opinions about what constituted a heated workshop.

"Ariel says you're in contact with Trevor."

Not this. She'd counted on the antagonism between Ben and Ariel to close down communication between them. In the past four days, school, her work, Ben's everlasting presence at the house and, yeah, her own procrastination had prevented Connie from having her own heart-to-heart with Ariel.

How to word this so he wouldn't think the worst of either her or Ariel?

"Connie," he whispered. "Please."

His head was bowed, his hands fisted in his front pockets. "I need the truth, Connie. Are you back with him?"

Connie felt as if he'd whacked her with one of his two-by-fours. "Back with— No! What exactly did Ariel tell you?"

His head came up; his eyes searched hers. "She said she found you and Trevor together. She didn't see anything pass between you two but she knew who Trevor was."

"She would. How she learned about him is beyond me."

"She said it wasn't hard."

Connie had to concede that. Ariel had probably figured out by noon on her first day who to buy drugs from. By day's end, she'd probably had Trevor's name and number.

"Connie," Ben said, "please tell me the truth."

"I am telling you the truth, Ben. I am not dating him. I am not dealing his drugs."

"You said you went to the school to meet with the vice principal. Is that true?"

Connie couldn't stand Ben's suspicion anymore. "Yes! I came across Trevor and Ariel by accident. I was taking the shortcut to her school when I overheard them in The Ditch. I came up with this big story about how Trevor is cutting me out of my portion and giving it to her to sell and she probably shouldn't trust anyone who will screw over the people he works for. She gave him back the drugs."

"So Ariel is selling drugs?"

"No, she gave them back. At least, I hope she did."

"But she was planning to sell?"

Connie drew a breath, stalling to figure out how to deliver the truth in the nicest possible way. "I think so, but you have to understand that she's gone through a lot and—"

Ben picked up a hammer and brought it down hard on the bench, sending shudders through the metal. "And so have we! My mom left me when I was eight, your dad died when you were twelve. We both had to pick up the pieces."

"I've got you, but she doesn't have anyone."

Ben's anger fell away. He tossed down the hammer and came to her. "You have me," he said softly, "and Ariel has you. But tell me, Connie, who do I have?"

This close to her, Ben's shirt pattern seemed extra-magnified, the lines of blue, green and gray intersecting straight and solid. "There is no one else, Connie. There never has been. It's lonely not to have the only one you love."

The pattern wavered before her eyes. She was breaking his heart, breaking her own, and the only right thing she could do was let it go on breaking until her redemption list was done.

"I have this crazy idea that you still love me," he said, "so you not choosing me is one thing, but choosing someone else, choosing someone who pulls you down, that's another. Fix your mistakes. Not other people's, or else you'll never be ready for me."

His way of saying she couldn't ever get Ariel and Miranda off the list.

"I know you think I'm being tough on Ariel," he went on. "We can both agree that she's gone through stuff we can't imagine. Even when you were at your worst, Connie, it didn't hold a candle to the situations she's waded through. Stuff like that will change a person. It has to. And you can want to help her. I'm not faulting you for that. And she can want help. And I'm not faulting her for that. All I'm saying is that maybe at this point in your life you have enough problems."

Her head dropped to his chest. "Yeah," she whispered. "Yeah."

His right hand slid from her shoulder and came around the back of her neck, warm and oh-so-good. Immediately it set to work, massaging the cords just as he used to do. "I don't want you to feel bad, but you already had plans. Good plans. Like your education. You passed your CPR course a few months ago. What are you planning to do with it?"

Well, since he could see that she was an unfit guardian, he might as well as learn that she was a pitiful careerist, too.

"Do you know why I was even on my way to see the vice principal?" Good thing his chest muffled her voice because she didn't trust herself to be coherent. "Sure, it was to follow up with Lakers-on-the-Go, but the real reason is that I was bored to absolute tears doing my homework for nursing. I didn't understand it and I didn't want to understand it. So, yes, I can save someone if they swallowed a bottle cap, but beyond that, this upgrading doesn't seem worth it."

"Living life well is worth it, Connie."

"Yes, but I don't know what that life is, okay?" This subject was too painful, too close to the truth. "What about you? It's not as if you're a millionaire. What are your ambitions?"

His lips pressed against her bent head. "My ambition is you, Connie. Creating a worthwhile life for you that includes me."

She couldn't help it. She drew back her head and erupted with a frustrated cry. "Ben, you always say the nicest things. It drives me absolutely crazy."

"I was thinking that I was saying some pretty tough things tonight. About you. About Ariel." He tugged on her ring finger. "About us."

She stepped back but her hands were somehow captured in his. "Tough but true." She pulled free a hand and poked him in his chest. "Like you."

He caught her hand and kissed it, glove and all.

Her heart tripped and tumbled. "Ben—"

"Would you rather I kiss you somewhere else?"

"No!"

"Liar."

"I'm not lying."

"You going to talk to Ariel tomorrow? About living somewhere else?"

She blinked at his subject switch. "Ben..."

"Because if you don't, I will come over and kiss you like you haven't been kissed in five years."

He would, too. Previous experience had proven he could kiss the spine right out of her, leave her in a pulpy heap, her brain mush, susceptible to all kinds of suggestions—like putting on a big, beautiful ring. But she wasn't letting herself take the easy way out anymore. Even if she spent the rest of her life striking the names off her list.

She drew what little breath she had left. "Tomorrow. I will talk to her. But I won't make any promises that you're going to like the outcome."

THE HEADBOARD WAS coming together. The wheels were inset and now he just had to think about the number of leaves he wanted. The largest in the center probably and then—

Someone pounded on the door. Likely Seth with one more wedding thing Ben must do right away or the world as we know it would implode. Except why didn't he walk right in as he usually did?

"Come in!"

It was Ariel in black and full scowl. No earbuds.

He read his phone clock. "It's one thirty. You're skipping."

"I have a spare."

"No, you don't." He didn't know one way or another, but given Ariel's nature, it was safe to assume.

"When else am I supposed to talk to you?"

She was skipping, then. "Do we have anything to talk about?"

Maybe up to seven leaves, but only if each had meaning…

"You might not have anything to say to me but I've got plenty to say to you."

Ben, his back still turned to her, rolled his eyes. Yes, no doubt.

The leaves could match the tree. Should he make them life-size?

"Auntie Connie admitted you are behind her talking to me about going into the system. You're not going to get rid of me so easy."

He'd make them life-size, keep them true to life.

"Are you listening to me?" she demanded. "Dad."

What? He spun around.

"Now I've got your attention."

"What are you talking about?"

"You know. My mom told me."

Ben wasn't falling for her goading. He turned back to his work.

"She told me before she died that you were my father."

Ben forced himself to breathe normally. To school his features so they didn't betray his heart misfiring. Only then did he face her. "Ariel. Your mother told Connie that she wasn't sure who the father was. If she wasn't sure sixteen years ago, why did she change her story during her last days?"

"She cleaned herself up, began remembering things she'd forgotten."

"Was she also on prescription drugs toward the end, too? Maybe making connections that weren't ever there?"

Ariel crossed her arms, which meant that he'd hit the nail on the head. "You're not denying that you could be the father."

Ariel wasn't stupid, and for all her faults, Miranda hadn't been, either. More the tragedy. "Then hear me now. I'm not your father."

"Because you know it for a fact or because you hope I'm not?"

"Both."

Her arms crossed tighter. "I want a paternity test."

The girl was crazy. "That's nice. You're not getting it from me."

"If you're so sure I'm not your daughter, then it shouldn't be a problem."

"I'm not going to all the expense of a paternity test when you can listen to me for free."

"The test is two hundred bucks. I already checked."

"Two hundred bucks too much."

"I'll tell Auntie Connie if you don't."

"Tell her what? That you think that I'm your father based on the ramblings of your crackhead mother on her deathbed?"

Ariel's jaw worked. "That was mean."

It was. The Miranda Effect flaring up again. "You're right. I am sorry." His second apology already to her.

Her arms dropped to her sides, she scuffed the sawdust on the floor. "Yeah, well, whatever."

He blew out every air particle from his lungs and tried again to convince her, slowly, logically. "You may not have met your father but you were very familiar with your mother. Was she capable of manufacturing a story? Did she ever lie to you?"

The whites of Ariel's eyes widened in anger, or pain. "Shut up about my mother. At least she was there for me, unlike you."

Ben focused on keeping his voice even. "I wasn't there because I didn't need to be. For the last time, I'm not your father."

"Then prove it. I'll even pay for the test."

Would she stop going around in circles? "I am not taking it because that means admitting to the remotest chance that I'm your father. Which I am not."

"You never...did it with my mother?"

"I never did." He was surprised at the smoothness of his lie.

"I don't believe you," she said. "I still want the test. But I'm willing to compromise."

This ought to be good.

"You talk to Auntie Connie. Say you've changed your mind and you want me to stay. In return, I won't tell her about Mom and you."

Connie had warned he might not like the outcome. "She's agreed to let you stay?"

"She has."

"Then what's it to you if I put my stamp of approval on what's between you and her?"

Ariel gave the sawdust another good scuffing. "Life's whole lot easier if she's not worried you're mad at her."

"I'm not mad at her."

"Yeah, well, Auntie Connie always was about trying to make everybody happy."

"That never works out."

"She'd feel happier if you were behind her."

"She say that?"

Scuff. "Does she need to?"

True. "You're not going to push for a paternity test because you don't want Connie to have to choose between the two of us?"

"Basically."

"Because I can tell you right now, she'd pick you. You hold all the cards, Ariel."

Up came her chin. "And it's my business if I want to play them."

Her mother had forced Connie to choose five years ago with disastrous results for Ariel. Today Ariel was creating a way for Connie to have them both.

Who was he to stand in the way? Last night, for the first time in three years, they'd touched. He'd carried the feel of her head against his chest, the warmth of her neck on his hand, the softness of her hair on his lips, carried the actual touch and smell of her to his bed last night. He was not going to have it torn from him again.

"Fine," he said, "I agree to your deal."

Ten minutes after starting her shift, the roughest, toughest, meanest dude Spirit Lake had ever manufactured walked in the doors of Smooth Sailing. Trevor McCready's brother swung himself up on a bar stool and inclined his head to Connie. She walked over, her heart sinking into her stomach. After the morning she'd had with Ariel, she wasn't ready for this.

"Hello, McCready," she said. "What's your first name?" He didn't blink. She'd always wondered what the first name of Trevor's brother was, but neither he nor Trevor had ever coughed it up. Trevor was always Trevor, and McCready, it seemed, was always McCready. She sighed. "What can I do for you?"

"We need to talk."

"Now?"

"I don't make appointments." He could talk without moving his lips.

Dizzy came up behind her. "Things won't be busy for another half hour or so. You go. I can cover." Dizzy nodded at McCready, and he regarded her without blinking, without moving a muscle. It was another of his unusual abilities to be so large and yet not move. He made a rock look like a vibrating ball of frenzy.

Outside, McCready crossed the street, leaving Connie little choice but to follow. He cut straight down the long slope by the promenade and stood in an area of melting snow and soggy grass and stared out over the lake. The lake was at its worst right now. In early spring, the water appeared frozen, but the ice had started to weaken—a white, pockmarked plain. Boring and deadly.

His gaze still on the expanse of the lake, he said, "You ever thought of getting back together with Trevor?"

It was a good thing he couldn't see her face because she was pretty sure she couldn't hide her sheer incredulity.

"I think that ship has sailed," Connie said with what she hoped was the right amount of blandness and finality.

McCready grunted. "My brother never knew an opportunity when he saw it."

Agreeing with him meant she was insulting his brother, which might not go over well. Connie settled on, "I guess we all make mistakes."

"You making one now?"

The big man was at last getting to the point. "I'm not dealing, if that's what you're wondering. I was just saying that to make the kid I'm taking care of steer clear of Trevor." Connie picked her way through the next bit to make sure that she didn't offend McCready. "The kid's mother was an addict out in Vancouver. Sold, too. I don't want the same end for her."

McCready turned his head just enough for him to see her from the corner of his eye. "Trevor let on who he's working for?"

Connie forgot not to sound surprised. "I assumed he was working for you. I acted as if I was working for you, too, but I didn't mention your name. The less the kid knows, the better."

McCready made a clicking noise with his teeth. Connie remembered that sound from when she'd met with him last summer and he'd wanted to know where his brother was. She'd told him—she did have some self-preservation instincts. She'd felt sorry for McCready having to discipline his brother, according to the rules of the brotherhood.

"Nope. No one with me deals where kids work and play. No schools, no playgrounds. No lake."

Which meant that Trevor wasn't working for his brother, and his brother's kind didn't tolerate free agents. Once again, Trevor was heading for trouble, and once again Connie felt for McCready, who had the unenviable job of getting Trevor back in line.

McCready's eyes shifted to a spot behind her. "You know why Ben Carruthers is staring at us?"

Connie glanced over her shoulder. Sure enough, Ben was sitting on a park bench at the top of the slope, not even pretending to look away.

Ben, please leave.

Instead he stood and began his own slippery descent to them. Connie bugged her eyes out at him, willing him to stop, stop, stop. He kept coming until he'd slung his arm around her shoulders and faced McCready.

"Hello," Ben said. "I'm Ben Carruthers."

McCready nodded, dipped his chin at Connie and walked off.

"Good," Ben said, low enough for McCready not to hear, but there was no guarantee that he hadn't, either. Leastways, McCready kept moving.

Connie whirled out of the curve of his arm.

"What were you thinking?" she hissed. "He can snap your neck."

"I kinda doubt he would do that right here and now."

"No, but he's a bit touchy. You coming down here and doing that alpha-male thing makes him think that you're just one more problem he's going to have to deal with. Besides, it's just not your business."

Ben shrugged. "Still."

That was his answer when he wasn't going to change his mind and he wasn't going to argue it, either. "What does he want with you, Connie?"

It was on the tip of her tongue to tell him not to get involved, but hadn't she promised to keep him in the loop about Trevor? "He wanted to make sure I wasn't dealing drugs independent of him. That's not allowed in Spirit Lake."

Ben watched as McCready got into his beater of a truck. "Do the police know about him?"

"I'm sure he has a deal with them."

"Our own are corrupt?"

Connie's feet were cold in her bar boots, her toes frozen through the thin faux leather. "No! It's just that… Look, I need to get back to work before Dizzy loses all patience with me." She didn't wait for his answer but slip-slid her way up to the promenade, Ben following.

Before she crossed to the restaurant, Ben touched her arm. "Ariel came by my workshop this afternoon."

"What did she want? Wait. This afternoon? She skipped school."

"It was during her spare," Ben said. "Look, she was pretty upset about me encouraging you to put her into the system."

"That's putting it mildly. How about a smashed coffeemaker and a boot hole in the new drywall?"

Ben winced. "I'll fix it."

"The drywall, yes. The coffeemaker, no. Frankly, the death of My Maker was the one good thing to come out of our conversation."

Ben's frowned deepened. "The thing is, she made some good points. It got me thinking that—that I was wrong. About her. About you."

Connie stared. "Are you saying that you changed your mind? That you want her to stay with me? Despite who she is? Who I am?"

Ben jerked his head in what she guessed

was a nod, though it looked more like he'd got an invisible slap. He clearly found it hard to admit he'd been wrong, probably because he was always right.

"What exactly did she say that changed your mind?"

Ben gazed out at the lake. At his truck. At Smooth Sailing. "She asked not to be judged by her mother's standards. She asked for a second chance. She asked for…a family."

Wow. "She said all that?"

"Not in so many words."

Trust Ben to see through the words of an angry teenager—and Ariel would've come on strong—to the hurt beneath them. Connie couldn't help herself. She wrapped her arms around his neck and gave him a hard hug. "Thank you," she whispered against his ear. "Thank you for believing in her. In us."

His arms came around her waist, tightened, then fell away. "Just—just trying to do the right thing, is all."

He was the right thing. Ariel had come to Ben because she knew that, too. Hadn't she practically ordered Connie to marry Ben? The girl had good instincts. Because any guy who could own up to his mistakes was a keeper.

She tugged on his hand. "Come on in. I'll get you nachos."

He hesitated and she gave another tug. "Come on. It's a celebration. We all get a second chance. Thanks to you." She leaned in. "Pretty please with no olives on top?"

He cracked a smile and she knew she had him. This time when she tugged on his hand, he came.

CHAPTER EIGHT

STANDING BESIDE SETH at the front of the church, Ben watched the woman he wanted for his bride walk down the aisle toward him. She'd explained several times during the past couple of months what she was wearing and why, but he hadn't paid much attention. Now, as she came along in this light blue, delicate, sleeveless dress, the form hugging her curves and her long legs stepping free from the gauzy curtains of her skirt to flash her long vine-y tattoo, her bare feet strapped to silver stilettos, her blond hair gleaming and abundant, he wished he'd listened so he could have trained himself to take full breaths.

Alexi, the star of the day, followed behind on Mel's arm.

Ben did pull himself together by the time they all faced the pastor, if only because he didn't want to blow his role as best man when he fully intended his position with Seth to be reversed next year, if not before.

Seth spoke his vows by heart, though it didn't help that Connie was mouthing them, too. Alexi's face melted under the words.

How was he ever going to top that? Didn't matter, so long as Connie said "yes" at the end.

When Ben's best friend and his new wife were presented to the assembly amid applause, his own heart was fit to burst from happiness for Seth and grief because it wasn't him.

A hand slipped into his. Connie's. She wasn't looking at him but gathering Alexi's kids around her to join the procession, her other hand in the clutches of four-year-old crowd-shy Callie. To everyone there, the joined hands must have seemed planned, part of "the look" of the wedding day. Ben stuck with the program and held her hand right out to the noisy receiving line, where Connie remained at his side in the same beautiful, radiant way that Alexi was beside Seth.

He would hope.

He would ignore Ariel who, in a black skirt and boots, was the only one there who didn't smile once.

He would not dwell on outcomes, especially as he shook hands with Luke and Derek and hugged their wives, who all appeared, except for Lindsay, the unsuspecting wife of Derek, to be playing their parts, too.

Today belonged to Seth and Alexi, but that didn't mean he and Connie couldn't find their own happiness, too.

CONNIE COULDN'T REMEMBER feeling happier. Because Alexi looked sen-sa-tion-al—dress, hair, makeup, all glammed to the max. Because Seth rocked the vows and sorta smiled over at her after saying them. Because the whole ceremony had gone off without a hitch, despite a frantic morning race to get a bride, four kids and a church ready, not to mention herself.

Because of Ben, who gazed at her as if she was the bride.

Her hand had slid into his of its own free will, and honestly, how could she pull away without it looking awkward? Even when they finally released hands for the receiving line, his suited sleeve brushed her bare arm, and then again when they rode together in the back of the limo. His fingers touched hers as they passed off flowers, phones, envelopes and granola bars. Simple, ordinary gestures that made her feel both chosen and at home.

Now with the reception complete, dishes cleared away and speeches made, the DJ began the first dance. Connie was on the edge of her seat. For the past two weeks, she had taken Alexi's part with her brother, coaching him through the steps. He had danced like his feet were cement blocks, but perhaps the secret lay in his partner. Because right now, with Alexi, Seth was a master.

Ben stepped behind her chair. "Time to join them."

A few guests at the assembled tables were looking their way. Lindsay, grinning, was one of them. "No, they dance the whole thing alone," Connie muttered through her own grin. "Tradition."

Ben didn't budge. "Seth's orders. He did not want everyone watching him trip over himself and Alexi's dress. He told me to get us out there as fast as possible."

"He's doing fine. Awesome, actu—" Her chair was tugged backward. "All right, all right. If that's what he wants."

As Ben's arm came around her waist on the dance floor, she caught sight of Seth's surprised expression. "Uh, Ben, I don't think this is what he wanted."

He drew her to within a finger's width of his chest. "Oh. I might have misunderstood."

Connie glanced back at Seth to communicate a nonverbal apology, but her brother's head was already bent to Alexi. "That was sneaky, Ben."

"Yep." He picked up the pace and Connie found her feet working on their own. She remembered she and Ben had found places to go dancing, teaching each other how to two-step and polka from videos. They'd gotten good enough to dance with each other and no one else. Not that she'd wanted anyone else.

Ben led her in a slow spin around the perimeter, a revolving moon around the sun of Seth and Alexi, their moves sending up a couple of wolf whistles and a smattering of applause. Lindsay gave a hoot and turned to Derek, just like in the wedding photo. Except this Derek, a decade later, was downing a beer. *C'mon, do the right thing*, Connie silently begged him.

Seth beckoned to the guests, and at once the four kids and Mel streamed onto the floor along with a few other couples and kids, including Luke and Shari.

Ben's lips brushed her ear. "You remember the first time we danced in public?"

"Yes. At Westerner Days."

"Nope. Your graduation, remember?"

Oh, crud, yes. The memory nearly tripped her, but Ben's hand and footwork got them back on track. He slowed their steps, which was fine as more couples drifted onto the dance floor.

Her mother had insisted Ben be her grad date. Connie had argued and fumed, ranted and raved, because the only reason her mom wanted Ben was so she could have someone checking up on Connie during the bush party that always followed graduation. Her mother had told her that if Ben wasn't her date, she wasn't paying a single penny toward her grad night, and so, because Connie had attached a hefty price tag to the event, she relented.

"I don't think I've ever said sorry to anyone as much as I did to you during that one dance," he said now.

She'd forgotten about that funny part of the grad. She grinned. "Three minutes and three rips in the dress. It's why this one is shorter," she added.

"That's appreciated. You're just as beautiful in this dress as you were in that one. More actually." There was a catch in his voice.

She forced herself to focus outside their little bubble.

She wished she hadn't. Derek's eyes were locked onto Shari—who was dancing in Luke's arms—with a look of raw, desperate love. Connie could see it from the dance floor. It must have been like a hot explosion to Lindsay, who stared at her husband in horrifying realization.

Connie moaned.

Ben pulled back. "What's the matter?"

"Derek. Lindsay."

Ben glanced at the couple, and for the first time in years, she heard him curse.

"Kinda ruins the mood, doesn't it?" she murmured.

"I hope not," he said, and pulled her tight to him. She let him because, on this of all days, she wanted more than just Seth and Alexi to have a happily-ever-after.

TEN THIRTY FOUND four-year-old Callie slumped over Ben's shoulders in a dead sleep and Connie herding the other three kids, who were practically sleepwalking across the parking lot to bed.

Bed tonight was inside an RV that Mel had rented for the occasion. Earlier, it had acted as a dressing room and rest spot, and now the kids could roll into beds nearby without anyone having to drive. It was ingenious and thoughtful and utterly Mel-onish. Connie was anticipating a few calm minutes in the RV before diving back into the loud hall. And yes, maybe a quick, quiet moment with Ben.

She unlatched the RV door and stepped aside to let the rest of the kids enter first, leading with seven-year-old Amy. The girl's scream yanked Connie up the stairs with Ben right behind. A woman's voice called out.

"It's okay, honey. I'm Connie's friend."

Uh-oh. Lindsay. Had the RV been left unlocked? Climbing inside, Connie made out Lindsay's low-lit figure at the dining table.

"Hey, Linds. Ben and I were just putting the kids down for the night."

"Okay," Lindsay said, but didn't move.

"C'mon, kids," Ben said, "beds and pajamas."

"I'll be right back," Connie whispered to Lindsay, and followed Ben to the bedroom at the back.

"No," he said over his Callie-free shoulder. "Stay with Lindsay. I'll handle this."

"I have to put Callie into her pajamas."

"Amy can help."

A reasonable solution, which left Connie no choice but to be a friend to Lindsay who still hadn't moved. Maybe nothing was bothering her. Maybe she just wanted a break from the events and the RV seemed like the natural, warm place to go.

"You knew about Derek and Shari, didn't you?"

No such luck. "Yeah, I did." Connie flicked on a light switch. Lindsay clapped her hands over her reddened eyes.

"Oh, sorry. Wasn't thinking. Do you want a water? Something stronger?"

Lindsay shook her head.

"Something hot? I can make tea." Why did she say that? How had tea ever helped a heartache?

"No. Thank you."

Which left Connie with no option but to sit across from Lindsay.

"When we talked about me and Shari in my office a couple of months back, you knew then. You didn't give me straight answers and that's not like you. Don't deny it. I've been sitting here for two hours, going over and over our conversation."

Connie dodged Lindsay's main point and

clung to a detail. “Two hours? You told me that—”

“No, I told Derek that the babysitter was sick, a lie, so I could get out of there. He’ll stay, because why come home with me?” Her words came out slow and hollow.

“You confronted him?”

“I told him that I knew about him and Shari, but that’s it. Not exactly the time or place.”

Deeper in the RV came soft thumps and mutterings of the kids as they figured out their sleep arrangements. Would Ben find all their pajamas?

“Why did Derek do it?” Lindsay’s dress rustled like wind in a bush as she slumped forward. “Is it because I’m fat?”

“What? No. Here, I’m making tea.” Connie popped to her feet and pumped water into the kettle, then set it alight on the stove. The blue flame glowed an eerie comfort. “You’ve had two kids, Lindsay, you can’t expect your weight—”

“Shari had three, and look at her. Not a pound heavier. I’ve gone up three sizes. Three! Can you blame him?”

“Yes, I can,” Connie said truthfully. “Cheating is no excuse.”

Lindsay's voice broke. "Then tell me, Connie, why? You did it. With Ben. Why?"

Connie froze, her ears—her every cell—tuned to the movements at the back of the RV. *Please, please, Ben, don't hear that. Please.* "I had...excuses, too."

Lindsay snorted, a wet sound of tears and shaky breathing. "Excuses? Is that all there is? No deeper meaning? Does he—he love her? Did he tell you that?"

"Uh, Lindsay, there is something you should probably know."

Lindsay looked at Connie, her eyes wide and wet, forehead rippled with hurt.

In a burst, Connie said, "Luke learned Shari was having an affair because she wanted a divorce. He and Derek talked about it over at Smooth Sailing. He just didn't realize that she was having an affair with Derek."

There was a long silence, a huge well of silence that Connie had no idea how to fill. Lindsay finally let drop two words. "I see."

"The thing is, I think the affair is over. Luke said a few weeks back that he and Shari were going to try to rebuild their marriage over the next few months, so what you saw today might be about the past and not what's going on today."

"They may have moved on, but Derek hasn't," Lindsay summed up.

Connie couldn't argue. A broken heart wasn't healed through more lies. "I'm sorry. I tried to tell you at your office after the Valentine's Day dinner, but I couldn't bring myself to do it. I hoped it would work out, and then when I found out that the affair was over, it seemed it had. I am sorry."

If Lindsay had slapped her across the face Connie would've understood. Instead, Lindsay did a wavy sort of shrug and smile. "It's okay, Connie. It's not your responsibility to solve everybody's problems."

Wow. She was forgiven. If only the names on the list were as easy to obtain forgiveness from.

"I don't want to look at him," Lindsay blurted. "I don't even want to be in the same house—why do you think I'm here?"

The kettle whistling saved Connie from answering. While she made tea, she fought with herself. She knew a thing or two about people escaping from their problems. After she and Ben had broken up, he'd disappeared for seventeen days. No one had any idea where he'd gone. After day nine, Seth had contacted Paul at the police department. Paul hadn't instigated a search because Ben was an adult, and a man whose girlfriend had dumped him.

When Ben had returned, he'd been thinner, quieter. To this day, nobody knew where he'd gone. Connie had learned all this through word-of-mouth because he'd never come to her. She'd never had to witness how much she'd hurt Ben. Sitting now with Lindsay, it hit her. Left her breathless at the sheer breadth and audacity of her cruelty.

"I am so sorry, Lindsay," Connie said again, bringing the mugs of tea over. "I can't understand how much Derek has hurt you. I do understand that whatever his reason, the fact that now he knows that he has hurt you and still doesn't come to you, that's doubly cruel."

Connie could still remember the breathless quality of Ben's one phone conversation with her. To confirm with her what he'd seen. The long silence, the extended breaths, like he was coming up for air after diving deep with each of his questions, with each of her answers.

"What should I do?" Lindsay whispered. "Where do I go?"

Ben had run away, but Lindsay with her two kids couldn't. From her purse, Connie fished out her house keys. She made a plan as she talked. "Here. My house keys. Crash on my bed. Pajamas are in the top drawer of the dresser. I've got a spare toothbrush somewhere in the bathroom drawers. Ariel might wake up." Connie had agreed to let her go to the house after an entire day of her sullenness. Ben had driven her back not an hour ago. "I'll send her a text saying that it's okay. I will tell Derek that you're not coming home tonight, and that he needs to be home with the kids."

Lindsay didn't take the keys right away, and when she did, her fingers were ice-cold.

Just then there were shouts from outside. The floor of the RV shook as Ben shot past. "Luke and Derek. Fighting."

OUTSIDE IN THE parking lot, Luke and Derek were facing off. As Connie wove between the vehicles toward them, Lindsay in tow behind her, she spotted Shari nearby between two cars, shivering in her dress. Ben slowed his steps as he approached his buddies and leaned against a parked SUV.

Luke was in his suit jacket, collar unbuttoned but solid on his feet. Derek had no suit jacket, a beer bottle in hand, and was unsteady on his feet. Connie could have knocked him over with a push of her finger.

Still, he was stupid enough to argue with his best friend and the husband of the woman he had cheated with. "You always have to have everything your way, don't you, Luke? You can't stand losing, can you?"

"Why don't you go home?" Luke said. A good question.

"How can I? No vehicle. Lindsay took it." Derek clearly hadn't seen his wife, and in fairness it was dark except for what light came from a couple of streetlights.

"Then where were you planning to go with Shari if you didn't have a vehicle?" Luke said, his voice low and way too calm. It was never a good idea to reason with someone who was drunk, especially one you were angry with. Connie glanced at the front doors. *Stay away, Seth.*

"He just wanted to talk," Shari said.

Luke kept his eyes on Derek. "Shari, enough. This is between friends." The last word was a low hiss.

Luke and Derek were heading for a fight. Connie started toward Ben. Her movement must have caught Derek's eye.

"Hey, that you, Connie? Yeah, you. Hey,

can I join your club? What is it? Cheaters-on-the-Go? I'm good for it. I got a witness, eh, Shari? You and me. Yeah, we can sponsor each other. Whaddaya think?"

Shari's opinion on the matter was never heard because Luke let fly with a hard right. Derek fell onto the hood of a nearby car. Beside Connie, Lindsay gasped. Connie glanced over at Ben, who hadn't moved from his comfortable spot against a SUV. Shari gave a little shriek and rushed to restrain Luke. Not a good idea.

He whirled on her. "What? You don't think he deserved that? You don't want me to hurt him? Whose side are you on?"

Luke made for Derek again. Thankfully Ben stepped between the two men. He lifted Derek by the shoulders off the hood.

"Let me get him out of your sight, Luke," Ben said, and then gave Derek a shake. "Derek. Your keys. Give them to me."

Derek tried to shake off Ben, looking like a blind guy beating off a buzzing insect. "I don't need to—"

Lindsay stepped forward. "Here, take mine." With shaking fingers, she unwound a key from her chain and handed it to Ben. She and Derek avoided eye contact. Lindsay spun away and ran. Connie let her go and darted to help Ben swing open the passenger-side door of Derek's SUV. Together they shoved the wasted Derek into the passenger seat.

Ben moved to Luke's side, put a hand on his shoulder and said so low that only Connie standing close could hear. "I know where you're at. Let me put some distance between the two of you. Okay?"

Yes, unfortunately, Ben would know.

Luke gave a quick nod.

Ben was reversing Derek's vehicle when Connie suddenly remembered something Lindsay had said and chased after him. He stopped. "Derek and Lindsay's babysitter. You might need to drive her home. Or better yet, maybe ask if she can stay over because Derek will be in no shape tomorrow morning. Lindsay is crashing at the house for the night."

"I heard."

And from the emotion in his eyes, she realized he'd heard more through the thin, particle board walls of the RV than just the conversation about the babysitter.

"Ben, I—"

He slowly reversed the SUV. "I'll see you back here."

She turned to find Luke and Shari staring at her. Probably because otherwise they might have to acknowledge each other.

Connie searched her brain for anything remotely fitting to say. "I'm going to check on the kids."

By the time she got them settled, Luke and Shari had long cleared out.

Seth met her at the door. "I was coming to find you and Ben."

"He's just driving Derek home."

"Yeah, Derek was knocking one back every time I saw him tonight. Not like him."

"Didn't Alexi tell you?"

Seth frowned.

Shoot, what was she doing, on their wedding day, making it seem as if there were secrets between the bride and groom? She rushed on, "Oh, never mind. I mean, ask Alexi. Look, it's not important for you to worry about on your wedding day, okay? Trust me."

Seth's frown deepened into skepticism.

"Fair enough. Just ask Alexi or Ben about it, but don't do it tonight, okay? Please."

Alexi opened the doors to the hall, still beautiful after all these hours. Seth regarded his wife. "Yeah, not tonight."

Then he gave Connie something she couldn't remember getting from him in years. A smile. A soft, conspiratorial smile like when they were kids and had found a way to get out of trouble. Or into it.

Seth took his bride's hand and they stepped into the hall. Alexi glanced over her shoulder. "Are the kids okay?"

Connie gave a little wave. "Yep. All good. Don't you worry about a thing."

As Seth and Alexi moved away, Connie let out a long, pent-up breath. If there was one good thing to have come from this day, it was that she had given Seth a string of beautiful memories. Time to get out her pencil sharpener.

"GET DEREK HOME SAFELY?"

Connie's question came at half-past three in the morning as she and Ben walked across the now-empty parking lot to the RV. All Ben wanted to do right now was fall flat on his back and snore his face off.

"I got him home," he said, not wanting to commit to the "safely" part because it probably hadn't been entirely safe to pitch the cheating jerk over the arm of the couch and leave him there.

Where a streetlight cut an orangey chunk from the dark parking lot, Connie placed her hand on his arm and tugged him to a stop. "Ben, after all that's happened today, especially with Luke and Derek, I think you should know something."

It couldn't be good because she was gnawing on her lip. "When I was talking with Lindsay, it came up. About you and me, about how I had cheated on you. She remembered that."

Ben didn't need the reminder. Somehow the whole town had learned what had happened, and when he returned from his trip to hell and back, all his buddies had wanted to take him out for a beer and bad-mouth the woman he still loved.

"I didn't realize until talking to her how humiliating it must have been for you that your friends knew the reason behind us splitting up. I didn't say a word, you have to believe that, but I can see how it must've hurt."

She bowed her head, her blond hair taking on a weird brassy glow under the streetlight. "The thing is, what you saw with me and the other guy was nothing. Nothing happened between us. I—I didn't ever cheat on you."

He'd promised himself that he would never

give up on her again. No matter what. Until right now, when he wanted to walk away fast and far. Or crawl away. That anybody had been preferable to him was cruel enough. But nobody? "Why?"

She lifted her head, frowning. "I thought you'd be relieved that there was nothing behind what everyone said, even though—even though I'd not stopped the rumors."

"Like I'd care what other people thought. I don't get why you made it all up."

"Because there was no other way."

"No other way? Maybe try telling me you wanted out? I mean, what kind of person pretends to cheat?"

"Someone," she said softly but with no hesitation, "whose boyfriend won't take 'no' for an answer."

Yes, he remembered her clutching his shirt-front, begging him to leave her, but always when she was drunk and not in her right mind. "Are you saying that the drinking, the partying…it was deliberate? To get rid of me?" It couldn't be.

Her face twisted, the same beautiful face that had smiled at him in the church, that had looked so…hopeful. "Some," she whispered. "Some of it was me wanting out. Some of it was you not letting me out. I didn't know what else to do. Even when I was bad, bad, bad, you behaved like I was something else entirely. You could never see me for who I really was."

"You could never see yourself for who you really *are*," he replied. She was shivering without a coat. He shrugged off his suit jacket and reached out to put it around her shoulders.

She backhanded the jacket to the ground. "This! This is what I'm talking about. Me being cold is my problem. I could've put on a coat but I didn't, so how about you let me suffer the consequences? If I was so stupid as to drink all those years ago why wouldn't you just kick my butt to the curb? Why did you go out and buy a freaking engagement ring?"

His jacket lay flat on the ground with twisted sleeves. He bent and picked it up. "Because I loved you. I still—"

Connie screamed, a piercing cry in the still night. "So what? I love you, too. I love you, I love you, I love you." She whirled away and strode off, her stiletto heels clacking on the asphalt, then suddenly she spun back. "But that doesn't mean I want to be with you. Or marry you. Right now, actually, it means the exact opposite."

Ben didn't know what to do. The love of his life had just confessed her love for him and yet—yet she didn't want to be with him. Had explained, in fact, that he had driven her to drink in his blind refusal to give her the freedom she had pleaded for.

He slipped on the jacket. A tiny rock was caught in the shoulder fabric. "Why," he said, shaking the jacket shoulder, "didn't you pack up and go? You lived in my house. Why didn't you leave me?"

She pressed her fingers to her temples. "Would you have let me go, Ben? Would you have left me alone? Or would you have chased me, wanting to know how to make it better?"

He would have come for her. Met with her at her work. Like he did now. Insisted he drive her home. Like now. Told her again he loved her and wanted her back. Like now. The tiny rock was biting into his skin. He dropped his hands from the lapels.

She understood his silence, as she'd understood them all. "Yeah, exactly. The only way out was to replace you. What other choice did I have?"

He didn't answer. He had turned her into

a cheater. A fake cheater, as it happened, but the effect had been the same. She had been shamed before her family, her friends, before an entire gossipy community. All because he believed he couldn't live without her.

Still couldn't, really.

He was no better than a stalker.

The ring was a thing of desperation, not love.

He was sick and broken. Not her.

"Okay," he whispered, "okay. I understand." Then, his lips and heart barely moving, he gave her what he could. "I withdraw my offer of marriage."

CHAPTER NINE

SLEEP FOR CONNIE had been more like getting punched out. Now she was coming to, ringed by four young faces firing questions at her head. Four shining examples of why singlehood was the good life.

The original plan—conceived a week ago when she'd been upright, in a quiet kitchen and with a coffee in hand—had been for her and the kids to have breakfast in the RV as a kind of campout. And because Ben was supposed to have crashed with her and the kids, he would've been there to help.

Except he'd gone back to his place last night.

She'd agreed that was for the best.

She needed coffee. A whole plantation of it.

Which, after enlisting the kids to hunt, she discovered she'd forgotten to pack.

"You're still in your dress, Auntie Connie," Callie noted.

"It looks like a piece of wrinkled sky," Bryn said. Kinda poetic for a nine-year-old.

She'd have to settle for the tea she'd made for Lindsay last night. Last night when—

She slammed the cupboard door on the tea. "Change of plan. We're driving to my house to get me some coffee before I eat you all for breakfast."

"We're going to drive the RV?"

"Do we wear seat belts?"

"Can we open the windows?"

"Do you know how to drive this?"

Connie navigated the house on wheels through the quiet Sunday streets, pulling it to a stuttering stop behind a strange car parked outside the house.

Oh, right, Lindsay. Ben would've given Lindsay her car key after dropping Derek off. "Okay, kids," she said, standing like a tour guide to face them. "Remember Lindsay from the RV last night? She stayed here at the house. Now, she might be up or she might be asleep. Whichever, just let her be."

"Do we say 'hello'?"

"Why is she at your house?"

"Is she homeless?"

"What's for breakfast?"

"Will Ariel be up?"

In answer to the last question: Connie hoped not. With the kids, Ariel was like a spooked cat. She disappeared at the first sight of them, not surfacing until all was quiet. With any luck, both Lindsay and Ariel were sleeping—or, after the kids broke loose inside, at least pretending to sleep.

Luck turned out to be manic-depressive. On the upside, there was the soul-soothing, smell of fresh coffee, which she rushed to get to in the kitchen. On the downside, in the kitchen was Ariel scowling at Lindsay for the apparent crime of making small talk.

"Connie!" Lindsay said in clear relief. At the influx of kids, Ariel hightailed it out of there.

The kitchen became a swarm of slamming cupboard doors, the fridge opening and shutting more than it had in months, the clatter of a frying pan and pots, and because Bryn insisted, the whirr of a popcorn machine, which had been left behind when the kids had lived there months ago.

Lindsay departed in the middle of it all, with a wave and a quick goodbye, deleting any chance for Connie to check in with her. Not that Connie could've done anything with the kids about.

It was a full hour before she'd scraped together a meal and could retreat to her room to change out of her maid-of-honor outfit. She'd never been so glad to get out of a piece of clothing before. It was dirty and reeking of last night.

She flung the dress on her bed, the blue sky now just a wrinkled rag. Instantly she picked it up, smoothed it, carried it to a safe place in the closet. It had been a beautiful day. She had given Seth and Alexi and the kids a day out of a magazine. The pictures would prove it. Pictures of her in this dress with them all.

How many would show Ben beside her?

And like Lindsay's with Derek, how many of them would be false?

No. Nothing with Ben had been faked. At least, on her part.

She still wanted him to stay away from her for both of their sakes. This time, though, it was a conscious, well-thought-out decision based on her worthy ambition to repair the damage of her poor life choices.

So if she'd gotten what she wanted, why did she feel so…robbed?

The door handle twisted down and Connie snatched Ben's shirt around her. A small, dark face appeared. "Callie. Honestly. I'm dressing, okay?"

"What are you going to wear?"

Fashion was a serious matter for Callie, an inheritance from her auntie Connie. Both Connie and Callie recognized that clothes were a business card. They conveyed your mood and opinion, and staked out territory. They made a statement, a question, an exclamation and started a conversation.

They could also hide a lot. And from what Alexi had confided to Connie about the years before she'd adopted the girl, Callie hid more about her past than anyone ever should have to. Connie wasn't privy to the details, but she could relate to the power of clothes to mask the hurt.

She held out her hand and Callie took it in her small dark one. It was like getting a key. "Pink," Connie said. "Today, I'm wearing a lot of pink."

Once she was dressed, Connie took Callie downstairs and emitted a flurry of orders to the kids, which she had to repeat ad nauseam as she herded them into the RV while throwing together stuff for herself. Connie had been granted the supreme responsibility of caring for the kids while Seth and Alexi were on their three-day honeymoon. On her way out, she took the ring box from the coffee table. She'd return the ring to Ben tonight when he came to the farm to check on Seth's livestock.

"Why are you taking the box?" Ariel surfaced from her basement room and was lurking in the hallway in her jumpy feline way.

"Why is it any of your business?"

"Because it's not something you usually do, that's why."

"That doesn't explain why it's your business. Since you're here, grab your things and get into the RV. We're going to the farm."

"Now?"

"Yes, now."

"No way. We agreed I only had stay there for the night."

Right, she'd forgotten. Now she'd have to come back into town to pick up Ariel with the RV and all four kids. "Fine. I'll be here for five thirty."

"No. Ten."

"Five thirty. Ten's too late for me to come into town with the RV and all four kids."

"Wait. The RV? No way. Ben can pick me up."

"No, he can't."

"Why?"

Halfway down the stairs, Connie stopped, remounted them and said to Ariel what she should have told herself a long time ago. "Ben Carruthers is not here to serve you. Put on your big-girl panties and be ready by five thirty."

BEN DROVE UP the farm's driveway after Connie had served up a supper of cereal and raw carrots to four, unimpressed kids and one surly teenager. The plan had been a meal of chicken nuggets, fries and carrots, but she'd burned the fries practically to ash and forgotten the nuggets in her freezer when she'd picked up Ariel. The carrots were only on the menu because they'd been in Alexi's fridge.

She watched from the kitchen window as Ben parked and walked straight to the barnyard without a glance at the house. Well... what else had she any right to expect?

"I'm supposed to help Ben with the chores," Matt, the eldest of Alexi's children, said. Seth had decided to become a farmer, which had blown Connie away when she'd first heard it because he had made the biggest point about not getting saddled with anything. Now on top of providing for a family, he was taking care of goats and cows, and talking about bringing in elk. Elk!

All the cows had calved, except for one. Matt had checked on her earlier and said she was showing no signs.

"Sure, go ahead and help," Connie said. "I can always pour you a fresh bowl of supper."

Instantly Bryn and Amy also wanted to go, and she let them. Ariel went off somewhere and Callie helped Connie tidy up the kitchen.

Connie shuffled and mumbled from sheer exhaustion, the power of pink having worn off shortly after lunch. It didn't help that the kids were on Easter break and thought their auntie Connie existed for their entertainment. Her three-day stint would be no Thursday night walk in the park.

Ben returned from the barnyard, the kids milling around him like women around a clearance rack. He stopped in front of the house, and for a panicked moment Connie wondered if he was coming inside. But no, they said their goodbyes. The kids veered to the door and Ben continued onto his truck.

Her gaze strayed to her purse. Maybe she should hold off on the ring. It might seem insulting.

But not returning it would show indecision and selfishness and weakness and greed.

She caught up with him as he was reversing his truck, his head angled to look out the back. She tapped on his window.

He braked and faced her, his sunglasses banding his eyes in a blue reflective glare. She held up the box, which in his glasses appeared very big and she very tiny.

Down came the window. His face was sunglasses and an unsmiling mouth. She would miss his mouth. It was just right for her finger to trace. What was she going on about? All these months, she'd not touched his lips with her fingers or anything else. He'd given her a ring but not a kiss.

"You gave me a ring but you didn't once try to kiss me. Why not?"

"I planned to kiss you once you put the ring on." The corner of his mouth twisted down a long ways. "Quite a bit, as a matter of fact."

Connie leaned against the door, the running motor vibrating through her hip. "I see."

"I figured I'd gotten the order wrong. This time, I planned it differently—ring first, then kissing." The corner of his mouth slanted down so far it nearly slid straight off his face. "Didn't work. Again."

In his glasses, she saw a warped, puckered version of herself, like she was a piece of scrunched-up plastic wrap. A freak. "Ben, I didn't mean—"

"I'm not saying this to make you feel guilty. The opposite actually. Another example of me deciding for the both of us how things should be."

He had made assumptions, except— "Wanting to become engaged first isn't a bad thing."

His lips hardly moved as they formed the words. "I take it you want to return the ring."

Connie unwrapped her sweaty fingers from around the box. "I know you said you wouldn't take it, but under the circumstances…"

"That's fine. I'll take it." He set it in a cup holder as easily as if she'd passed him a bottle of water for the road.

"Okay. Thanks," she squeezed out, and stepped back.

He threw the truck into gear and then braked. He turned to her. "You can take my name off your list." He tilted his head to the box. "You paid up."

No—it was too quick. Like a Band-Aid ripped off when the bleeding hadn't stopped. "I was just giving back what I hadn't taken in the first place."

He shook his head. "You have to take my name off your list, Connie. I need you not to owe me anymore. After last night, you keep me on that crazy list of yours, and both of us will forever be trying to make it up to each other. Give me this."

She'd thought she'd spend a lifetime paying him back, instead he made it seem as if crossing off his name was doing him a favor. From the ragged edge in his voice, maybe she was. Maybe the kindest thing she could do, the only thing she could do, was not to make up for the past, but put it to rest.

"Okay. I will," she promised.

His truck started to move and she found herself with a death grip on Ben's door. "Could I see it? The ring? Just once."

He braked once more and handed her the box.

She took it, fingering the lettering as she had the day she got it. She drew a breath and heard Ben do the same. *Just do it, Connie.* She flipped it open.

It was empty.

No. How could she have lost it? She should've locked her door. Hidden it. Put it in a safety-deposit box. *Something.*

Ben stripped his glasses off and they both stared at the white padded slit.

"Ariel" was Ben's one-word answer to Connie's unspoken questions, and he parked his truck, his hand on the door latch.

Connie's instincts flared. "No. Don't. Let me handle it."

"Theft, Connie. Theft."

"You don't know it was her."

"Who else?"

"Please, Ben. I'll get your ring back. Only let me do it. I promise."

He went still. "Don't promise me anything anymore. We agreed."

"We agreed that when we thought the ring was in the box. Same deal, I return your ring first."

"For the record," he said. "I don't need the ring for my name to come off."

"I lost the ring. It's only fair that I give it back."

"It serves no purpose."

"It may again."

"What are you saying? That you and I are going to be a couple again?"

"No. For you. Going forward—"

"Find me the ring and it ends there. Deal?"

She snapped the empty box shut and squared herself to enter the house. "Deal."

CONNIE THREW OPEN the front door of the farmhouse, shouting for Ariel.

She was curled in a ball on the living room couch, while the kids ricocheted around the room. "All right, the lot of you. Auntie Connie didn't pack her meds and the pink's worn right off. You need to get in your pajamas, pee, wash hands, brush teeth, wipe faces, clean feet, get in bed—all within fifteen minutes or I keep the prize." She flipped up her hand at the first squawking. "You know the rules. No questions, no backtalk, or you're disqualified. Go."

They were off at the post. Connie turned to Ariel and flipped open the empty box. "Where is it?"

Ariel's face, through her thick Goth makeup, lit up. "You lost it? You lost the ring. Suh-weet." She crowed laughter.

Connie snapped the box shut. "No. I didn't lose it. It was stolen from me. I want it. Now."

Ariel looked her in the eye. "I didn't take it."

Direct eye contact had nothing to do with honesty. "Then you know who did. Either way, I want it back."

"Or what?"

Connie could play this game. No one better than her at it, Miranda's daughter or not. "Or you're out. I will refuse to be your guardian, and you're on your own."

Ariel stretched out her legs, her boots on the cushions. "This again."

"This again. Boots off couch."

She didn't move. "You'd trade me in for a ring?"

"Isn't that what you did when you took it? Decided that the ring was more important than living with me? Not your couch, so boots off."

"Look, if I could've gotten away with taking the ring, I would have, but it's pretty stupid to steal from the person who's feeding you."

"Stupid but not impossible."

"I'm neither."

"Take those boots off the couch, or I will tell the kids you destroyed their prize."

"Like I care." She dropped her feet to the floor.

Connie behaved like a grown-up and didn't smirk. "Now. If not you, give me a name."

Ariel shrugged. "As you know, I wasn't the only one in the house last night."

Lindsay. It just didn't make sense. Lindsay was a friend, more than a Facebook one, too. Then again, she hadn't been in the best frame of mind last night, and she'd practically bolted this morning.

"I'm going out once the kids are down. You have to watch them."

"You can't make me. I've got rights."

"Yes, you do. Be sure to pack them when you leave for foster care."

Ariel rose up off the couch, ready to launch herself, probably at Connie, when the kids tumbled back down the stairs.

"We're done!"

"What's the prize?"

"Bryn's feet are still wet."

"They're wiped. What's the prize?"

Connie grabbed her coat, purse and RV keys. "Your prize is Ariel. She's going to show you funny cat videos on her phone for a half hour. Then, to bed."

The kids gathered around a stormy Ariel, who had no place to run. Welcome to family.

LINDSAY LIVED IN the newer part of Spirit Lake, where big houses had been packed in with smaller ones and town houses. Lindsay's house, it turned out, was one of the big houses with absolutely no parking spots available. Connie motored the RV up and down the nearby streets before she finally moored in the nearby school parking lot three blocks away. She really needed a car, especially now that Ben wouldn't be driving her around.

Her phone pinged a text message. Alexi. Everything all right?

Absolutely! Kids are in pajamas and heading to bed. Eventually they would be.

I called the house but there was no answer.

Connie crossed a street, texting like a teenager where truth was a spectrum. I must have not heard it. All's good.

Okay. Thanks again for making my day so beautiful.

My pleas—

Ping. Seth. Ben not answering. He w/ u?

Crud. She'd forgotten that as far as Alexi and Seth knew, both she and Ben were staying at the farm. Clearly Ben hadn't informed Seth otherwise. Which made sense, given that

Seth exploded if their names were mentioned together.

No. Everything is okay. He checked the cow. She paused and made an assumption. The cow is fine.

Tell Ben she needs to be checked 2/3 a.m.

"You got to be kidding me," Connie muttered. She was pretty sure Ben would not be driving out to see if a cow was dropping a calf at two in the morning. Would Mel? Yes, but that would start a whole line of questions from him. Besides, it wasn't fair to haul him out of a warm bed when she was right there.

If anything happened to that cow, she was back in the doghouse with Seth.

Got it. Go enjoy your honeymoon.

There was no immediate reply, and she turned up the walk to Lindsay's house.

Lindsay's red door was a set piece in a wide frame of stained glass patterned with vines and flowers that bordered the sides and top. Nice. She could do that with her renovations. No, Ben's renovations. Ben's house. She was not only breaking up with him, but her house, as well.

Her knock was answered by a boy about Callie's age with wet hair and in Power Ranger pajamas.

"Who are you?"

"Hi. I'm Connie. Is your mom or dad home?" *Please, not Derek.*

The child blasted, "Mom!"

Connie breathed out. But Lindsay's tired face was not easy to take, either.

"Yes?"

Connie had not imagined where the conversation accusing Lindsay of theft would occur but in a doorway with her small child observing was awkward.

" I was wondering, when you were at my house last night, did you—if you happened to notice—was there a ring box on the coffee table? In the living room?"

Lindsay tilted her head, as if she hadn't heard correctly. "A ring box? I don't know. There might have been. I wasn't in the living room."

Connie believed her. "And you didn't see it anywhere else, by chance?"

"No. Why do you ask?"

"There was an engagement ring in that box. And now it's missing."

Lindsay sucked in her breath, her eyes widened. Correct reaction. "Oh, no. It went missing? Yesterday?"

Possibly? For all Connie knew, the ring could've gone missing the day after she got it. Maybe it had never been there in the first place, and the whole thing was a big joke on Ben's part. No, he'd never been more serious.

Still, she had no description of the ring, no time for when the crime was committed and an owner who was not motivated to get it back.

"I think so," Connie admitted.

Lindsay's tired face redrew itself into one of sympathy. "Sorry, Connie. Alexi must be beside herself."

Connie had to think that one through. "It's not hers. It's—" She couldn't say "Ben's" because that would unleash a pack of rumors and, for the same reason, she couldn't say it was hers. "It belongs to a friend." All hail the shadowy concept of friend, a true friend to liars and teenagers. "I was keeping it safe for him until he could give it to his girlfriend."

"Oh, okay." A frown creased Lindsay's forehead. "I don't know if it means anything, but when I got in, I heard voices downstairs. One of them was a man's voice. I thought Ariel was watching TV. She called out when I entered the house, and I told her it was me. I went straight to your room after that. I didn't hear any more voices but I wouldn't have from the other side of the house, right?"

As you know, I wasn't the only one in the house last night. Uh-huh. Time for round two of interrogations. "Definitely a man's voice?"

"A male voice, anyway. Like I said, it could've been a show. I'm not sure."

Except Ariel didn't have a TV and she always used earbuds with her phone, even when she was alone. "Okay. Thank you." Connie had her hand on the door handle before common decency kicked in. "How are you doing?"

Lindsay shot a look at her boy and said with great cheer, "Fine. Thank you for asking."

"Oh, that's nice," Connie replied with equal heartiness. "Let's keep in touch."

"Yes, let's."

They waved goodbye under the bright porch light, and as the lovely red door closed, the little boy said, "Mom, you should've asked her where Dad is."

CHAPTER TEN

ARIEL WAS WHERE Connie had left her, on the couch but with no kids, earbuds in. Connie flicked them out.

"Hey!"

"Kids in bed?"

"Where else would they be?"

"Who was with you last night?"

"Uh, she was your friend."

Connie activated mother mode—hands on hips and a sharp tongue ready to cut through lies. "You are in a very vulnerable position right now, Ariel. I wouldn't push it if I were you."

"I don't know what you're talking about."

"Yes, you do. My friend heard a man's voice. Who was it?"

"She heard wrong."

Lindsay had suggested that possibility but Connie could smell Ariel's deception like a hastily extinguished cigarette. She was covering up for herself and for the guy she was with. Ariel said she didn't have any friends, girls or boys. And she hadn't brought anyone home, despite Connie repeatedly inviting her to do so.

"Not a man, then. A boy?"

"Not a boy."

"Back to a man. Who—" The identity hit Connie like the taste of sour milk. "Trevor McCready."

Ariel was not quick enough to hide her guilt, and Connie ran with her instincts. "The scumbag came to the house, didn't he? He knew I'd be away at the wedding."

"I didn't invite him. He showed up. What was I supposed to do?"

"You were supposed to slam the door in his face, and then call me. Here, give me your phone. I'm calling Trevor."

Ariel scrolled through her phone list and handed it to her without a word. Did Ariel regret not slamming the door in Trevor's face? Not that her cooperation mattered. Trevor was apparently not in the mood to take calls, even from teenagers he was taking advantage of. Ariel stared up at the ceiling in a good presentation of boredom.

On the sixth ring, his voice mail kicked

in. "Hello, Trevor. Connie here. I understand you're not taking calls from this number because Ariel has already contacted you, warning you that I know you were with her last night and that you've taken my engagement ring."

Ariel's boots hit the floor, boredom dropped for indignation. Connie pushed on. "You're not dragging Ariel or me into whatever you've got yourself caught up in, you understand? You are to stay away from her, her school and my home. You go against me, and I will have all kinds of law coming at you."

Connie ended the call, her hand shaking. She was beyond tired, far worse than after a hard shift at Smooth Sailing. Then, her shins hurt, her bones hurt and her right eye twitched. Now, it was all this plus a hollowness in her gut.

She tossed the phone at Ariel. "I'll deal with him and the ring tomorrow."

There was, however, one thing she didn't want to put off. Connie drew a breath, not sure she had the strength for the answer... Man, what her mother had gone through to raise her. She sank to the couch beside Ariel. "Did Trevor try anything with you?"

Ariel screwed up her face. "No! Gross. He's, like, your age."

Connie was too relieved to feel insulted. "He's three years younger but he doesn't moisturize as much as he should. What did you two do then?"

Ariel leaned over to brush something invisible off her boot, her hair hiding her face. "He brought me a cupcake. For my birthday."

Her birth— Of course, she was born in April. Her first birthday without her mother. Connie groaned. "I'm so sorry, Ariel. I completely forgot… The wedding…" That explained Ariel's grumpiness. Sweet sixteen and no one had wished her a happy birthday.

She placed her hand on Ariel's back. "I'll make it up to you. You could've told me, you know."

Ariel shrugged and her back rippled under Connie's hand. "You were busy. We all were. It was just…Trevor remembered, was all, and I'd only mentioned it to him once. Anyway, my birthday was just an excuse for him to yammer on about his latest, greatest plan and you. Real boring topics."

"Latest, greatest plan? For stealing a ring, maybe? You fencing drugs for him?"

"I'm not selling, I'm not buying. So long as

you keep me, I won't." Ariel turned her face away. "And I don't know about your stupid ring. Not like I'd get in the way of you marrying Ben, anyway. It's win-win."

Win-win? Connie fell back against the couch. "Since you're so interested in my relationship status, you should know that Ben withdrew his offer of marriage."

She might as well have injected Ariel with adrenaline. The girl leaped to her feet and began pacing, the motion lulling for Connie's tired eyes. "Oh, no, he's not. He's not getting out of it this time."

"I agreed with him, Ariel. It was—" Connie searched her brain, which was already powering down, for the right word "—mutual."

Ariel snorted. "He can't get rid of me. He's my father."

Connie figured her exhausted brain had slipped into a dream zone, the surreal space that exists during drifting off or waking, when images and words of the day collided with scenes from the past. Right now, for instance, Ariel was mixing up Darth Vader's famous lines with something about why Ben couldn't get out of marrying her. "Okay," she mumbled.

"Mom told me before she died. She'd blocked

the whole thing out of her head, but toward the end, she did some therapy. She's sure it was Ben."

Ben and Miranda? But—

"Why was she so sure?"

"We both turn our heads the same way or something, and we've got the same eye color."

This had to be a dream. Connie closed her eyes, ready to give in to it.

Ariel's voice came loud and undeniable at her ear. "Ben knows. I told him."

No. This did not fit into any vision of her Ben. Her head came off the couch. "What? When?"

"The day I skipped school I went to see him at his workshop. He denied he was my father but—" she gave a dramatic pause "—he didn't deny that he'd slept with her."

Connie sat in the dark, in her brother's house, listening to a sixteen-year-old ruin her life. Ben. The best man ever.

"I asked for a paternity test but he said he wasn't doing it."

No. Not her Ben, not the guy who never forgot to pick her up from work, who had practically taken care of himself since he was ten. He'd never deny his responsibilities. He would not *not* do it. "I'll talk to him, okay?" Would she ever.

Ariel bit her lip, a tooth worrying her lip ring. "If you don't marry him but he's my father, what happens then? Who do I live with?"

Ben had read Ariel right. She wanted a family. Ben, too. Only not one with her.

IT FLEW IN the face of all her girlieness, but Connie loved the smell of McCready's garage: the loamy smell of oil and grime with its overlay of metal and the added metallic tang of paint. Loved it, though she preferred the wood scent. And its feel. Ben could make wood feel like skin.

She didn't dare touch a thing in McCready's garage. He had a low tolerance for anybody in it. But since Trevor, his brother, was not picking up and she didn't know where he was holed up these days, she had no choice but to track the bear to his den.

He was bent over his workbench, which was littered with bit and bolts from what she assumed was the Harley parked next to him. He cast a glance her way when her booted heel clicked on his cement and then returned to his work. She said nothing and waited for him to acknowledge her. A highly irritating ritual, but that was how McCready operated.

She waited as he fiddled with parts. She waited while he blasted the silence by revving the bike's engine until the pipes were a vibrating blur. She waited as he polished tightly coiled metal. A shock, maybe?

She waited until she thought she might as well pick up the kids from their playdate with another family and try this another day when McCready leaned against his bench, still polishing the thing that could be a shock. "You still being here means it's important."

Finally. "I need your help."

"Figured you weren't here to offer it."

"It involves your brother."

Silence. Was he waiting for her?

"I have reason to believe that he stole my engagement ring."

McCready squinted at the coil and polished on.

"Trevor was trying to get the sixteen-year-old girl in my care to sell drugs at the high school, and I found out that he was at my house the other night. Then I discovered the ring has gone missing."

"A ring went missing off your hand?"

"No. It wasn't on my hand. It was in a box on my coffee table."

"Why was it in the box and not on your finger?"

"Because I'd not yet accepted the proposal."

"What does it look like?"

"Not a clue. I never saw it. Diamond, I assume."

McCready snorted. "There's a big ol' diamond ring in a box and Connie Greene couldn't be bothered to sneak a peek? Hard to believe that."

"Yeah, well, by the time I got around to it, there was nothing to see."

"If you never saw the ring, what makes you sure it was there in the first place?"

"Who proposes with an empty box?"

"How would I know? I never met the guy."

Connie drew in a deep breath of metal and oil and open roads. "Look, it's Ben, okay?"

"The girl could've taken it."

"No. Ariel has no reason. Trust me if I say her life is easier if I wear the ring."

"Why would Trevor take it?"

"Me. He wants payback for the beating he took last summer. This is all part of it, I'm sure."

McCready grimaced. He straightened into a

force bigger than Ben or Seth, Luke or Derek, or any man she'd ever served. He set down the coil and said, "I'll deal with it."

Her skin prickled at the way he said that. Calm and easy, as if he had nothing better to do than press on his brother to return a lady's engagement ring. "You don't have to," she said. "Just point me in his direction, is all."

He took one step toward her. "I said I'd deal with it."

Connie stepped back. "Thanks. I'll...go now."

His silence followed her out.

BEN WAS PAINTING the living room walls of Connie's house—or his, whichever—when there was a knock on the door loud enough to bust it down.

He couldn't see who it was from where he stood, so he had to set the roller in the tray, carefully, collapse the extendable handle, carefully, remove his gloves sticky with heat, carefully, and step across the drip sheets, carefully, before he could make it to the front door.

It was McCready. He filled the open door frame, causing a man-made eclipse. "Connie here?"

"No," Ben said. "And I wouldn't say otherwise even if she was."

McCready grunted. "I have what she wants."

Ben wiped the sweat from his paint gloves on his jeans. "You're not the first man to think that."

McCready grunted again. "Mind if I step inside?"

Ben let him in, because McCready wasn't the kind of guy who would stay outside if he wanted in, anyway. Once he'd maneuvered his body into the front entrance, McCready reached inside his jacket pocket and held up, between his thick thumb and forefinger, the engagement ring. "She lost this."

Ben fought the urge to make a grab for the delicate jewel that had ridden in the man's pocket, probably along with lint, knives and chewing tobacco. "I suppose there's no point asking why you have it."

"She could tell you."

"She never told me that she'd gone to see you, so I doubt it." They hadn't spoken or texted all day, which was not unexpected but it felt strange, as if he was forgetting to do something.

McCready shrugged, which looked more

like he was dealing with an itch between his shoulder blades than responding to Ben. "The thing is, the temporary owner of the ring claims she has something of his." He gave another roll to his shoulders, and his muscles cracked like splintering wood. "One hundred pills, to be exact."

Ariel and her drugs. Dragging her bad business into Connie's home. Wait until he got ahold of her. Ben nodded at McCready's index finger, where the ring was now tight on the first knuckle. "Keep it." As if they both didn't know that was already going to happen. "I'll see to it that his...stuff is returned. You okay with me coming by with it?"

"Not for you to get involved."

Connie must've told him they weren't engaged. "Since I own this house and there's a good chance the pills are on my property, and because that ring belongs to me, I'd say I'm involved."

McCready rotated his head to glance around at the renovations. "You own this place?"

No papers had yet been signed, but there'd been no change to the understanding between Connie and him, either. "We have an agreement."

"How much you planning to sell it for?"

Where was McCready going with this? Ben did some rapid calculations and fired off a number.

McCready nodded. "Property's nice. You know if the town will allow a triple garage in the back?"

Ben answered, and they went back and forth like that until Ben finally had to say, "Thing is, McCready, I don't really intend to sell."

McCready shrugged. "Just keep me in mind should things change." He crooked his ringed finger. "She seemed pretty determined to get this back."

"I guess she felt it was important."

"If she got me involved, she must've thought so."

Ben couldn't resist asking, "She owes you a favor now, I take it?"

McCready's mouth thinned. "She's been good to me."

What kind of good could Connie have done this biker?

"Some people," McCready said, "don't last pass their warranty. Others are built to last."

Was this some kind of biker philosophy? And what exactly had this situation to do with Connie's expiry date?

McCready slipped the ring back in his pocket and opened the door for himself. "We can both agree," he said on his way out, "that Connie's built for this ring."

"Tell her that," Ben advised the closed door.

QUARTER PAST THREE that afternoon, Ben zipped his truck around the corner out of eyeshot of the house and locked the front door to make it seem that he wasn't there. He didn't want to give Ariel any reason to avoid coming into the house, and if he knew her at all, an empty house was the most inviting trap of all.

Sure enough, at 3:42, he heard the lock turn and he rose from the bar stool in the kitchen to meet her, his socked feet silent on the smooth floor. She'd sluffed off her backpack and was leaning against the door, eyes closed, face smooth, lips moving as if in prayer. Ben almost felt something other than deep abiding annoyance with her.

"Hey, Ariel."

Her eyes snapped open, and her expression reformed into its usual Goth scowl. "What are you doing here?"

And he was back to his usual annoyance.

"Renovating, in case you haven't figured that out."

She pushed off the door and climbed the stairs. "What's the point now that you and Auntie Connie aren't getting married?"

Ben leaned on the top post, blocking her. She stopped on the step below and bugged her eyes out at him. "Excuse me."

Ben knew she was running on fumes. There was no hungrier time than immediately after school. It was universal. Twenty years on, just seeing a school bus in the afternoon made his stomach growl. He'd eaten a muffin and a coffee while waiting for her.

He didn't move. "For one hundred pills, I will."

She rolled her eyes. "English, Benji. English."

"Your buddy, Trevor, took the ring. No surprises there. You hand over his drugs and he'll give back the ring."

Her eyes shot side to side. "You talked to him? When?"

"A message was relayed to me."

"Who?"

Ben thought of McCready, of his size and of where his loyalties lay. "Not for you to know."

"I don't have any drugs." She retreated down the stairs. "I'm going to my room."

"Sure," Ben called after her. "Begin your search there. Holler if you find anything."

Ariel hit the landing. "I'm not doing a thing." She started down the short flight to her bedroom.

He followed her. "Then I will."

It was her turn to block his path. "Stay out of my room." She grabbed his arm. He stopped and stared her down until she released it, then he continued on, Ariel close behind. She pushed past him to reach her door first and slam it in his face.

Easy enough. He opened his pocketknife and sliced through the plastic sheeting. He stepped inside square onto a book. There were books everywhere. Not textbooks but novels, upside down, spread out like flopped birds. Books and pens and paper. With drawings of fantasy characters. Ones with pointy ears and fire for clothes and waterfalls spilling from hands and all of them looking peeved and dangerous. The exact expression on Ariel's face right now.

If she was anybody else, he would've said that the pictures were brilliant. As it was, he shook her quilt and sent a book flying.

"What are you doing? Do you think I sleep with the drugs?"

He didn't answer but stripped off the pillowcases. When he cut the pillow open with his pocketknife, only hypoallergenic fluff swelled out. She shrieked, "You're freaking crazy! I'm texting Auntie Connie right now."

He waited until she'd pulled her phone free from her jacket before he knocked it from her hand and snatched it up. "She doesn't need more of your lies."

"Lies? You think all I got is lies? How about this for the truth? You don't have a thing on me, and you know it. In fact, you've admitted it's the other way around."

His grip on the pillow tightened. "I've done nothing to get you away from Connie. I've kept my end of the bargain."

"Changing your mind about marrying her is interfering."

"You're taking a personal matter between Connie and me and turning it into something about you. Which it isn't and never was."

He threw open her top dresser drawer and saw her underwear. Slammed it shut. No way was he going through that.

"Auntie Connie's taking it seriously. She

promised me you would take the paternity test."

She'd told Connie that he was her father. Worse, Connie had believed Ariel enough to want it proven. She didn't trust him. He didn't look at Ariel because he couldn't and not smash something, everything.

He needed to get to Connie. Their engagement was off the table, but that didn't mean he wanted her thinking the worst of him. Two sides to every story, right?

But first, Ariel.

He walked to her mattress, got a good grip on it. "In case you didn't notice, I became an adult long ago. I make my own decisions." He hoisted it up in one smooth move. Nothing there. He let it drop with a deadened whump.

He scanned the room for more possibilities.

"Are you done?" Ariel pointed to the dresser. "Can I have my phone back now?"

He picked it up. Her wallpaper was a pic of her and Miranda, a close-up selfie. Miranda's face was thin, her hair scraggly, her skin papery. The only big part of her was her smile. Her head rested on Ariel's, who had her cheek mushed against her mom's shoulder.

He felt Ariel coming, and he twisted away

before she could strip the phone from him. "Give it back." And then, "Please."

Tears hung wet in Ariel's eyes, and Ben felt a surge of regret. He handed her the phone. Her tears convinced him what her room with its books and fantasy drawings had already told his gut. She didn't have the drugs.

If—and this was a big if—she also didn't know where they were, then the only logical conclusion was that Trevor had somehow misplaced them or they'd been stolen from him, and now he was trying to lay the blame at Connie's feet until he could locate them.

Or he had deliberately planted them on Connie so that—well, so that what? Ben leaned against the dresser, which was about the same height as his workshop bench. Why would Trevor plant drugs and then ask for them back? Was he counting on Ben and Seth and everyone else believing that they were Connie's? Make his point, and then exchange them for the ring? What kind of weak revenge was that? Ben remembered the Trevor that night at the bar. A man in love who'd felt wronged. Ben recognized the feeling well. Only his faith in Connie had prevented him from going down the same dangerous path of vindictiveness.

Something didn't add up.

Best find the drugs fast and clear them out of the house.

"I'm going to Connie's room."

He felt a jolt of surprise when Ariel's boots clomped behind him on the wooden stairs.

Ariel's room was a Spartan prison cell compared to Connie's. He'd forgotten how much she could fill a space. There were traces of her on every square inch. In the textbook on the floor with a nail file as a bookmark. With the half a dozen shirts and skirts on her bed. Or the jewelry boxes with bling spilling out. Her scent, too. Caught in her lotions and nail polish and makeup and bottles. It was like burying his face in the crook of her neck.

"Where do we start in this mess?"

Ariel had a point.

He strode to the bedside table and yanked open the drawer, sending a collection of lotion and creams tumbling together. Inside was other typical Connie stuff—a loyalty card to a manicurist, hair elastics, a few pocket-size steno pads, a wedding invitation—then, tucked to the side, was a Ziploc bag, folded and taped with a pile of small, mud-green pills.

Taped up. Which meant Connie wasn't using but didn't confirm whether or not she knew about it. He held it up for Ariel. "This it?"

If possible, under her Goth makeup, Ariel paled. She took two hesitant steps toward him, her gaze fixed on the bag like it was a dangerous, alien creature. Squinted.

She stepped back and cursed.

He held up a warning finger and she glowered. "You'd swear, too, if you knew what that was."

"How about we test that theory? What is it?"

"It's not Trevor's."

"Okay," he said, drawing out the word expectantly.

"It—it—" Ariel stumbled and dropped to Connie's bed, sending one of Connie's books thudding to the carpet.

Ariel's eyes were wide with what in anybody else would pass as panic.

"It means they've found me."

"Who? Out with it, Ariel."

She shook her head and her face crumpled.

"I need to see Auntie Connie. I need to see her." She spoke like a kid wanting her mother or an arrestee requesting a lawyer.

Or someone who feared for her life.

CHAPTER ELEVEN

Ariel wants to talk with you. Bringing her now. McCready has the ring. There in 15.

CONNIE READ THE text and then looked at the four faces turned to her at the dining room table. They'd been about to start crafting a Welcome Home, Mr. and Mrs. Greene banner for Seth and Alexi's return the next day. She'd rustled up glue, construction paper, tissue paper, markers, string, tape and more tape and these ultra-awesome fake gems with a super easy peel-and-stick backing.

This banner was her humble offering to the kids for having slouched off for most of the day. After motoring Ariel to school that morning, she'd intended to give them a full day of nonstop excitement, but she'd fallen asleep on the couch during the puppet show they'd specially prepared for her. She'd woken an hour and a half later to a silent house and torn outside, screaming her head off. All four kids emerged from behind the barn, where they were constructing an outdoor village from the recyclables heap.

"I'm sorry," she said to Matt, who would've had to keep an eye on all of them. "You could've woken me."

He'd shrugged. "'S'okay. Not much into puppets."

Right now he didn't look as if he was into banner-making, either, if his fists in his cheeks was anything to go by.

"So, Ariel and Ben are coming out right now," Connie said, as if this was the news they'd all been waiting for, "and I'll need to speak with them for a little bit. Are you guys all right to start on your own?"

Her answer was slumped shoulders and pouty lips. From outside, she heard the crush of gravel under the wheels of Ben's truck. "I owe you one," she said to Matt, who held up two fingers. "Fine, two."

On the porch, the wind sliced into Connie's skin, though any thought of returning to the house for a jacket scattered after at the sight of Ben and Ariel. She appeared ready to puke on her boots and Ben—well, Ben looked like the reason for Ariel's state.

He climbed the stairs, his heavy step vibrating through the wood and into the soles of her feet.

"Where are the kids?"

"Inside. At the dining table. Making a craft."

He positioned his back to the kitchen window. From his pocket he withdrew a sandwich bag of green pills. Fentanyl. Connie whipped to Ariel, who gave her a murderous glare.

"McCready came by with the ring," Ben said. "He said he'd give it back in exchange for these. I found them in the drawer by your bed."

"In my—" Connie grabbed the bag and examined it. Bands of masking tape over the seal protected against easy tampering and doubled as a label. "100" and "XOXO" was written on the tape. Hugs and kisses? What was the bag doing in her drawer? She opened that drawer every day because of the list. Except, other than the morning after the wedding, she'd not been home for two days. Two days in which her already rickety life had come tumbling down.

Connie thrust the bag out to Ariel. "Trevor gave you these?"

She shook her head. "No."

"But they are his?"

She dragged her fingertips from the corners of her eyes down her cheeks, her black eye makeup scoring lines down her face like tear trails. "Maybe. But they're not his stuff."

"Talk."

Ben crossed his arms and squared his feet, a physical mirror of Connie's demand.

Ariel banded her arms across her stomach. "Mom and me, we went to Calgary in November when she ran into trouble in Vancouver. We moved into this fourplex, and it had a reputation for being kind of a drug house."

"What do you mean 'kind of—'" Connie peeked at the kitchen window for big ears "—'a drug house'?"

Ariel shifted from one black boot to the other. "Customers came and went, okay? One of the apartments was the warehouse and then they sold out of the one above."

"They?"

Ariel pointed to the "XOXO." "Hugs and Kisses."

"There's a gang called Hugs and Kisses?"

A bit of the normal sarcastic Ariel poked through with an eye roll. "Yeah, the guy who named the gang thought it was 'ironic' because he liked to think they were really tough. Anyway, he was as good at running the operation as naming it. He was wrecking it for everybody and it was set to blow up in all our faces.

"Round about then, Mom checked herself into the hospital. So, I stepped in. There wasn't much else to do. School was not going to happen, not with Mom so sick and me having to do strange hours. And I needed food. I couldn't steal everything all the time, you know."

Connie didn't know, hadn't ever really known. She'd always had somebody. She had chosen to run wild; she'd never been forced. She glanced over at Ben who wore an unreadable expression. Surely, he had to feel something for this girl who could very well be his daughter.

"Anyway. It didn't take long for me to get in with them. Not even a month, and everything was passing through me on the way to the *da boss*."

Connie shook the bag. "This stuff?"

Ariel shrugged her "yes."

"You know what this stuff does to people. It kills them. Sooner or later."

"Yeah, well, starvation kills, too," Ariel flashed back. "And stealing is a crime, too.

And I didn't make the customers buy this stuff. They came to me!"

"There were places you could go where you could've got food and shelter."

"Yeah, and they'd tell me I couldn't see my mom." Ariel's mouth twisted. "She was dying, all right? The hepatitis had damaged her liver and turned cancerous. Mom had no money. I needed to live somehow. Not everything is pretty like how Alexi and Seth make it for those kids." She pointed with her chin to inside the house.

Connie had heard only bits and snippets from Alexi and Marlene about foster care, but she'd gathered it wasn't all rainbows and unicorns. The foster parent could mean well, but the kids knew they were ultimately a paycheck. Ariel must feel like that now. Living in a place where she didn't belong. Guilt washed away Connie's anger. First thing when this was all sorted out, they'd put up proper walls in Ariel's bedroom. Even if Ben wouldn't be putting them up.

"I take it you got into trouble with the gang," he said to Ariel.

"The hospital called. I had to get there fast but I was waiting for our supplier to bring our order. I turned it over to the best guy there.

I showed him the money to give, how many packages it was for. I told him twice and then I left."

Ariel spoke in hollow, precise words. "When I got to the hospital, they'd put Mom in a room by herself, and I knew what that meant. I asked and they said, 'Soon.' Hours? Minutes? And they said, 'Yes.' All I could do was swab her mouth and make sure her oxygen was okay.

"I fell asleep without even meaning to. I woke up to the nurses taking off the tubes. I saw her hand, not her face, and there was a nurse beside me. And I knew." Ariel scrunched her face, pain compressed to every line.

"They let me look at her, like it was my duty. I did, and, yep, she was dead. I couldn't afford a funeral. So I left her there."

Connie hugged her. It was like wrapping her arms around a statue. No give. Ariel didn't turn into her, or put her arms around her. She stepped away.

"You could afford an obituary. It said your mom was cremated," Ben said.

His quiet voice held an accusatory edge Connie didn't appreciate. Ariel answered tiredly. "I paid for the obit because it would be my only proof to the world that she lived.

I said she was cremated because that's what she'd wanted. I don't know if that's what happened."

Connie hugged the Ariel statue again. "When this is all over and papers are finalized, the next step is to find your mom, okay?"

Ariel gave a shrug and a nod, the long side of her hair shielding her face. Connie released Ariel, and Ben seemed to interpret that as a signal for him to continue his interrogation.

"You went back to the gang," he prompted.

"Yeah. The deal had gone sideways. The guy hadn't counted right. He took one more package—" she jutted her chin at the bag Connie held "—than what was agreed on. And because I only had the exact amount of money, it wasn't like he paid for it, either. It looked like we stole it. My second dead body that morning."

"You were blamed?"

"Technically, I was in charge, so yeah. This kind of job doesn't allow for personal emergencies but I had to take the risk. And lost."

Ben made a disgusted noise and looked away, as if he couldn't stand the sight of Ariel. "And you brought your mess with you?"

"I didn't exactly leave a forwarding address. Hugs and Kisses deals in the city. In the north end. Some of those kids haven't even left the city in their whole life. I figured they wouldn't chase after people who leave."

"And yet they're here," Ben stated.

Ariel shifted on her feet. "The guy who runs the gang, he might've heard Mom and me talking about Spirit Lake. He might've figured out that I'd come here. It wouldn't have been hard for him to connect with Trevor." Ariel's fingers, with their chewed nails, raked down her face again. "He wants to become a one-percenter—you know, with a biker club—and he might've found out that Trevor's brother is one so he'd work even harder to get in with Trevor."

Connie fought to track Ariel through her twisting tale. "This gang—what? Leader?—put them in my drawer?"

"He might have, or Trevor might have. Either way, the reason's the same. To tell me that they know where I am, that—that there'll be payback."

Ariel's fingers tapped against her ringed lips, as if thinking. They were also trembling. Connie wanted to hug her again.

"You did bring your mess here," Ben said flatly.

What was the matter with him? Why keep badgering Ariel?

"There is nothing wrong with a daughter wanting to be with her dying mother," Connie snapped. "There is nothing wrong with someone trying to run from a bad situation. There is nothing wrong with someone running to the only person she knows who might give a flying flip whether or not she lives or dies." She stepped in close to him. "You, of all people, should understand what that feels like."

He stepped in even closer. "And you should understand what it is to take care of family."

"Auntie?" Callie's face was at the window. "Do you have glitter?"

"We'll deal with this later," she directed Ben and Ariel. "Ariel, go inside."

Ariel wordlessly obeyed. Callie's disappeared from the window.

"I'll deal with this now," Ben said. He held out his hand. "Give them to me." She hesitated and he said, "Connie. You can't have those around the kids."

"And you can't have them, either."

"I don't intend to keep them."

"Take them to the police."

"With your record?"

She bit her lip. Everyone, especially the

police, knew she was to blame for the charge Seth had taken on himself. She was guilty of a lot of other juvie stuff, though. And she'd been a recreational user who'd associated with dealers. It wouldn't look good.

"And even if they're persuaded to believe it wasn't you, then they'll blame the girl. And as much as I really don't appreciate how she didn't care to fill us in about the trouble she was in—"

"She was scared, Ben. Of what we might do."

"Such as go to the police?"

Okay, point taken.

"She kept secrets but I don't want her in trouble with the police," he said.

She smacked the package into his open hand. Ben shot down the porch stairs.

"Ben!"

He didn't break stride until he was at his truck. She caught up to him as he swung his door shut. Ben stashed the bag in the glove compartment, beside the packet of Kleenex, a tape measure, a box cutter and her hand lotion. Was it not a week ago that she had used the lotion while driving home? A relic from a safer, saner lifetime.

"We need to talk, too," she blurted. "You and me. About Ariel. About—about Miranda."

He gave her a long, level look. "I'll take the paternity test, if that's what you mean."

No, she wanted to know why he'd been with her in the first place. How he could've slept with someone he claimed he'd never liked. How that someone was her best friend.

Except her right to ask assumed that she and Ben were in a relationship.

She stepped back from his truck. "Yeah, that's what I mean."

He gave a short nod and drove off.

Connie had never taken so long to climb the four porch steps.

She found Ariel right in there with the other kids as they decorated the Welcome Home banner.

Connie let her go for it. Scented markers and glitter were their own kind of therapy.

McCREADY'S GARAGE WAS locked down solid when Ben arrived, as was the door that led to the biker's upstairs apartment. Ben pounded on it and the garage bay door in case the big man of mystery was hunkered down inside. No answer, no surprise. The truck and Harley were gone, too.

He'd have to come back later or tomorrow; neither option suited Ben. He wasn't interested in bringing home a bag of drugs, especially if Trevor was plotting his next dirty deed.

All he wanted was to unload the drugs and get the ring.

He would show the ring to Connie and she would strike him from her list. Then all would be fair and square between them. Except for the white elephant of what had happened between him and Miranda.

The girl had thought that by telling Connie, she'd get a father. A family. All she'd done was drive the nail into the coffin of that dream. Positive or negative, the test would do nothing to bring them together because Connie no longer trusted him.

Frustrated, he kicked the door to McCready's apartment. There was a security camera mounted over it. Did McCready monitor movement? Maybe, maybe not.

Another more direct and effective method to message the biker occurred to Ben. If his day had gone even slightly better than it had, he might've reconsidered. As it was, he strode to his truck, retrieved his ten-pound hammer from his truck toolbox and smashed the camera. The alarm went off instantly. He put back his hammer and waited by the door amid the shrieks.

Less than seven minutes later, McCready swung his truck full speed up to Ben, pulling to a stop inches from him.

He strode past Ben, twisted a few wires and the alarm fell quiet. Underneath McCready's one-percenter jacket Ben caught a glimpse of a dress shirt collar. McCready, in a quiet, almost offhand way, said, "You did this?"

Ben was still riding high enough on a mix of frustration and vicious disappointment to say, "Yes. I'll replace it tomorrow. We need to talk."

McCready grunted. He unlocked the door that led into his garage and walked in, leaving it open. Ben took that as an invitation to enter so he did, only to be met by McCready on his way out, wielding a tire iron.

He strode over to Ben's truck and smashed the windshield. He said to Ben, "Now we'll talk."

Fair exchange for his own willful destruction of property.

He followed McCready inside where he was tapping on his phone cradled in his big hand. Why make a call now when he'd already said they'd talk?

McCready put the phone to his ear and turned his back on Ben. He took the hint and walked to the far side of the garage. Still, in the quiet of the room, the big man's soft voice drifted over to Ben.

"Yeah, yeah, I'm okay. Some knuckle dragger was dropping off parts and thought he could deactivate the alarm."

He was talking to a woman, Ben realized. McCready had a girlfriend? Well, sure, it was possible.

"Listen, I gotta stay and deal with him. Just talkin'. I don't know how long I'm going to be."

His voice was tender, intimate. Ben didn't think biker chicks were usually treated so well.

"Me, too. Call you when I can, hon."

When McCready was done, he raised his voice. "That call was not where I saw this night heading so this had better be good."

Ben tossed the bag of drugs onto McCready's workbench. "As good as it gets."

McCready joined him at the bench. "Where was this?"

"Connie's bedroom. Bedside drawer. We both know she didn't put it there."

McCready raised his hand. "No, I don't know that. You found it on her property, in her stuff, so if it looks like it and smells like it, then it is, to my way of thinking."

"Except why was I searching for those drugs in the first place? Because you said Trevor wanted them. So the worst she's guilty of is possessing what he's dealing in."

McCready flipped the bag back and forth between his hands, held it up to the light coming through the windows. "Trevor doesn't deal fentanyl. It isn't his."

"As far as you're aware. But we both know your brother has a bad habit of biting off way more than he can chew."

McCready set the bag on the bench, flexed his hand open and shut. Ben wouldn't last if McCready turned on him right now.

The biker opened the top drawer of his tool chest, the narrow one where nuts and bolts were kept. He dropped the bag in there, picked out something and flicked it onto the bench. The ring pinged against the metal bench surface.

Ben swept it into his pocket. "Thanks for taking such good care of it."

"Any idea why," McCready said, "Trevor's got this stuff?"

Either McCready really was clueless or he wanted to check the facts against Trevor's version, which made sense, given Trevor's track record for manufacturing the truth.

"Trevor got his hooks into the girl that Connie's in charge of."

"Ariel."

"You know her name?"

"Connie told me."

"Yeah, so the girl has reason to believe that the drugs came from a gang she was involved with in Calgary. She fell out with them and moved up here, thinking she was clear of them. Only now—" he pointed to the drawer where McCready had deposited the bag "—they've tracked her here. Trevor doesn't care about the drugs. He wants us to understand he can sic this Calgary gang on Ariel any time he wants. He controls the girl, which means he controls Connie."

"Not here to rescue them."

Wasn't that what Connie said herself? Except— "You got the ring back for Connie. You must think you owe her somehow."

"I got the ring back. So no, I don't owe her anymore."

Ben decided to put Ariel's theory into play. "The guy who runs the Calgary group probably wants to get in with your people. He's using Trevor to do it."

McCready didn't blink. "Trevor's an adult. He can think for himself. This has got nothing to do with me. And when you leave tonight, we won't be seeing each other again."

McCready was right. He was in no way tied to these events, a bag of flushable drugs notwithstanding. But he had made one mistake, and Ben knew what love could make a man do.

"Your little brother isn't your problem. Would you say the same about the woman you were just talking to?"

McCready drew himself up. "You won't be dragging her into this."

"I won't," Ben said. "But can you say Trevor won't?"

McCready said nothing, and then finally, "Get out."

Ben took his truck down the back alley and turned it to face the rear of McCready's garage. Through the splintered windshield, he watched to see what the big biker would do.

Not a quarter of an hour passed before McCready appeared on his bike, motor gunning, at the entrance. He gave Ben one long look and then roared off. Ben didn't follow. It was now up to McCready.

As for him, he had a ring for Connie to see.

All was darkness when Ben pulled up to the farmhouse except for the glow from the porch light. Connie sat underneath it, bundled in a deck chair. She was cocooned in a full quilt wrap and wore a toque, with only her hands exposed to hold her phone. The kids would be asleep, so finally he could have her to himself.

He parked and as soon as his foot hit the gravel her interrogation began. "Why are you driving that thing?"

He'd brought his other truck, the first truck he'd ever owned, given to him by his father. It was a beater, more rust than metal, and every year he debated renewing the registration and insurance. He did it for sentimentality, which tonight had a very practical side.

"The other's in for repairs." It would be tomorrow.

"Repairs? You were just driving it."

"Still."

"You just had it in for servicing before the wedding."

The good thing about Connie was that she remembered every detail of his life. The bad thing about Connie was that she remembered every detail of his life.

"Rock to the windshield." He climbed the steps and parked his butt on the freezer-cold seat.

"When? Tonight? After you left?"

"Yes." He stuck his hands in his pocket for warmth and touched the reason he'd come. He withdrew the ring and dropped it onto the flat screen of her phone.

She went rigid, then her slim fingers lifted the ring, the overhead porch light catching on the many facets of the diamond.

A beat passed. Another. Was she reconsidering his proposal? Should he make it again?

"This," she whispered, "is the most beautiful thing I've ever seen."

He decided to test her waters. "It was built for the most beautiful person I've ever seen."

She swung her arm like a boom toward him, the ring on the end. "Ben. A ring this nice needs more than a beautiful person to wear it."

He didn't take it, even though it was six inches from his nose. "Like a beautiful person who also loves me?"

Her hand with its offering stayed put and her voice stayed firm. "Like a beautiful person who loves you and trusts—"

He knew what she was about to say. *You. Trusts you.*

He took the ring, his fingers brushing her cold ones, and slipped it into his pocket again. Later, he'd drop it back into the wood box in his workshop. He might as well leave. Except he couldn't. After a day like this one, he couldn't bear going to a dark, empty house without the hope of Connie. He sat in silence, the chill air seeping into his body.

She shifted and her hands disappeared into the wrap. "I'm glad you got the ring back."

"Yeah," he managed, and then when he was sure he could say more, he added, "My name comes off your list, right?"

Silence.

"Right?" he repeated.

"Right." The single word was a soft exhalation.

Nothing more to be said. He needed to lever himself out of the chair, fire up the old beater and clear out. He pressed his hands on the chair arms to start the process when she said, low and fast and breathlessly, "Could you tell me what happened between you and

Miranda? So I understand. Please. I wasn't an angel but you—well, you were."

His time of reckoning.

He didn't owe her an explanation, and from the way she framed the question, she knew it. If the paternity test produced the expected results, his mistake could stay buried and Connie would never hear the ugly details.

Never hear and yet believe the worst. He would forever see the suspicion in her eyes. They weren't meant to join in holy matrimony, but she needed to know that it had always been her for him, and never her best friend.

He sunk back into his cold chair.

"You were in grade eleven."

He let her do the math. She'd been seventeen, Miranda a new eighteen and Ben twenty-one. A three-year gap that meant nothing now but was a generation at that age. Twenty-one meant he'd been out of school and working and living on his own. Twenty-one meant that you didn't chase high school girls.

"You dated guys, and I guess Miranda did, too. And I stayed away from both of you. Because you told me you weren't interested in me, and I wasn't interested in Miranda. Only—only that didn't stop her. Or me."

Connie didn't say a word. She didn't need to. He could see her censure through her careful neutrality.

He continued, "You know better than me that her family life wasn't great. My big tragedy was that I didn't have a real family. Hers was that she had one, right?"

If possible, Connie huddled deeper into her cozy wrap and gave a quick nod. "She never wanted me to come over to her house. So, once, I followed her back to her place. She lived in the old town houses, the ones they demolished two, three years ago? I took her music player, so I could have a reason to come over. Ben. There was nothing in the house. Nothing. There were kitchen chairs in the living room. There was a mattress in the first bedroom. No bed frame. Nothing. I didn't go any farther. And her dad. He was lying on the floor, sleeping, snoring loud as a train. I saw her face. It was beet red. I said I would see her tomorrow and I promised myself I would always be her friend. Only I wasn't, Ben. Maybe that's why it's important I know what happened between you two. Because

I need to be her friend and stand up for her now, when I should have years ago."

He suddenly realized what she must be thinking. "Listen, what happened between Miranda and me wasn't the smartest thing I've ever done but it was consensual. Nothing happened that she didn't agree to. She wasn't ever drunk or high with me. All right?"

"I— Okay," she breathed out. "It's just that with Miranda—well, she often went out high or drunk."

"Yeah," he said, "I always knew when she might come over. Usually Wednesdays or Thursdays. When she'd turned up for classes, dried up, tried to be some kind of normal."

"What? She came over to your place. She never told me."

"I don't think either of us told anybody. Least of all you."

She shifted around inside her wrap. "Yeah, okay, I can see I might have made things difficult for you two. So, she came over...and you two had a relationship?"

"Relationship is a bit of a stretch," he said. "Things weren't good for her at home, so I gave her a place to go for a while. We'd stay inside, watch a movie. She liked action ones, which suited me fine. It got to be that I'd rent one early in the week, knowing she'd probably be over."

"But Seth was always at your place, too. Didn't he notice her there?"

"A couple of times. Miranda would hide in the bedroom."

"You made her hide in the bedroom? Like she was something to be ashamed of?"

"Connie. Miranda would run there herself. She didn't want that trouble with your family."

"Fine. Carry on."

"What can I say? After a movie, and pizza—I'd always get pizza because otherwise she'd eat raw onions if I let her—she'd go home. Once, she seemed a bit sadder than usual. I reached out to her…and it became something more."

He wasn't proud of himself. He should've just given her a hug and driven her home, even if she said it was only a ten-minute walk. And now, from what Connie had just said about where Miranda lived—

"She loved you, you know." Connie said it softly, rolled it out there like a grenade.

No, not Miranda. "I was just someplace to go. Food and shelter. And a bit of comfort one night."

Connie lifted her knees to her chin, bunching herself into the wrap, pulling the ends tighter around her face. "No. She always wanted you, Ben. Since the day she met you."

Ben had had no idea. He couldn't recall the day he met Miranda. Probably Connie was there, and therein lay the problem. When Connie was there, he couldn't see anyone else. "Wanted me?"

Her wrap ballooned again. "Are you really that dense? She wanted you like you wanted me. For love, for a future, for someone who'd remember her birthday and take her places, someone she could dress up for, someone who called her just to say 'hi.'"

She'd come to him, straight and sober. For food and a warm home—and him? "Why didn't you tell me?"

"Miranda didn't want me to. I think it was pride. She didn't want you to be nice to her because I asked you to. As it turns out, you weren't a very nice guy."

"I was," Ben said, desperate to defend himself, "a twenty-one-year-old guy who had an eighteen-year-old girl come over. And yes, that one night I wore a condom. Having sex with someone you don't love is not a crime.

If it was—" He stopped. Nothing good could come from finishing that.

Connie did, anyway. "I'd still be in jail."

"You, Miranda and half the town," he said.

"You never went out with her? Maybe took her to the movies? Or out for pizza?"

"No," Ben said. "She didn't seem to want to. She never asked to go anywhere."

"Would you have taken her, if she had?"

"Probably," he said, and then to keep it honest, he added, "Maybe not. It wasn't her that I wanted."

Connie twisted her mouth. "You got me in the end."

"Yes."

"She never came to you? Confronted you about her pregnancy?"

Ben shook his head. "I told you. We used a condom. Besides, the timing doesn't quite match up. She knew I wasn't the father."

"Then why did she tell Ariel you were?"

"Would you want to tell your kid you didn't know who her father was? Or worse, you did know, but didn't want your child to have anything to do with him? Wouldn't you want to hope for that point-one-percent chance the condom was defective?"

"She always made the identity of the father a big secret."

Ben quietly said the ugly truth. "It could've been, even to her."

Connie flinched. "We can't be sure of that."

Also true.

But there was one final piece to his story Connie didn't yet know. Maybe the most important part. "She came to me again. One night, a couple of years later. Drunk this time. Came on to me. Tried to drag me down the hall to bed. I refused to go, told her to sleep it off on the couch or go home to her kid. She wouldn't let up and I lost it. I lifted her up and tried to throw her out. She started crying then and begged me to let her live with me. Her and Ariel. She said she would be good. And Ariel, too. I would see. Just give her a chance.

"I didn't believe her. If she hadn't already turned herself around for her daughter's sake, why would she now? I refused."

Ben didn't look at Connie.

"From that point on, she hated me. You remember what she was like. I couldn't do any good in her eyes, and after a while, I didn't care if I did."

"She hated you more than she loved me," Connie said. "Otherwise she would've stayed.

Hated, too, that you picked me instead of her." Sadness dulled her voice, sharpened his guilt.

He fumbled on. "Now, thinking back… with everything that has happened, I wonder if, maybe if I'd let her stay, if things would've been different. If we could've found a way for all of us to be together."

"I dunno," Connie said. "You hated her, too. I always thought it was because you figured Miranda was a bad influence on me."

"She was. And I did. But if I'd known that she had genuine feelings for me…I might've treated her better. We might not have seen each other as the enemy. She might not have forced you to choose between us."

He expected her to cut him down. Wanted it, even. Instead, she sighed. "I have my own list, remember?"

He finally understood how Connie felt. The need to come clean. How could he with a dead person? Connie had picked Ariel as her way to make it right with Miranda.

He'd do the same. Even as her father.

CHAPTER TWELVE

BEN CALLED FOR a DNA testing appointment the next morning and—whaddaya know?—there'd been a cancellation, and would he be able to come at two? He snapped up the time, not knowing if Ariel was free. She was probably at school and he didn't have her number to text. He could go through Connie, but given last night's conversation, the less he had to inflict himself on her, the better for them both.

On a hope and a prayer, he stopped at Connie's house during the school lunch hour.

"Hello?" he called out, entering.

A kitchen chair scraped against the tiles and Ariel came to the top of the stairs, a pepperoni stick in one hand and her phone in the other. "Auntie Connie's not here. She's at the farm."

Weird to have this hard-bitten teenager give Connie a childlike tag. "It's you I want to see," he said. "I have an appointment at the DNA clinic for two in Red Deer. Can you come?"

She didn't move. "You serious?" When he nodded, she said, "I've got a science test this afternoon. I don't know if I can get out of it."

"Can you get Connie to say you're sick or something?" That way, Ariel could be the one to tell her about the appointment.

"I'll try," Ariel said, and for the next while, she and Connie fired texts back and forth, while he leaned against the door and waited. At last, Ariel slipped her phone into her pocket. "She said she'd do it."

"And in return?"

Ariel halved the length of her pepperoni stick in one big bite. "I have to clean her bathroom if I fail the test." She began chewing contentedly. "Which I won't, because I've got an eighty-five average in science right now."

Ben experienced a shot of pride. No, it couldn't be that. Relief, then. Relief that Ariel's academics were not yet one more problem for Connie. "A high mark like that only proves I couldn't be your old man."

He'd meant it as a compliment, but the smile fell from her face. "I guess we'll see."

"Guess so," he said, and checked the time on his phone. Too early to go, not long enough to leave and come back. How to kill time? "You need to bring ID."

"What kind?"

How was it that everything he said triggered a new complication? "I dunno, birth certificate, learner's permit, social insurance number, whatever you got that proves you are you, I guess."

She thumped in her combat boots down the stairs, skimming past him as she rounded the staircase to her basement. "This'll take a while."

"Perfect," he said, because it was.

"Oh, and I'm the sarcastic one," she said over her shoulder.

He leaned against the door and kept the peace.

ARIEL DIDN'T SAY a word during the entire twenty-minute ride to Red Deer, which suited Ben. She sat straight and tilted a little forward, looking all around like a kid on a field trip. Maybe for her, it *was*. She'd moved to Spirit Lake two months ago, and how often had she gone into Red Deer since then? How often had she gone anywhere? Even in an old beater like his. It didn't sound as if Miranda had had a car, given her lifestyle, and from what Ariel had said, none of the gang kids she hung with were well-traveled.

Twice he felt her gaze on him and braced for whatever she might fire his way. But then her attention slipped away to a hawk in flight or a moving tractor in a field, and he relaxed again.

Once, she winced and cupped her hand over her jaw. He remembered her first night here when he'd taken her for a sub. "Your tooth still hurt?"

"A little."

A tooth didn't hurt a little for two months. By now, it probably hurt a whole lot. "Tell Connie about it. She'll take you to the dentist."

"It's fine." Ariel pulled her hand away but not a minute later her hand crept back. Fine, he'd say something to Connie himself.

In the waiting room of the clinic, the probabilities from late-night internet searches spun in his mind. He tried to look calm, indifferent. He glanced at Ariel, who seemed to be pulling off what he was aiming for. Either she'd achieved it, or they were both faking it.

In the end, the whole procedure from entering the private room to the mouth swab and out again took them under fifteen minutes.

In two or three business days, they'd know if they were family or not.

Getting back in the truck, Ben got a text from Connie. Seth's cow is in labor! Get out here! And in a second text, Please.

Ben groaned. What did he know about calving? The closest he'd come to a cow that wasn't in his burger was these last couple of days checking Seth's cattle, and each time he'd checked on the pregnant cow, he'd hoped she'd stay that way until Seth returned. No such luck.

Once again, he felt Ariel looking at him. This time, she spoke. "What's the problem?"

"Seth's cow is calving."

"So?"

"So I don't know anything about calving. He said to call the vet if the cow was in trouble but I'm not sure I'd be able to tell."

"Oh."

"Yeah. Oh."

He still had no clue as he observed the cow in the barn pen. The animal was lying down on the straw, her back end bulged and lifting as her muscles and the calf worked together. She looked fine.

A whole lot better than Connie, in fact. She

had lifted Callie into her arms, her face paler than he'd ever seen it. "Will she be okay? Should I call Seth?"

"No. He'll just worry and I don't know yet if there's anything to worry about."

"You don't need me here? I can go?"

The cow bawled, long and low and almost in surprise. Connie squeaked in terror and burrowed her head against Callie's shoulder, covering the little girl's own head with her hand, as if the barn roof was caving in.

"You can go," Ben said. Connie was off like a bullet, still holding Callie, back to the house, where she'd ordered the other kids to stay put.

He leaned on the gate. The cow had shifted around so that her back end was now on full display. He wanted to run after Connie. "Now what?" he said aloud to himself.

"I think we wait."

Ariel. He'd forgotten she was there. He'd brought her straight out to the farm with him, and had barely registered that she'd followed them to the barn. She turned her phone screen to him. It was a video of a black-and-white cow lying in straw, calving. "The front feet are the first to come out."

"Does it say how long that'll take?"

Ariel unmuted the video, and the soft voice of the narrator—the cow owner apparently—drifted into the barn. Not a minute passed before Ariel said, "She keeps cutting the video, so I can't tell."

Ben rested his arms on the top railing of the gate and his foot on the bottom one, and settled in to wait. Ariel came up beside him, leaned her arms on the second railing from the top and rested her chin on the top one.

"You don't have to stay."

"I know." She didn't move.

Okay, then. They watched the cow's back end bulge and retract, bulge and retract. Once she got halfway up on her hind legs, then folded down again and returned to the bulge-and-retract pattern. If this was farming, Seth could have it.

"Do you have a family?" Ariel asked.

The question had come out in a rush, a quick birthing of what she'd probably wanted to say on their drive to Red Deer.

"I'm an only kid," he said. "My mom left my dad and me when I was eight, and my dad eventually moved to Fort McMurray. Haven't seen him in nearly five years."

"You and him don't get along?"

Ben rubbed his thumb along the railing,

worn smooth from sixty-plus years of hands and arms doing much what he was now. No amount of sanding could replicate the slow wear of time and touch. "We don't not get along. We're just not interested in each other. He signed over the house to me, all paid for, before he left for Fort Mac and that was that."

His father had also given Ben fifty-seven thousand and six hundred dollars, an odd number, as if he'd drained the account to the nearest dollar. His father had written him the check on the truck hood warm and vibrating from the engine chugging underneath. He handed it over and said, "That enough?"

Ben had understood what he was really asking. *Is this enough for me to leave you in good conscience?* Ben told him it would do, folded the check once and put it in his shirt pocket. Then he'd shook his dad's hand and wished him a safe drive, his usual sendoff since he was ten. His dad had reversed out of the driveway; they'd waved to each other as they always did, shine or snow. His father had driven off and Ben had headed around the corner of the house to his workshop. And that had been that.

"Why did your mom leave? Was your dad beating her?"

What? Her expression was deliberately neutral, as if by assuming a horror she'd given him permission to lay on whatever the truth was. "No, he wasn't. Far as I can gather, she was bored. Of marriage, of being a mother."

"Wow. Cold."

Exactly what Connie had said of him. Was apathy inherited? From both sides?

Ariel seemed to believe so. "That explains your lack of interest when it comes to me. You didn't have any real parents so you think I don't need them, either."

"You get top marks in psychology, too?"

Ariel fixed her attention back on the cow.

"I had parents enough," Ben said. "Mrs. Greene and, until he died, Mr. Greene. Shirley and Jim." Even now, saying their names comforted him.

"I had parents in a way, too. Mom and Auntie Connie."

Ben knew where she was going with this one. "Until I came along and ruined it, right?"

"They weren't like how Alexi is with her kids," Ariel said. "Both of them burned the food all the time. I remember Mrs. Greene actually. She taught me how to use the toaster and cook an egg in the microwave. I made my own breakfasts because a lot of mornings they were too hungover."

It couldn't have been easy for Ariel. "I think," he conceded, "I came out ahead when it came to parents."

"Yeah, well, I've made it this far," she murmured.

She had. By the skin of her teeth, but she had. This time, he didn't deny feeling proud.

The cow stood and began to turn in the small space, moaning.

Ben straightened. "What's happening?"

Ariel lifted her chin off the railing and tilted her head to inspect the cow's rear end. "I see the feet!"

Sure enough, two hoofs protruded out, but then disappeared back inside the cow. Ben jutted his chin at Ariel's phone. "Is that normal?"

Ariel played more of the video and Ben watched it with her. It was. So was wrapping chains around the front legs and pulling the calf out.

"Should we do that?" Ben said.

"Might make it easier on the cow," Ariel said.

But not on him. "Let's wait."

The cow seemed to think Ben was talking to her and laid back down.

"What's going on with Trevor and the bag?"

By now, Ben was used to Ariel speaking out of the blue. How much to tell her? "I gave it to a guy who knows Trevor. He will talk to Trevor."

Ariel looked at him as if he'd gone insane. "Who is this guy? Does he understand who he's dealing with?"

Ben recalled how expertly and indifferently McCready had applied the tire iron to his windshield. "Believe me, he understands. I don't know how these gangs or dealers work, I'll be the first to admit that, but he does, okay?"

"If he doesn't get it right, and they get ahold of me—" She stopped, her teeth scraping her lip ring.

He said it for her, softly. "They'll kill you."

Her lip paled where her teeth had bit down so hard on it. "Or worse," she whispered.

That had never occurred to him. All kinds of ways to get even.

The cow rolled up on her heavy udder and began to pant. Out came the hooved feet again. Ariel stiffened. "Okay, I think she's close."

The hoofs disappeared again, leaving behind a red membrane-y balloon. Ugh. Connie would've puked if she'd seen it. He was having to swallow hard himself. The cow was panting now, her muscles flexing and straining. Minutes passed. The hooves didn't appear again.

Ariel strode over to a hook by the barn door and lifted off a long chain with a padded noose. "The kids said this is what Seth uses on the cows."

"That can't be right."

She began to unhitch the gate.

No way was she going to do his job. "I'll do it," he said. To cut off her arguments, he added, "I'm stronger and you need to tell me what to do."

That seemed to suit her fine—had she counted on him to react that way?—and he found himself kneeling on the straw, groping with his bare hands inside the cow for the feet.

"I got 'em," he said.

"Okay, so pull them out—gently—and then slip the rope around them quick before they get back in. Then you have to pull on the chain so the feet don't disappear inside again."

He did it and, while holding the tension on the rope, said, "Now what?"

She instructed him to pull in time with the contractions. When the calf squelched out onto the straw minutes later, she walked him through how to check the calf's breathing passages and how to wait for the cow to lick her calf dry and then to nudge the calf to the cow's engorged udder.

Good. Done. "When you get the results, will you tell Auntie Connie?"

He should've known he wouldn't be clearing the pen without at least one more question. "I'll give you my number now. I'll text you and Connie at the same time."

"How long will it take?"

"Two to three business days." He'd opted for the rush service.

"How long after you get them will you forward it to us?"

"Within twenty minutes. You can text me after three days if you haven't heard."

Ben was closing the gate when Ariel lobbed her last question.

"If it turns out not to be you, do you know who else it could be?"

What a thing for a kid to have to ask. Ben rolled off a strip of paper towel from a dispenser on the wall and wiped his hands as best he could.

"No," he said, giving her the most honest answer he could. "I don't."

"I guess you're my one chance, then," Ariel said.

At family. At what every lost and lonely kid, in combat boots or riding a bicycle, secretly wanted.

The calf's mouth latched onto his mother's teat and the tail became a wagging blur of bliss. The cow, her lashes long, blinked at Ben in clear dismissal.

Job done. He opened the gate and closed it behind him.

"Thanks," Ben said, "for helping out." He paused and then said, even though it sounded way too heavy, "I don't know if I could've done it without you."

Ariel pushed off the railing. "We didn't have a choice. Auntie Connie was as useless as teats on a bull."

CHAPTER THIRTEEN

AT SUPPERTIME, SETH and Alexi arrived back home from their short honeymoon. The kids instantly mobbed them, and Connie stood aside and let the family become a big cluster of hugs and kisses. Besides, she could never get enough of Seth going soft with his ready-made family.

He sat on the front porch, strung with the kitschy Welcome Home banner, two kids on his lap, two more pressed to his shoulders and a cat circling his legs. He was handing out gifts like Santa Claus. Even Ariel, off to the side as always, brightened when he tossed her a small present. A pack of cards. It twisted Connie's heart to see Ariel's quick blush and casual thanks. Who, except maybe her mother, would've bought her anything out of the blue? Connie still had to buy her a birthday gift.

Alexi came alongside Connie. "The kids look really happy. Thank you."

"Oh, they were great," Connie said. "No problems whatsoever." They might have a different story about her.

Alexi tipped her head. "But...?"

But I broke up with Ben, the kid in my care has a drug gang chasing her and my ex seems to want me hurt or killed or convicted. "I should start cooking the rice."

"Might as well call Mel and Ben," Seth said, his fingers already working his phone screen. Great. All she needed was to have to pretend that she and Ben were happy.

Amy thrust her arms into the air. "A family reunion!"

"Technically Ben isn't family unless he marries Auntie Connie," Bryn said.

"Which isn't happening," Seth cut in with a warning look at his new stepson.

As far as Seth was concerned, she was still not good enough for Ben. Alexi departed into the bedroom with the luggage and Connie pulled out her phone to do...something, anything, check Facebook.

There was a text from Ben. Ariel has a sore tooth. It's been like this for two months.

Two months? Why hadn't Ariel told her? How had Ben learned of it?

"Mel can come over," Seth said. "Ben's busy."

Busy telling her what she should have known, apparently. "Does Mel know I'm cooking?"

"Cooking? Whatever. You got the chicken from Sobeys and salad in a bag."

"Hey, the rice is all me. Speaking of which—" She should cook it.

Seth set to work on his phone. "I'll tell Mel to pick up fries from McDonald's. It'll satisfy his need to bring food and save you the trouble of burning another pot."

The kids had definitely told a different story. "Don't you need to milk a cow or something?"

Seth rose to his feet, kids and cats falling away from him like rocks down a hill. "I better make sure the new calf's okay. Honey?" he called to Alexi through the open kitchen window. "I'm going out to the barn. Callie and Amy went upstairs and I'll take the boys, all right?"

"All right, sugar," she chimed back.

Sugar? Connie mouthed to Seth. He glared and quickly left with the boys, who were happily beating on each other.

Connie picked up the crumpled wrapping paper and tried not to think of Ben. They hadn't been in contact all day, which felt like months and months. *Well, girl, get used to it.* She wanted the distance, in fact. Only—only—what was that stupid Chinese proverb? *Be careful what you wish for because you might get it.*

No. Stop with the regrets, Connie. Keep moving.

She shoved the last of the paper and ribbons and plastic into a bag and tied the handles. Now, time to shake out a salad.

As she entered the kitchen, Alexi appeared at the bedroom door adjoining the dining room. "Connie? Could you come here?"

She said it in a way that made Connie wonder if she'd left her dirty underwear lying on a pillow. She was sure she'd picked everything up that morning.

As soon as she entered the room and followed the direction of Alexi's gaze, she realized the one important piece she'd forgotten to pack. The ring box. It sat on the bedside table for all to see. Well, for Alexi and—thankfully—not Seth.

"Yours, by chance?"

"Uh, yes." Connie slipped the box into the leg pocket of her cargo pants. What was the story she'd told Lindsay? "A friend's actually. Friend of a friend, from Smooth Sailing. He lives with his girlfriend and he doesn't want her accidentally finding it and ruining the surprise, and he works up north and doesn't want to take it there into the camps."

Alexi frowned. "There's no ring in it. I checked."

Right. Ben had it. She must've looked as desperate as her thinking because Alexi touched her arm. "I'm sorry, Connie. I assumed Seth had put it there. That's why I opened the box. Do you know where it could be?"

"Oh, yes. I put it in—in a safety-deposit box."

"Why didn't your friend do that?"

"Uh, why didn't my friend do that? Well… you see, he, uh…"

Alexi took on the mother stance, hands on hips, head tilted, eyebrows raised. Connie remembered her own mother had assumed that position daily, if not hourly, with her. She herself had used it on Ariel. "Who gave it to you?" Alexi said.

Connie slumped to the bed. "Ben."

Alexi dropped down beside her. "Ben proposed to you?" The faint squeak in her voice shifted her out of her mother role into something else. Dare she call it friend mode?

"Yes."

"Wow." Alexi nudged Connie with her elbow. "Was it the wedding?"

"Ah, no. He'd proposed way before then. On Valentine's Day."

"Valentine's Day! And you two have kept it a secret all this time?"

"Yes, well, I didn't accept his proposal, and then he withdrew it." Because she'd told him that he suffocated her, except that since the wedding night, she'd felt as if she hadn't drawn a proper breath.

"Oh," Alexi said, and fell silent.

Connie was absolutely not going into Ben and Miranda and the whole paternity test thing. She drew on another truth. "He can do a lot better than me."

"You know what I thought when I first saw you?"

Connie cringed. She'd been Alexi's landlady at the time and she'd dressed herself in solid pink to muster the courage to kick her and her four kids out of the only home they knew. "That I made the evil queen in Cinderella look as—" she glanced around for inspiration and pointed "—cuddly as that stuffed animal?"

Alexi tucked the stuffie, a green moose

with scales, in her lap. “There was that. But also that you were the most beautiful woman I’d ever seen.”

“I am beautiful. That’s a fact. Like grass is green and birds have feathers.”

“Humble, too.”

Connie twisted to look at the other woman square-on. “It’s not as easy as you think. People make assumptions. I can’t tell if men want me for me or my body, and women are jealous and catty. You’ve no idea.”

Connie realized how that sounded at the same time Alexi whacked her with the moose. Oddly, it felt good. Normal. What a good friend would do when insulted.

What Miranda would’ve done when they’d been best friends and convinced her that nothing or nobody would get between them.

“I’ll have you know,” Alexi said, “that *two* men have proposed to me.”

Eager to keep the subject off her, Connie asked, “Honest now, whose was better?”

Alexi burst out laughing. “You wouldn’t believe Seth’s. It was the absolute worst. He probably—”

“—doesn’t want you telling his sister,” Seth said, pushing open the door, scowling.

"You have to admit it was pretty bad," Alexi said.

"You have to admit I made it up to you," he said.

They began to make bedroom eyes at each other.

Connie bounced off the bed. "I've got a big important salad to not make."

Later, after supper, Connie whispered to Alexi as they loaded the dishwasher, "Did you tell Seth?"

Alexi rattled in the last of the silverware and closed the door. "About what?"

Connie started to remind her when she caught sight of Alexi's face. "Brat," Connie pronounced, and snapped Alexi's leg with her dish towel.

Alexi grabbed another towel. "Game on."

And they—like friends, like *sisters*—were off—laughing, snapping, circling, while Mel and four kids cheered them on. Seth and Ariel rolled their eyes and went back to their poker game.

FROM THE MOMENT Seth insisted that he would drive Connie back to her house, she knew that her brother planned to have a word with her. Except, once in the truck, he hesitated, apparently having overlooked the presence of Ariel, who sat between them, gnawing on her lip ring and fiddling with the strap on her backpack.

"Oh, just spit it out," Connie finally said. "Ariel's heard it all."

"Heard too much," Seth said. "Whatever I have to say can wait."

"That's a first."

Seth pointed his finger at her. "Don't start."

Fine. She wouldn't. It had been a long, long time since she'd had so much fun with family. She'd counted three times that Seth's smile had included her, and once he actually laughed at something she said. Ben would have thought—

No. Move on.

She moved onto Ariel's bulging backpack. "How much homework do you have?"

"I have to read a story for English, that's it."

"Uh-huh. That bag's pretty full for one story."

"It's a long story."

"Hey," Seth said. "Connie just wants the best for you."

"Yes, Ben," Ariel muttered.

"What's that?"

Before Connie could stop her, Ariel said, "Ben goes on about how Auntie Connie is just taking care of me. Every day after school, he asks about homework like I'm his kid, which—"

Connie swatted Ariel's thigh and glared a warning. But even without the whole paternity matter, Seth had plenty to go on. "Why's Ben over there every day after school?"

"Fixing it up. He bought the house," said Ariel.

"No," Connie said. "He has not. He offered to buy it, but he hasn't."

"Well, you agreed to sell it to him. I was there, remember?"

"The deal fell through."

Ariel snorted. "Yeah, like the proposal."

Seth yanked the truck to the curb and parked fast. He switched on the overhead light. "You're right, Connie. Ariel *has* heard it all." His voice was hard, cold, not happy. "Ariel," he said with false cheer, "tell me about this proposal. I take it Ben asked Connie to marry him?"

Ariel shrank against the seat, and now—now she decided to keep her mouth shut. Time for Connie to open hers. She spoke fast. "Yes, Ben proposed, and I refused and he refused to accept my refusal. At first. Then he withdrew his proposal, took back the ring and now we're good. Okay?"

"What did you do to make him change his mind?"

Connie threw up her hands. "What makes you think I did something wrong? Maybe, just maybe, Ben figured out on his own that it was over between us."

Seth shook his head. "Three years since you two broke up, three years of him eating where you work, three years of getting sad when you started going out with someone else, three years of me never talking about you around him because it's such a sore point, and then he up and backs out of a marriage proposal to you? No. Something doesn't add up."

All the happy noise from this evening, all the repairs she'd done to their relationship, were ripped away. Nothing left but him, angry and suspicious. As always. Everything, the wedding, taking care of the kids, working on her stupid course, none of it had worked.

"What can I do," she whispered, "to make you stop hating me?"

He stilled. "I don't hate you."

But his words were too quick, too hollow-sounding. She pressed back against her seat and looked out the window at the darkened trees. She'd bail out of the truck, except that Ariel was right there, and if a sixteen-year-old could deal with freaks hunting her, then she could take a little truth from Seth. And maybe he could take some from her.

"I can't do nursing, Seth. I tried. I was okay with CPR. It made sense. But all this chemistry and statistics… I mean, I can do it, I know I could get through it all, but out in the real world? I nearly fainted when the cow was calving. I ran away. Ariel ended up helping Ben. It wasn't that it was gross, but all I could think about was all the ways it could go wrong. What kind of nurse does that? I'm just not that interested in sick people. I know me saying this is a big disappointment to you and I'm sorry. I'm really sorry. You got a criminal record for me so I could make something of myself and all I did was screw up and here I am again flat-out telling you that I can't do it. I'm sorry, I'm sorry, I'm sorry—"

"Connie," Seth said, "shut up."

Between them, Ariel made a sound Connie had never heard. A whimper of fear, a quiet plea for them to stop.

As one, Seth and Connie slumped against

their seats. Seth reached for the gearshift behind the wheel, then pulled back. “I forgive you.”

Connie gasped. Like a drowning person who surfaces and takes in their first air.

“And you don’t have to make it better. If you don’t want to go into nursing, you don’t have to.”

She sucked in another breath.

“I went into farming. What guy pushing forty gives up steady money to go into something he knows next to nothing about? Especially when he has a family to support.”

She hadn’t realized he was so worried about his decision. “It’ll work out.”

“All I’m saying is that if you want to do something other than nursing, then I can hardly blame you.”

“Except I don’t know what I want to do.”

Ariel loosened her hold on her backpack, and a small smile played at the corners of her mouth. “Party.”

“That’s so not true. I work, I volunteer, I help with the kids, I take care of you. I don’t even remember the last time I went to a party.”

“The wedding.”

"My *brother's* wedding. That's an occasion."

"A party." Ariel turned to Seth. "And there are posters all over the school for a huge year-end event she's planning for all the kids. Hundreds of kids. A summer kickoff. I call it a party."

"I call it a party, too," Seth agreed. He switched off the overhead light and headed the truck down the street. The discussion was over for him. Apparently, he and Ariel thought her life was one big party after another.

"It's not like before," she said. "It's just people together, having fun. That's all, I swear."

"Connie," Seth said quietly, "I know. I was at my wedding, remember?"

The wedding where Luke and Derek, drunk, got into a fight.

"You organized a great party, everyone had fun, the drinking didn't get out of hand and it was perfect."

A compliment, finally, but one she didn't deserve. "Well, actually—"

Ariel swatted Connie's thigh and glared. Pulling up to the house, Seth caught the movement and glanced at Connie.

"As I was saying," she said. "there were

lots of people who helped with the wedding. And yes, including you, Ariel."

Ariel bit her lip, this time to hold back a smile, and sweetly dipped her head. "Thanks, Auntie Connie."

"You're welcome," she answered, and hopped out of the truck. Ariel slid out and continued up the walk to the house. Connie turned to Seth.

"All right," she said. "You can say what you've been itching to tell me."

"I forget now." Seth hitched himself in his seat. "I don't hate you, Connie." He smiled a little and then it grew big and for her alone. "In fact, it's probably the opposite."

She matched his smile. "I love you, too, bro."

She quickly shut the truck door and walked away to ease his embarrassment.

IN HER OWN bed for the first night in four days, Connie reached into her bedside drawer and pulled out her current steno pad. Very carefully, she drew a line through Ben Carruthers's name because she'd promised him she would.

As soon as she finished, she wanted to undo it. She felt as if she'd cheated. Ariel had told her that Ben would let them know about the results of the paternity test. She'd said that the test had gone "all right." Helping Ben with the cow had also gone "all right." She'd also let drop that Ben had passed the bag of pills to someone who she figured out was McCready. That had also gone "all right."

Connie ached for details about Ben's meeting with McCready but that would mean talking to Ben, and while she could claim a right to know based on Ariel's involvement, last night's revelations had left them both tender and raw.

Best to leave him alone right now. She had no right to demand that he give her space and then not give it to him.

She drew a second line through Seth's name and felt good about that. She hovered her pen over Miranda's name. Close, but she needed to ensure Ariel's safety from the gang first. And her own, for that matter.

She didn't even consider Trevor McCready's name.

CHAPTER FOURTEEN

"EIGHT CAVITIES?"

Connie stared at the dentist and down at Ariel. The girl was stretched out on the dental chair, looking as shocked as Connie felt. Eight times two hundred was sixteen hundred bucks. If Ben turned out to be Ariel's father, she knew where the first child support payment was going.

"The good news is that five are tiny pinholes." Jeremy Dillard, the dentist, sat on his stool on the other side of Ariel. "They can wait for a couple of months."

Five-eighths of Connie's stress disappeared. "And the other three?"

Jeremy bared his pearly whites in a sympathetic grimace. "I could put off two for a few weeks but there's one—" he tapped a dark splotch on the X-ray up on the computer behind Ariel's head "—here. I might have to do a root canal."

Ariel twisted around to view her teeth, all

transparent and gray and garish. "What's a root canal?"

"The cavity has reached down through the tooth and touched the nerve," Jeremy said. "Inflammation happens. That's why you've been experiencing soreness."

"Pain," Ariel said. "Pain."

"Uh, yes," Jeremy said. "So to repair the cavity, we need to go deeper than we normally do and work at the level of the nerve."

Ariel turned to the wall where a picture of teddy bears on a bench hung. "Okay."

Jeremy switched to Connie. "I have a cancellation this afternoon. I could do it right away, if that works. We'll just put it into your current account plan."

"No!" Ariel lifted her head. "I just said 'okay' to what you said. I didn't agree to it." She squirmed to get out of the chair, not easy given she was sloped backward.

Connie clamped her hand over Ariel's arm. "Jeremy, can you give us a minute?"

"Sure. I'll have someone come by in a bit," he said, already exiting.

Connie pushed aside the overhead light and scooted her chair close to Ariel's head. "All right. What's up?"

Ariel stared at the ceiling. "Nothing's up.

I've had enough of being poked for one day, is all."

"Not buying it," Connie said. "You've been on extra-strength ibuprofen for…what? A week, a month—24/7? You've got the chance to end the pain right now. What's the problem?"

Ariel's arm was as stiff as wood. She closed her eyes, her long lashes a thick fringe. Miranda had had the same unbelievable lashes. "They'll give me a needle, right? For the freezing?"

Okay, the needle. Understandable. "No one likes them, Ariel. But it'll last for a second and then—"

She stopped. Of course. A needle. Miranda had shot up, probably in front of Ariel. Ariel had seen someone she loved, the only person she'd loved, die from using a needle.

"I get it," Connie said. "I get it. Listen, they have what they call 'sedation dentistry.' Do you want me to check into that?"

Ariel shook her head. "That costs too much."

"That's fine," Connie said. It would be if Ben was her dad. Otherwise she might as well have Dizzy sign her paycheck directly over to Jeremy. "Here. Let me ask at the front desk, okay?"

No dice. Ariel would require medication ahead of time, which meant losing out on the present opening, and Connie really didn't want Ariel going through five more days of pain. Somehow she needed to get Ariel through her fear.

When Connie broke the bad news to Ariel, tears pooled in her hazel eyes. Tears from the same girl who'd stuck it to an entire gang. The girl who described her mom's death without a single lip tremble.

"Hey, hey, it's okay," Connie said. Keri, the dental assistant, peeked around the divider at them and looked as though she was about to speak when she spied Ariel. Connie mouthed, *Ten*, and she nodded and disappeared as if patient breakdowns were routine here at the Dillard Dental Clinic.

Her tears spilled out, and Ariel gazed at Connie with the pleading look of a small child. *Make it stop. Make it all better.*

Connie planted the box of tissues from the counter behind Ariel on her lap. She stripped out a handful and wiped Ariel's cheeks, first the right, then the left and back to the right. "You let it out."

"I don't want to cry," Ariel said in a tearclogged whisper. "I want to get my tooth fixed but…but…"

"Okay. You don't need to say it, sweet pea," Connie said, stripping out tissues and wiping, wiping. "I get it."

How to do the filling without strapping Ariel down? "What we're going to do," Connie said with absolute confidence, "is throw you a party."

"What?" Ariel said. "You can't make me have a party I don't want."

"Hear me out. When was the last time I threw you a birthday party? You were, like, eleven, right?"

"Yeah."

"See? I'm way overdue."

"I don't want a party. I want—"

"Your tooth fixed." Connie caught sight of Keri and waved her down. "We want to get a tooth fixed here."

The assistant took her cue, and Connie moved to let her take the chair. Connie quickly sat on Jeremy's stool. Ariel's grip on the armchair tightened but she said nothing. "All righty, then," Keri said, and smiled at Ariel as if she was the prettiest thing on earth and not snot-nosed and red-eyed and strung out.

Connie could've kissed her. "Let's take care of you."

Panic began to widen Ariel's eyes. "I don't want—"

"A party," Connie said, practically taking apart each sound of each word as she spoke. "You want to get your tooth fixed."

Ariel's eyes rolled to Connie. "Don't leave me."

Except Jeremy would need his stool back. To insert the needle.

"I'm not going anywhere," Connie said. "I'll stay here. We'll talk about the party. I like to start with the venue. The house?" Someone pushed another stool from the reception area into the cubicle. Was someone monitoring from the other side of the divider? Connie snagged it and settled herself directly behind Ariel.

Jeremy came in, the needle discreetly at his side. These guys were good. Maybe they ran drills for this sort of thing. Watched reenactments. Were they being taped? A debriefing to follow after-hours?

Jeremy slid into his seat and asked Ariel what she had planned for the rest of the day.

Wrong move. Ariel lifted her head and shoulders clear off the chair and glared at him. "Don't screw with me. I know what you have."

Connie eased Ariel back onto the chair and cupped her hands around Ariel's face. She half expected the rebel to bat away her hands but instead she nestled her cheek, the side with the bad tooth, against Connie's hand.

"Auntie Connie."

"Yes?"

"I want—I want…you to help me get my tooth fixed."

Connie didn't move her hands. "I can do that."

The needle went in as Connie babbled about cakes, balloons, books, prizes, guests, music, presents, housecleaning.

When the freezing took, Connie withdrew to Ariel's feet, while Jeremy and his beautiful assistant did their magic show.

Once on the street, they walked home like zombies. Ariel said, "I know you were just talking about a birthday party to distract me. You don't have to do it."

Ariel didn't seem fazed by the procedure, but Connie was sure the whole side of her face must feel as big as a beach ball. "If you want a party," Connie said, "I'll help you get through it."

Ariel scraped a tooth on her numbed lip. "I got through a root canal. I guess I could survive one of your birthday parties."

BEN ATE PIZZA alone in his workshop. Connie was probably working her first shift at Smooth Sailing since the wedding. Him eating there wouldn't work on so many levels, and he didn't have the energy to sit alone anywhere else. So his workshop it was, downing pizza straight out of the box. Pizza he had to pick the olives off because he'd forgotten not to order them.

A shadow passed by the workshop window, activating the motion detector light. McCready? Trevor? Ben crossed his shop and threw open the door.

A man stumbled, and his foot crunched the gravel at the entrance to the workshop. "Ben. That you?"

Derek. A very drunk Derek.

"It is. Come in. Have a seat."

"Sure," Derek said, drawling out the single word. "I've got a bit of time." He negotiated the doorway and Ben quickly unfolded a lawn chair. Derek fell into it. The frame caved and splayed but held.

"So," Derek slurred, "what have you been

up to?" He looked around, probably for something with alcohol. Had the man sobered up at all since the wedding?

"Not much," Ben said. Not much he would admit to, anyway. "I kept an eye on Seth's farm while he was off on his honeymoon."

Derek scrunched his face. "Oh, yeah. He's married." He gave a short, harsh laugh. "The last to swing from the old marriage noose."

"I'm not married," Ben reminded him.

Derek's laugh grew louder. "Face it. You and Connie have been married since you were kids. You just don't have the matching rings, is all."

Ben held out the pizza box to Derek. "Pizza?"

"Sure." Derek began to rise but Ben got to him first. He lifted a piece heavy on the olives and offered it to the other man. "Here. Sorry I don't have a plate. Or napkins." The pepperoni topping was sliding off before Derek snagged it in his mouth.

Solid food would do him good. Why had he shown up here? They'd never hung out together separate from Luke and Seth. Then again, Derek wouldn't be spending time at Smooth Sailing with the way things stood between him and Luke. Maybe he and Derek did have something in common.

"Hey, what's that?" Derek meant the headboard. The bedsheet had slipped off it at some point into a heap on the floor.

"That? A…a couple ordered it."

"Oh, yeah?" Derek got himself upright and walked toward it with his drippy pizza. "You did all the woodwork?"

"Yeah."

Derek squinted. "Leaves. Wheels. Baseball bat. Oookay. Wheels. What are these wavy lines?"

"Hair. Waves. Wind."

"For newlyweds?"

Why not? "Yeah."

"Aha." Derek pointed a wavering finger somewhere in the direction of Ben. "It's a wedding gift for Seth and Amanda."

Let him think that. "Alexi."

Derek had gone back to studying the board. "Hey, you know what's missing? Rings."

If Ben didn't see another ring for the rest of his life, it would be too soon.

"Rings are like…like the ultimate symbol of marriage. You don't have a ring—" Derek waved his bare left hand deep into Ben's face space "—then you don't have a marriage."

Finally, a perfect lead-in to guide Derek away from the headboard. Ben bent and picked up a corner of the sheet. "I take it you and Lindsay haven't worked things out."

Derek remained rooted too close to the headboard for Ben to pull the sheet across without making it into a big production.

"Things couldn't be better," Derek answered, cramming the last of the pizza into his mouth. "We're finally having open, honest communications. Open and honest until I tell her what I'm thinking and then she yells at me. Not saying I don't deserve to be yelled at. But her yelling and me—well, me not feeling much more than sorry for her doesn't make for a marriage."

Connie's sad, pitying eyes from two nights ago rose to Ben's mind. No one wanted to be pitied. "Aren't you even going to try to make it right with Lindsay?"

Derek plunked himself on the sawhorse directly in front of the headboard. Maybe now that Derek's attention was diverted, hiding the headboard might not matter anymore. Ben dropped the sheet.

"Haven't you heard a word I said?" Derek launched into his troubles. "Before the yelling was the talking. And this is where it gets complicated. You see, I love Shari and

I thought she loved me, but in the end she chose Luke."

The corner of Derek's mouth pulled down. "No surprise there. But it kinda sucks for me because I can't be with Shari, and no one can do anything about that. And nothing I can do about the fact that Lindsay loves me and I don't love her back." Derek pointed his hand at Ben. "And that's when the yelling starts."

Ben understood Lindsay's need to yell. He'd kicked and yelled at a lot of things after his breakup with Connie, although he'd been by himself and far away when he'd done it. Ben hoped Lindsay had tucked her kids away before she'd started in. Except Connie had faked her affair, so why then—

"Explain to me why Shari had an affair with you if she loved Luke."

Derek leaned in conspiratorially, so far that he had to move his foot from the sawhorse to the floor to brace himself. "That's the thing. The one thing I'm better at than Luke is loving his wife."

A competition? Derek had ruined his marriage and a friendship, not for love but to prove who could love better?

"But Shari," Derek continued, "being Shari, has decided that it's better to love than be loved, or loved not quite as much. Which took me a whole lot of beers to figure out."

"I see that."

"Which is why—" Derek pointed at the engraving "—you need to put rings on that thing."

Back to this. "The couple doesn't want them."

"Seth and Amanda will want them."

"Alexi. They don't."

"Here." Derek came off the sawhorse and set his finger on a blank spot in the wood exactly where Ben had once considered adding rings. "Put them here."

"Look. Derek. I'm telling you—"

"You don't believe me. Let me show you." He picked up a chisel Ben had left on the sawhorse.

No. "I'll take that, Derek." Ben reached for the tool but Derek lifted it away.

"I got it, I got it. Let me just shape it in for you. Show you what I mean."

Derek shouldered up to the headboard, blocking Ben from the chisel and the engraving.

"Stop it, Derek." Ben tossed the sheet at the headboard, hoping to intercept Derek.

Instead, Derek knocked the sheet away

with his elbow, the sharp move causing the chisel to drive straight into the wood, the blade scoring the wheels, leaves and a mermaid tail.

Derek swayed in front of Ben. "Oh, man, I'm sorry."

Ben didn't realize he was planning to punch Derek until the impact of his fist on Derek's jaw shunted up his arm. Derek reeled back against the headboard. The sheet of wood skidded and crashed to the cement floor, Derek landing on top of it.

Derek tried to stand, stepped on the soft pine, splintering the wood.

This time when Ben drove his fist into Derek's face, he knew exactly what he was about.

Hard hands gripped his shirt at the shoulders and pulled him off Derek.

"Ben!" It was Seth. "Easy. Easy."

Ben breathed hard, forced himself to say, "Get him out of here."

Derek, nose bleeding, was again trying to scramble to his feet. Seth released Ben and steadied Derek, moving him toward the door and handing him a box of tissues. All the while, Derek mumbled, "Sorry, man, sorry for the headboard. Just wanted to get the rings on. You know what a symbol they are. Oh, man, I screwed up."

Seth almost had him out the door when he stopped and said to Seth, "Look, buddy, it's been bugging me. I'm sorry for getting into that fight."

"No worries—"

"No, that wasn't right. Not at your wedding. That's just bad luck. I've, like, cursed your marriage."

Ben flew at Derek again, but Seth more or less heaved Derek out the door first, disappearing with him. Hopefully to carry on where Ben had left off, though he doubted that. Seth was not drunk or angry or hurt. He was happily married to the woman he loved and who loved him back with all her heart.

There was no fixing the headboard. A fitting end to his campaign to win Connie. He should be thanking Derek for doing what he would've had to do, anyway.

The door opened and Seth walked in again. "I got him sitting on your back steps, dealing with his nosebleed. I'll check on him in a bit."

Seth picked up the headboard and leaned it against the wall. He drew the white bedsheet slowly, respectfully, over the board, like over a murder victim. He settled himself on the sawhorse where Derek had sat, except facing Ben at the workbench, and said nothing.

Ben knew Seth would sit there all night, if need be. Like the way Ariel had stayed with him in the barn. He might not have the woman he wanted but he did have two people who cared enough not to leave him alone to deal with his problems.

"Things were pretty intense," Ben said, and leaned against his workbench, "while you were away."

"Sounds as if it started before then."

"Yeah, Connie figured out back in February that Derek was sleeping with Luke's wife." Ben picked his next words carefully. "Him and Luke got into a bit of a fight in the parking lot during the wedding. But listen, Derek's drunk. Your marriage isn't cursed."

Seth shifted his butt on the hard wood. "I know that. He's just feeling guilty. I'm good." He paused. "It does explain a few things."

He paused again, clearly waiting for Ben to fill in the rest of the details, but Ben didn't want to bring up the topic of Connie.

"All right," Seth said. "I'll say it. Reason I came by tonight was because Connie says you two talked about getting married."

"It was my idea," Ben clarified. "She convinced me otherwise, so we're good, back to the way things were."

"All right."

That quick acceptance wasn't normal for Seth. Usually any conversation about Connie included an apology, a rant, a warning. "I know you're all right with it," Ben said, "but for the record, it wasn't because of anything she did. It was me."

Ben really didn't want to tell Seth about Miranda, but between Connie and Ariel, it might come out. Seth deserved to hear it straight from the one he'd chosen as his best man.

He spilled his guts to Seth. About Miranda. About Connie resisting his proposal. Even of her fake affair. Of putting his house up for sale and his plan to move into Connie's. With every pent-up worry and secret released, Ben experienced the wash of contentment that can only come with a heart-to-heart with a longtime friend. Other than a few questions, Seth stayed quiet. When Ben declared himself done, Seth tipped his head toward the headboard. "I take it that was for you and her."

Was. "Yeah. A gift to go with the ring. She doesn't know about it. Just as well."

Seth shifted a bit more on the sawhorse. He cleared his throat once, twice. Preparing to remind Ben about Connie, to deliver his best buddy "I-told-you-so" about his wild sister.

Instead, he said, "You? A dad?"

"I seriously doubt it."

"Still."

"Could be worse. Could be four kids."

"Four of mine equals one of yours."

Given the trouble Ariel was in, Seth was probably right. "Listen, I don't want you thinking badly of Connie," Ben said. "She's changed. Or maybe it's that she's gone back to the way she was when she was a kid. You know, friendly to everyone, wanting to fix all the damaged souls. I mean, remember the Polar Dip. Out there, half naked to earn money—"

"Yeah," Seth said. "I was there. That's when I knew for sure she had changed. Man, I was so relieved. I thought I'd done permanent damage."

"What?"

"After Dad died, I rode Connie hard about everything. No wonder she never felt good enough. Especially when it came to you. I made it pretty clear she was to keep her hands off you. It used to get to me that, with you, she could do no wrong. But I was worse. With me, she could do no right."

Seth winced. "I shouldn't have got in the way. I acted like you two couldn't figure out how to be together for yourselves."

They hadn't figured it out, but stating that would only invite Seth to become involved. Still, there was one area of Connie's life Seth needed to know about.

"Remember Trevor?"

Seth stiffened. "What's he done to her?"

Seth was pacing tight circles between the sawhorse and door by the time Ben got him up to speed.

"I was worried about Connie and Ariel staying in the house alone last night," Ben said. "I drove by their place at three in the morning."

"It's all the other hours I'm thinking about."

"You and me both."

"I should be there. Just the idea of Connie in danger means I won't rest."

But wasn't that the point she'd tried to make to Ben at Seth's wedding? There never had been anyone else. There had only ever been him. She was as alone as him. He'd only heard part of her message about not wanting him. He'd missed the part about not wanting to need him.

He'd deal with Derek. Let him sleep it off on his couch. Or his bed, since he'd no plans to use it tonight.

Ben tossed the pizza box into his garbage. "You go home to your family, Seth. I've got Connie covered."

THE WEDDING PHOTO was gone from Lindsay's desk in her office at the town hall. Instead, it was covered with paper, sticky notes and a take-out burger wrapper, a paper coffee cup… and deodorant? Lindsay swept that last item into the open maw of her purse as Connie sat.

Lindsay's wedding ring was also gone from her hand.

The half hour meeting about the year-end event stretched into a full hour with both her and Lindsay riffling through piles of paper to locate the correct form, only to riffle in a different direction for another one. Forms Connie had completed and emailed back to Lindsay months ago. Now today, when everything should've been in place, Lindsay couldn't find any record of them on her computer and was hoping to find them in the paper mess.

"I'm so sorry," Lindsay said for about the millionth time. "I'm usually not so disorganized."

"No worries," Connie said, "we all have days like this." She shook loose a sheet from the pile. "Is this it?"

"Yes," Lindsay said. "How did you do that?"

"Practice. You should see my bed. At any one time, you can find thermal socks and my bikini."

Tears welled in Lindsay's eyes. "My bed is empty."

Lindsay blinked fast and furious, and Connie dived for the door, closing it so Lindsay could fall apart in private.

"Hey," Connie said softly, coming around the desk. "Want to talk?"

Lindsay breathed in and out, in and out, pointlessly smoothing the edge of the desk with her fingertips. "It's over. We've agreed to that."

"Oh." Derek was a jerk, but he'd been Lindsay's jerk. "Oh. I am sorry."

"He told me that he had loved her for a long, long time. Since before she and Luke got married. He said he liked me, thought he loved me, at least enough to make a family, and so he did. But a year ago she gave him an opportunity and he took it.

"It's ironic, really. I can almost sympathize with him. I know what it is to love somebody who doesn't love you back to the same degree."

"Ouch."

"He laughed when I said that and left."

And ended up at Ben's place. He had told her about Derek's visit when she'd come home from work to find him stretched out on her couch. Derek was sleeping it off on Ben's couch, and Ben had decided he'd be camping out in her living room every night until the issue of Trevor was settled. Ariel was sleeping downstairs and fine with the arrangement.

Ben had also confessed that he'd told Seth about Trevor, and that if Ben wasn't on the couch, then Seth would be, and no one wanted that, right? Then he'd wished her good-night and flicked off the lamp. Connie hadn't argued—couldn't, really—and she'd slept better than she had in ages. Slept straight through Ariel leaving for school and Ben leaving for…somewhere. She'd no business knowing.

Connie covered one of Lindsay's restless

hands with her own. "You will find someone who will love you, and you alone."

"You mean like how Ben loves you?"

Connie withdrew her hand and sucked in her breath, every bit as deeply as Lindsay had. "Yes."

"Why don't you love him? I don't get it."

"I do love him."

"Do you love someone else more?"

"No."

"Well, then?"

"I need to deal with things from my past before I can move on. Otherwise I'll screw it up again."

"So? Who said you have to be perfect at love? Who said you even have to be good at it? You just have to keep showing up." She lifted her eyes to Connie's. "Practice."

Practice makes perfect.

She'd struck Ben's name from her list. Was she ready to practice with him again? Not while Trevor was on the loose. She promised herself and everyone on the list she'd stick to it, and she would. Not giving up was her new way to love. Lindsay pushed back her chair and stood. "I'm quitting."

Connie blinked. Had she missed something? "What?"

"You can take my job. You're better at it than me, anyway."

"No. Lindsay. Listen—"

"You're right. I need to deal with things, too. I've practiced all the wrong things. I've just been thinking that if I kept at it, if I kept being friends with Shari, she'd be friends back. If I worked hard, I'd be a good mom. If I looked nice, Derek would love me. None of it worked. Even my kids—" Lindsay took in a breath deep enough to suck all the oxygen out of the room "—even my kids blame me for their dad leaving."

Lindsay bent and picked up her purse. "You're right, Connie. Love's too important to just hope it'll work out. Look at me, look at you." Lindsay's voice had risen to a squeak. She dropped her fat purse on the desk and began to toss in random stuff.

"Linds, I get that things are bad right now—"

"Things are no worse now than they were on Valentine's Day when I thought Derek loved me." Into her purse went a chunky earring and a paisley mug. "Except now I know the truth." She stuffed in a pen topped with a giant daisy and the mouse pad printed with Live, Love, Laugh. "I'm not faking it anymore." Then the framed photo of the kids. "I'm not."

Lindsay swiped away her tears and gripped her Mary Poppins of a bag. "I'm leaving."

Which she did, with a terrific slam of the door.

The force lifted a sheet off the desk and it drifted to Connie's feet. A request for security—the one form they still needed.

Wow. How perfect was that?

CHAPTER FIFTEEN

When the email with the paternity results popped into his phone, Ben's courage failed him. No way could he fire off a text to Connie and Ariel and leave it at that. The outcome, either one, mattered too much. He drove over to the house and walked inside.

Connie was perched on a stool at the kitchen island, her laptop open in front of her. She wore pink flannel pajamas, her hair scrunched in a high ponytail with the big pink tie-thing he well remembered.

All that pink was not good.

She took one look at him and reached for her phone. "I'll tell Ariel to come home as soon as she can."

"She'll skip school if you do that."

Connie's fingers didn't stop moving over the keypad. "Nearly home time, anyway." Message sent, she pointed to the fridge. "Pick your poison."

Ben cracked open a can of Coke and wondered if it was the last time he'd drink as a man with no family obligations. Parenthood was like getting conscripted into a job for which he had no qualifications, but failure resulted in human tragedy.

"Why are you in pink?"

"I'm getting my résumé ready." She'd returned to the laptop and was squinting at the screen, pressing on the keys.

"What? What!" She exploded at the screen. "Line up, will you?"

She stripped the pink hair tie from her hair, rustled the blond mass into a wild stack Ben's fingers twitched to smooth out and then she bunched it all back together into its original shape. The whole operation took about thirteen seconds, and he remembered it well from every time she'd been frustrated since she was ten.

Ben rounded the island and glanced at her screen. "Looks good to me."

She pointed her pink-tipped finger at the page. "No. See. This diamond should have the same spacing as the one above it. I got the other one to work but this one is an ab-so-lute pig."

"Try hitting the tab key."

"I have! It makes it worse."

Fresh out of ideas, he changed the subject. "What are you applying for?"

"The position of event coordinator for the town opened up."

Something in her voice, with its studied flatness, put him on alert. "Isn't that Lindsay's job?"

"It was. She left it."

"Left it. When?"

"Today. Two hours ago. During my meeting with her. I was helping her look for a form and she told me that she and Derek were done and she was quitting. Then she suggested I'd be better at her job than she was, and then… and then…"

Connie did the thirteen-second hair trick again.

"Derek says she yells. Did she yell?"

Connie's phone pinged. "Ariel. She's on her way."

"Did Lindsay yell at you?"

"She got louder, yeah." Connie thumbed out a text, presumably to Ariel. "That's fine. I understand."

But it probably accounted for the color of her outfit.

"Connie," he said, trying to sound as if it

were a point of interest only, "did you wear pink when we broke up?"

"What? No." She scowled at her screen, then with a growl pushed it away and lowered her face into her hands. "I *ate* pink, okay? I ate buckets of strawberry ice cream and berry popsicles. Strawberry milkshakes. Cupcakes with pink icing. And *ham*. Straight from the package. It was gross. To this day, I can't stand ham."

"You regretted it?"

"No. I didn't eat anything else, so I didn't gain a pound."

Ben bit back a smile. "I meant, did you regret breaking up with me?"

She spread her fingers and peeked out at him. "I did and I didn't."

"Because you felt free."

"Because I finally wasn't taking advantage of your love. I finally did something nice for you."

"It didn't feel that way."

She shut her fingers up tight. "I know."

"I forgot to eat," he said. "I drove south and fueled up the truck, but skipped meals. Days would go by." He paused. "I didn't gain a pound, either."

Her fingers dug into her forehead so hard

they'd leave marks. "I'm sorry, Ben. I know I already said that but I have nothing else to say."

"Don't forget about how I wouldn't let you go, either." He tugged her hands away. "Let's just say we both made mistakes and leave it at that." He didn't want to leave it at that. He wanted to pull her close and breathe in her mussed hair and ask—beg—her to forgive him for Miranda, to take him back. But he didn't want to put her in that position.

The front door flew open. "I'm home!"

Home. He and Connie exchanged smiles.

They triangulated themselves around the kitchen table, Ben's phone in the middle.

"All right," Connie said, her eyes on Ariel. "How about we all agree that no matter what the results are, we all have to stay seated at the table for a full five minutes afterward?"

Ben took in Ariel's cornered look and the blush that now suffused Connie's cheeks. "Sure, but as for the sixth minute," he said, "I plan to flip the table and flop to the floor."

Connie narrowed her eyes. "Open the email."

He stretched his arm out full length and tapped on the attached document. They all leaned in, heads inches apart. Ben began reading as soon as the words sprang up, until he came to the only one that mattered: *negative.*

He should've felt total relief but instead there was a sliver of…disappointment.

Ariel's face was stone. "Well, I guess that's that." Her chair scraped like nails as she pushed away from the table.

Connie pointed at her. "You promised."

Just like that Ariel dropped onto the hard-wood chair. She looked at Ben. "I guess you were right."

He held her gaze. "If I were wrong, I wouldn't have minded."

"Yeah, well, me, neither." She began to trace the wood grain on the table with her finger.

Connie held up her hands, palms out. "All right, guys. Enough with this big dramatic display of emotion. Let's just coolly, calmly discuss our options."

Ariel rolled her eyes, and for the second time during his visit, he worked hard not to smile. This was the Connie he knew and would always love.

"Nothing changes," Connie said. "I'll still keep working to get custody of you. I got a terrific job opportunity today, so we'll be all right. It has health benefits, so you won't have to worry about your teeth."

"I'm not worried about my teeth," Ariel muttered.

"You're not, but I am," Connie said.

Ariel circled a knot in the wood grain. "Thanks, Auntie Connie."

Connie didn't miss a beat. "You're welcome. Now, could you please help me with my stupid résumé?"

Shoulder to shoulder at Connie's laptop, the two main females in Ben's life began gently bickering their way through the problem at hand. They were set for life, those two.

Providing Trevor didn't screw it up for them.

He waited until Ariel explained about tabs and headers and then had gone down to her room with a muffin before starting in.

"I spoke to Paul at the police station about Trevor. He's on their radar, but they're not saying where he is, if they know. McCready's our best shot. Right now, he's our only shot."

"What about the Calgary gang? What did Paul say about them?"

"He wasn't aware of them, and I didn't have much info to give him. He said to call it in if any of us noticed anything or saw anybody suspicious."

Connie stripped out the hair tie and started in on her hair again. Thirteen seconds was all it took for him to come to her and tug her from her bar stool into his arms. Man, she felt good in her soft pajamas and—

"You smell pink," he said.

She wrapped her arms tightly around his waist, and she flattened herself to him. Even her cheek was pressed against his shirtfront. He allowed the rightness, the goodness, of the moment to soak into him. This. Forever. No matter what.

"Let me love you, Connie."

Her arms tightened hard enough to leave an imprint. "What if Trevor hurts you?"

"Take me to the hospital."

"If you die? And don't tell me that can't happen. It can."

"Then you get everything."

"What?" She lifted her head and searched his face.

"Who else?"

Her eyes widened, took on a hunted look. He cupped her face. "I'm not asking you to marry me. Not that I'd refuse if you asked me. All I'm saying is that when you 'take advantage of me,' as you put it, I feel good. I don't feel used. I feel useful."

Her pink lips parted. "That's a very dangerous idea, Ben. Especially in this house, which needs a ton of fixing."

"So…you're letting me in?"

"Trevor's on my list. Not yours."

"How many are left on it?"

"Trevor and Miranda, but if I deal with Trevor, that means Ariel's old life is behind her and I'll feel square with Miranda."

Then am I in? The question he desperately wanted to ask, the question that made him weak to ask.

She stepped back and he let her. She looped her thumbs in his side belt loops, an old, casual act that had always been hers. "I get that you like feeling useful, Ben. Except with me, a guy should only have to take so much of that. I don't want to be a chore, an obligation. Someone you're constantly having to fix. I want to be a joy. The kind of person that I am with everyone else. But with you and Seth and everyone else on my list, I was ugly, a broken piece of—"

"I never thought of you that way."

"But *I* did. I figured that if I could cross those names off my list, then I would be good to move on. I could say that I'd changed. I really want that—I said it before and I still mean it. But now, with Trevor, I don't know what it'll take to clear him off the list. So where does that leave you?"

In their good days together when she'd ask questions that made him doubt their future together, he'd pull her hard against him and tell her nothing she did would make him leave her. Then he'd kiss her senseless.

He still felt the same way, wanted the same result. Except now, he drew her hands from her belt loops and gave them a quick squeeze before releasing them.

As he headed to the front door, he answered her question. "Where does it leave me? Sleeping on your couch. Fixing up this house so I can make a few bucks off it. Roofing with Mel, now that the season's starting up. Helping out with Ariel."

He opened the front door. The grass in the yard was greening up, and his truck with its new windshield was parked in the driveway like it belonged there. "Getting ready for us."

DIZZY WAS ON a rampage. In fact, she'd been on a rampage since Connie had come back from taking care of the kids five days ago. From tight-lipped glares when Connie slid into Smooth Sailing not even five minutes late, to clipped orders about tables and menu changes, to a cold shoulder during after-hours downtimes, Dizzy was a whirlwind gaining speed and blackness.

Even the regulars were starting to notice.

"Don't look now but I think Dizzy's making a Molotov cocktail back there with your name on it," Marlene said when Connie brought over a double order of Wednesday's Wings.

"It's getting worse each shift," Connie said, refilling Marlene's water glass. She turned to Mel sitting across the table. "You okay to share the wings or do you want to order something separate?"

"I'm not okay to share the wings," Marlene said.

"You said you were," Mel said. He appealed to Connie. "You heard her, didn't you?"

Connie couldn't be sure, but she had always stood up for Mel. "Loud and clear."

"I share my food like I share my bed. Which is to say, I don't. Order for yourself."

Mel handed his menu to Connie. "I'll have my usual." That was code for Connie to choose for him. "Ben coming by?" That was code for wanting to know how things stood between Connie and Ben.

Connie aimed for truth that wouldn't entail commitments. "Maybe later. Not sure."

Marlene picked up a wing. “You keeping the kid, then?”

“Yeah,” Connie said. “I am.”

Marlene shook her head. “Hope you’re assigned a decent caseworker. Unfortunately, it won’t be me. Conflict of interest and all that.” Marlene’s eye caught something behind Connie. “Speaking of conflict—”

Dizzy was giving Connie the evil eye from the island bar. She jerked her head toward another table in Connie’s section. Connie waggled her fingers at Marlene and Mel. “It’s been fun.”

Mel returned the finger waggle and Marlene waved her off.

At the two-seater bar table sat one. “Hey, Derek. What can I get for you?”

She took in his empty beer glass—his third, and they’d only been open an hour. He’d come on foot from Ben’s place, and Ben confirmed that Derek’s truck was indeed back at his place. So if he asked for another she could serve it. *Ask for the bill, Derek. Ask for the bill.*

“I’m thinking about getting another beer.”

“If you’re only thinking about it, you’re also thinking about just getting the bill, too.”

Derek made a throaty rumble of agreement, his eyes still on the empty glass.

"Speaking as a recovering alkie, I'd go with the bill," Connie said.

Derek's eyes didn't shift. "I ruined everything for everybody."

Hard to argue that one.

"No idea how to make it better."

Didn't she know the feeling. She'd tried to become a better person, but had she really succeeded? Or was it that she'd just accepted the help and the forgiveness of Ben and Seth because she'd never be better?

Connie picked up Derek's basket of dry rib bones, his greasy napkins, the squeezed lemon wedges. She took his empty glass from him, too. "Be the best person you can be." Miranda with her scrawled amateur will, a messed-up plea for a new life for her daughter. Connie's mother fighting to keep her daughter safe from her own stupidity. Alexi seeking assurances from Connie about her kids while on her honeymoon. "For your kids?"

He nodded once at the now-empty table. "The bill, please."

Connie grinned. "I'll be right back."

The cash desk was part of the bar where

Dizzy was polishing the already-gleaming bottles of her specialty collection. Connie kept her head down and tallied up Derek's bill.

A crash of glass splintered the air behind Connie. Twenty-five-year-old Glenfiddich pooled amid bottle chunks. Dizzy stared at the mess with anger and horror and despair.

She threw back her head and howled a curse.

Her establishment fell dead quiet. Only the sizzle of the kitchen grill reached Connie's ears.

Then Dizzy was gone. A whirlwind out the back door. Connie gathered bar towels and a roll of paper towel and an ice-cream pail from under the counter and got to work. Without a word, another server filled in at Connie's table. Mel's head appeared over the top.

"I can finish up here," he said. "You see to Dizzy."

Connie kissed her brother on both cheeks. "You make me believe in God and leprechauns."

But not in her power to talk to Dizzy. She half hoped as she opened the door to the alley that Dizzy had left for the night. But in the last couple hours of evening light, she caught sight of her on the other side of the hedge that bordered the alley, puffing hard on a cigarette.

Connie ducked through the hole in the hedge, acquiring a pebble in her spiked heels and a scratch on her arm from a branch.

"I'd forgotten how dangerous that little portal is," Connie said conversationally.

Dizzy blew a long stream of smoke into Connie's face. Connie ached to pluck the cigarette from Dizzy's hand and finish it for her. Six months after going cold turkey and the craving was as strong as ever.

"Okay, boss, what's up?"

"I don't want to talk about it. Especially to you."

"It sounds like I'm the problem." Connie shook her foot, hoping to dislodge the pebble. "So I'm the one you should probably dump on."

"I don't want your help. Leave it alone. And while you're at it, leave everybody else alone. All you ever do is interfere, expecting others to fix your problems."

Did she mean Ben? "I don't think—"

"*Not* thinking is your problem. But if you need rescuing, you'll Barbie yourself into getting a search party, won't you?"

What? Connie wormed her foot around to draw the pebble into the curve of her arch. Her phone in her back pocket beeped a text, which she ignored.

"I don't know what was in my head," Dizzy said, waving her hand and cigarette ash at the back of her restaurant, "calling this place Smooth Sailing. It's been anything but. That's me. Stupid dreamer. You make the mistake of caring, and all you get are lies."

She funneled another stream of smoke at Connie, who sneaked in a bit of an inhale. She immediately started gagging. Dizzy smirked. Connie had never seen this side of Dizzy, but she recognized the bitterness, the despair, the self-recriminations.

This was not only about her. Her and who else? Not Ben, not Ariel.

"Has Trevor been around?"

Dizzy dropped her cigarette, ground it into the graveled lane. "That tool is worse than you. He'd kill his own grandmother for a buck."

Trevor had never done anything to Dizzy, had he? The list of people with beefs against Trevor was long, including her, Ben, McCready… A memory rose up, of McCready giving Dizzy a long, quiet look the day he'd come into

Smooth Sailing to talk to Connie. And Dizzy, doing the same, not smiling like she did with her regulars.

"McCready. You and McCready." Connie's phone beeped a second time.

"Not a word," Dizzy hissed, "not a word. His brotherhood finds out he's not with someone in the life, it won't go well for him. It's enough his brother is causing him trouble."

Dizzy was talking about a world Connie knew little about, and what she had learned last summer made her want to stay clear of it. "Listen, Dizzy, I won't say a word. I promise."

She twisted her mouth. "Your Ben already figured it out."

Another secret? "He did? He never told me."

Dizzy seemed to realize she'd stuck her foot in her mouth. "I thought he would spill to you the first chance he got. Solomon—McCready—had to leave me one night because, as it turns out, Ben insisted on making trouble over Trevor."

When Ben had delivered the pills and recruited McCready to deal with Trevor. "I doubt McCready discusses his love life with anyone. You're too important to him."

Dizzy shoved a shank of her hair behind her ear. "Look, I get that we all make mistakes and we all deserve second chances. It's why I hired you when no one else would. Sol—McCready wants the same thing for himself. He wants to leave the life, has for years, but Trevor and you keep dragging him back into that swamp. Leave him out of it. Understood?"

"Understood." She paused and then, unable to resist, added, "Solomon?"

Dizzy raised a warning finger. "Not a word."

"Not a word."

Connie's boss set her hands on her hips and her gaze on the back door of her restaurant. "I guess I have a mess to clean up."

"You will probably find it's done for you," Connie said as her phone beeped again. "Though Mel might appreciate a beer on the house."

Dizzy pointed at Connie's pocket. "You should deal with that and get back to work yourself."

Dizzy was at the back door when Connie opened her messages. One look at them and terror choked her. She wasn't returning to work.

CHAPTER SIXTEEN

Time to pay up. I've got Ariel. This is Trevor. Call me.

I mean it. Now.

Now or I will hurt her bad.

WHAT WAS THE idiot up to? Connie was about to call Ariel's number when a video came through. Twenty-seven seconds. She played it.

The camera wavered at first on a head-and-shoulders shot of Ariel and then steadied. A wide, black scarf was wrapped over her eyes. Trevor's background voice told her to go and she started speaking.

"Auntie Connie. The people from Calgary, they got me. They decided they want to make things right, so this is the deal. If I want to leave them, I have to get jumped out. You know what that is, don't you, Auntie?"

Connie gasped. Yes, she did. To leave a

gang, you gave the members permission to beat the crap out of you.

"I can't make them accept it any other way," Ariel rushed on. "It's what they want. But Trevor has another idea. He wants you to take it. For me. Don't, Auntie. You don't need to pay for my mistakes."

The video stopped there.

Trevor had gone completely insane.

She needed to see if McCready knew what his dumb brother was up to. Before him, though, she had to speak to Ariel in person. Her phone rang. Trevor had beat her to the punch.

"So, what's it going to be, Con? Her or you?"

"Trevor, what are you doing? This is serious. This is *kidnapping*. Let her go and I won't call the police. We'll talk. Work something out."

"I know what this is. I'm not stupid. You won't call the police, either. Otherwise they'll take Ariel from you. I figured it all out."

Connie grabbed her hair in frustration. "Trevor, don't you get it? Of course I'll call the police if it means Ariel will be safe. I don't care what happens to me."

"Then take the girl's place."

It was like talking to a recording that would only accept one answer.

"I want to speak to Ariel, please."

"Give me your answer first."

"After I speak to Ariel," Connie said slowly as if speaking to an English-language learner. "Then I'll give you my answer."

"I don't have her with me."

"In that case, I guess we don't have a deal."

"You come to me. I'll call them and let you talk to her."

"Fine. Where are you?"

"Meet me in the parking lot by the library."

"Why there?" she asked.

"It's public, and don't even bother trying to track her phone's GPS. I turned all that off. And I wouldn't involve your pretty pet dog of a boyfriend, either." He ended the call.

As if she would. No way was she dragging Ben into this mess. Call him, and she might as well put his name right back on her list. Except—

She'd promised to keep him informed about Trevor. As a friend.

Also, not telling him was plain stupid.

First, she'd get hold of McCready, then Ben. Only she didn't have McCready's number, and it was too far to walk to his garage.

A taxi? Or no, call Ben to take her there. But what if McCready wasn't home? Then what? And Trevor was waiting.

Of course!

Dizzy was setting a pitcher of beer in front of Mel when Connie rushed up to the table.

"I need…his number. You know whose. It's an emergency."

"Good to see you finally showed your face," Dizzy said. "This lady would like another order of wings."

Marlene arched an eyebrow at Connie and delicately patted her mouth with a greasy napkin.

"Dizzy. Please," Connie whispered into Dizzy's ear. "Trevor called. He's kidnapped Ariel."

"What?"

"So you see—"

Dizzy pulled away. "Call the police."

That got the attention of Mel and Marlene, and the tables on either side of them. Dizzy hustled back to the bar.

"Anything—" Mel began.

"All good!" Connie called out cheerily, and then booted after her boss.

She cornered her at the cash station and spoke fast. "I will call the police if I have to, but what happens after that? It will make adopting Ariel doubly hard, if not impossible. Did I say I was trying to adopt her? Anyway, I am. It will look really bad."

Dizzy whirled on her. "You know exactly what you're doing. You found out something about me in confidence and not ten minutes later you're trying to exploit it. I already told you what would happen if I found you making trouble. Keep him out of it. Keep me out of it."

"A phone call. That's all I'm asking. From you. He'll pick up for you."

"I'm not taking advantage of him."

"You're not! You're making him feel useful."

Dizzy gave Connie an incredulous look. Okay, Ben made it sound a whole lot better. She tried again. "Besides, how do you think he would react if he found out I had to send the police out on his brother because when I asked you to call him you refused?"

Dizzy threw her an absolutely foul glare. "That's a real low blow."

"I know," Connie said, "I know."

But her boss did as Connie asked, and seconds later Dizzy was talking to McCready.

She handed the phone to Connie and pointed to the back.

Connie took the phone and followed Dizzy's silent direction.

McCready gave her an opening line. "I hear Trevor's got Ariel."

"Him and that stupid gang from Calgary." She hit the back door and kept moving, filling McCready in with what she knew. "What should I do?"

"Go to him. I'll meet you there. Stall him. I'm in Red Deer."

"Red Deer? That's almost twenty minutes away."

"Twelve, my way. Stall." He hung up.

Connie came through the restaurant again, grabbing her purse from the closet off the kitchen, and handed Dizzy's phone back to her. "As you might've figured out by now," Connie said, "I'm leaving for the night."

Dizzy slipped her phone into her pocket. "You going to tell me what's going on?"

"I'm meeting with him and his brother. Don't ask me. I'm just doing what I was told."

"That's a first." Her boss yanked frosted mugs from the bar fridge and opened the tap. "Go." And then, "Don't be stupid."

For the third time that night, Connie headed

out the back door. She'd call Ben on the way. She ducked through the hedge and nearly walked smack-dab into the open driver's door of a white sports car.

Trevor.

"WHAT ARE YOU DOING?" Connie asked.

"You didn't show, but then I realized you'd be walking, so I came to pick you up."

"To take me to the parking lot?"

"No. To take you to Ariel. Get in."

If he didn't take her to the parking lot, then nobody would know where she was. She needed to stall him here, until she could figure something out. "Not until I talk to her. That was the deal."

Trevor leaned his arms on the open door and thumbed a number into his phone. Connie couldn't help notice that he'd scored a really nice car.

"Yeah. I've got her. She wants to talk to the girl first…Because I said she could…What's the big deal?…Yeah, yeah, understood." He passed his phone to Connie and she pressed it to her ear.

"Ariel?"

"Auntie Connie?" Her voice was small and frightened. Connie's mouth went dry.

"Are you hurt?"

"No."

"Do you have any idea where you are? Say it fast."

"Down a gravel road. The place seems empty. It might be—" A shout and she heard the phone being fumbled.

"Hey." It was a male voice. Young. One of the gang. "Give the phone back to Trevor."

She did, and all Trevor said before ending the call was, "I'll bring her."

"That's presuming a lot," Connie said, glancing around for…anything.

"I can't see you letting her take a beating."

She couldn't see *herself* taking a beating, either. "Listen," she said, "I probably shouldn't take my purse. Those guys you're with will steal everything. Let me pop back inside—"

She moved and he grabbed her arm. "You'll go tell everybody. How stupid do you think I am?"

Not as much as she hoped.

"I'm not bringing my purse with me. That's stupid. Here, I'll stick it in the hedge." She moved to drop it in there.

"*That's* stupid," Trevor said. "Anybody can

see it." His face darkened. "Which is exactly what you want, isn't it?"

He grabbed her purse. "Let's go. Now. Your phone. Give it."

She'd given up on calling Ben, but as long as her phone was on, the police could locate her. She could say no, but then what? He'd overpower her, bruise her up and, in the end, take it, anyway.

As she handed it over, she tried one more angle. "Have you told your brother what you're doing?"

Bad move. He took her upper arm in a punishing grip and hauled her toward the passenger door. "Leave my brother out of this. Did you call him? Did you?" He shook her and she stumbled on her high heels.

"No, I didn't. I don't even have his number. Check my call history yourself."

He did. Still holding her arm and her pink purse hanging off his other arm at a jaunty angle, he skimmed through her call log. Apparently satisfied, he powered the phone down, flung open the passenger door and pushed her in, slamming the door behind her.

He dropped her phone into her purse and chucked it into the back.

And they were off.

Sort of.

The car was a standard, and Trevor only knew stick shift from watching her drive her old car. He jolted them into third gear, down the alley. He stalled turning onto the street and again at a four-way stop.

When he conked out crossing the tracks, Connie lost it. "Why did you get a manual? You suck at it."

"Shut up. I got it this far, haven't I?"

Got it this far? That was an odd turn of phrase. "This isn't yours?"

Trev revved the engine and lurched them forward as he switched to second. "No, it's the other guy's."

"Ah, Ariel's 'friend,'" Connie said, making air quotations. "He's obviously done well for himself on the backs of his workers."

A jerky revving and Trevor switched the car to third. "Meaning I haven't?"

"You and your ego, Trevor. Would you quit comparing yourself to everybody?"

"You mean to my brother, right? Just say it." He wrenched the gearshift into Neutral but didn't hit the gas before double-clutching into first. There was a grinding and the third stall in three blocks.

"Don't. Say. A. Word."

Connie didn't because it was all pretty obvious.

"Okay, you drive." He stared straight ahead as did Connie. "You will not try anything because Ariel is still in trouble."

No kidding. She waited until he was out of the car before lifting herself across to the driver's seat. She started the car and slipped it into gear.

"Where to?"

He gave her directions that led south of town. She tried to think of all their old haunts, but nothing came to mind. She needed to come up with a plan. Run the car off the road in front of a farmhouse and then make a run for it? That might work.

"If you don't volunteer to take the beating, they'll just turn on Ariel."

"How do I know they won't, anyway?"

Now that Trevor didn't have to coordinate his hands and feet, he relaxed against the leather cushions. "Because the guy who heads it up doesn't care what happens to Ariel. Not really. All he wants is what I can give him."

"Your brother. And what your brother's connections can get him. Fame and fortune."

Trevor twisted in his seat to face her. "How did you figure that?"

"Ariel's not dumb. I wouldn't be surprised if we got there and she has them all tied up."

Trevor stroked the screen on his phone. Was he going to call just to make sure? "Is that the reason you're not freaking out about the beating? You're counting on a kid to rescue you."

She remembered telling Alexi about what a pain it was to be beautiful. Ha. She wondered idly if her teeth would be knocked out. She could get implants, of course. But they were, like, five thousand dollars apiece.

"No, I'm not," she said quietly. "Otherwise I wouldn't be in this car."

They'd probably break her nose.

And ribs, but those healed up well enough.

"It's me who arranged all of this. They hurt you and then I introduce them to McCready. My brother's high up, you know. He lives in Spirit Lake but he's got connections across the country."

"I see," she said quietly.

"What? What did you say?" Annoyance lined his face. His left ear. She'd spoken to his deaf ear.

"I see," she said louder. "Trevor, if I do this, if I take this beating, can we call it even?"

He stared straight ahead. "Turn right at the mailboxes."

She began to slow. What a beautiful ride. At least she'd be going out in style.

"McCready didn't stand up for me. He's senior. He could've pulled weight."

Connie eased the car onto a graveled road, stones crunching under the tires. "It could've gone worse for you, Trevor."

"People always say that. 'It could be worse, Trevor.' What about this?" He bared his teeth on the right side. Sure enough, a molar was missing. "The guy ripped it out of my head. It's humiliating to smile. I smile and look ugly to everyone."

Connie let the car roll along in second gear on the grassy shoulder. Trevor didn't seem to notice. "McCready's named after our dad. You know who I was named after? The guy our dad lost a fight to. Our dad had to name me after him as part of some kind of payback. I never heard the full story. McCready has, I guess."

Trevor had never told her this detail of his past. She did know that McCready didn't like to admit to being Trevor's brother, whether from embarrassment or to protect him, she wasn't ever sure.

"I figure my payback will be you getting your pretty face smashed in. And for the fun of it, I'm doing it because of your pretty Ben."

"What did he ever do to you? I'd broken up with him long before you. You and Ben were completely separate."

"And joined by our stupid love for you."

Love? "I—I—"

"Yeah, yeah, you didn't know I loved you. As you can see, I got over you. Benny boy, not so much. Bought you a ring, which you carry around but won't put on. Fun to dangle him, isn't it?"

Good thing she was driving so slow or she would've driven off the road. "For your information, I gave him back the ring."

"Then—" he reached into her purse "—what's this?" He held up the ring box she'd been carrying around, forgetting to give it to Ben. How had he known it was in her purse? Right. At the restaurant, he must've seen it when he opened her purse to put in her phone.

"The box is empty. See for yourself." Once again she'd prove him wrong.

He flipped it open.

"Look—" she began. The ring. It was there.

"Watch it!" Trevor yelled, and Connie yanked the car onto the road again.

"I swear, I didn't know the ring was there. Ben must've put it back. He didn't tell me."

"Yeah, right." Trevor shook his head and smiled, his ugly smile. "And that is why you need a good thrashing, woman."

She'd no idea why Ben had planted the ring in her purse, but she was pretty sure it wasn't to guarantee her a beating at the hands of a drug gang. Trevor really had gone insane.

"Just to confirm, I go through with this and we're even. Done. Agreed?"

"Done. Agreed."

She slipped the ring out of its box and onto her ring finger. Its weight grounded her, connected her to Ben, pointed her to a shining future.

"That's stupid," Trevor said. "One of the guys tonight might take it from you."

Connie shifted the car up to the next gear. "Over my dead body."

Trevor smirked. "That could be arranged."

McCready stood in Connie's kitchen, his massive size reducing Ben and everything in it to hobbit dimensions.

"He must've taken them to some remote place he's found," Ben said.

"Yep," McCready said. The man had already stated that possibility after filling Ben in on what had happened, what *was* happening. Ariel and now Connie had been kidnapped. Kidnapped by Trevor McCready to be taken who knows where to be beaten. *Beaten.*

Ben leaned on the island. "You must have some idea where he'd take them. Where has he been hiding out?"

"Checked there. Gone."

"Friends?"

The corner of McCready's mouth tightened. "None."

"He paints bikes. His clients?"

McCready's mouth tightened more. "No."

"You know people—" Ben refrained from lumping McCready in with them "—who have places to go for these...kinds of things. Could you ask them?"

"I could." McCready shifted. "But those guys want my brother, too. They would've already checked all the same places."

Anger ripped through Ben. "So you're choosing to protect Trevor? He wants to hurt Connie. Hurt her because he blames her for the beating your people laid on him. That's what this is all about."

McCready didn't move. "He's my brother."

Ben slammed his hand against the island, the instant pain almost restorative. "I gave you a chance to deal with him brother-to-brother when I brought back the pills. Whatever you said to him didn't work. Trevor is beyond help."

Ben reached for his phone. "We're done. I'm calling the police."

From the other end of the island McCready withdrew a knife. "Don't."

Ben slid open his screen and touched the phone app. The knife crashed against his phone, knocking it to the tile floor. Ben cursed and bent for his phone, only to have McCready's boot smash it to bits.

Ben stayed in his crouch and rammed McCready, propelling them both backward against the fridge. McCready shoved his booted foot against Ben's collar and knocked Ben back to the floor. Ben scrambled to get to his feet before the big man came at him again.

"Don't." McCready's single, repeated word held a warning but something else, too. A request.

Ben moved into a squatting position and waited. McCready nodded once.

"I'll find Connie and the girl. The rest…the

rest comes after. No police. Or else I won't get the help we need."

Ben wasn't convinced that excluding the police was the answer. And how could he be sure that McCready wasn't making this deal in order to delay locating Trevor? Then again, Ben wasn't equipped to do this alone. No use involving Seth, either, because he was as clueless as Ben when it came to Trevor's whereabouts.

"Yeah. All right."

McCready stepped back, giving Ben room to rise.

McCready opened his phone, and made a call. Then another, and another. With each one, Ben listened to McCready offer deals, make concessions, confirm loyalties—and, slowly but surely, sell out his brother.

After the sixth call, McCready returned his knife to his jacket. "Let's go get your girls."

CHAPTER SEVENTEEN

TREVOR HAD CONNIE drive to the end of a narrow gravel road and park beside a field covered with stubble from last year's crop. Stubble was a good name for the old grain stalks, rough and bristly like a man's unshaven cheek. Or wait, was the facial hair named after the straw? And why was she even thinking about this?

Trevor ordered her to cross the field to a giant metal shed set on a grassy patch in the field, probably used to store farm equipment or something. What did she know?

Her heels sunk into the softened earth and dirt immediately piled between the soles of her shoes and her bare feet. The least of her worries. So, too, the chill evening air that pebbled her bare arms.

Just let Ariel be safe.

Trevor fell silent as they crossed to the shed, which allowed Connie to steel herself against whatever was on the other side of the metal walls. They crossed in front of the closed bay doors and rounded the corner.

A teenager sprang to attention from where he'd been lounging beside a side door. He fumbled for something inside his jacket, his right hand busy holding his smoke.

"Easy," Trevor said. "Just us."

"Don't scare me like that," the guard said.

Trevor pushed him aside. He rapped on the door. Two old cars were parked against the shed facing out. The getaway cars. Trevor clamped his fingers around her arm.

"At this point, I'm not going to try to make a run for it," Connie said, and twisted her arm free just as the front door opened.

To another kid. Okay, maybe he could pass for twenty. He held a gun. Connie couldn't help it. She looked at his knuckles. His hands were pretty unmarked for someone whose eyes held the distant coldness of a killer.

The kid took in Trevor and widened the door for Connie to enter. As soon as she was inside, Connie scanned the gloom of the largely empty shed for Ariel. She was at the far end of the enclosure, still blindfolded, and with her ankles and wrists bound, her right leg quivering.

Arranged around the room were seven

young men. All looked young enough to be ID'd at the bar. The gang, Connie supposed. A bunch of bad kids not yet twenty with garish hair and tattoos. She might have dismissed them as wannabes, if Connie hadn't identified three with guns. Guns! They were all pointed to the floor at the moment, but the boys held them with a carefulness that convinced Connie that the guns were ready to use.

A boy, or young man, or whatever his age made him, detached himself from the group and came to them. His T-shirt and jeans draped from him, and his entire frame was emaciated. Was he a user as well as a dealer?

"You Ariel's aunt?"

Connie made a stab at diplomacy. "Yes, Connie Greene. And you?"

He sneered, as if he figured she was pulling a fast one. "You know what you need to do?"

"I understand the principle," she said slowly so her voice didn't shake as badly as her insides were. "I'm to take Ariel's place so she can get jumped out of your organization."

He took another full step toward her. "We are going to beat you until we decide we're done, and you're not going to stop us. Got it?"

"Bare fists."

He blinked.

"Bare fists," Connie repeated. Diplomacy was over, but negotiations were still open. "No bars, no iron, no rings, no knives. Fists or open hand only."

"What are you going to do if we don't?"

"Then it's not happening."

He shook his head, like she was full of it, but she could see his hesitation.

"No," Trevor said, and cut between them. "We had a deal. It was the refrigerator."

Refrigerator? She glanced around and located it in the opposite corner to Ariel. Its solid whiteness was almost lunar in the deepening darkness of the shed. Wait. She knew that fridge.

Trevor crowed in laughter. "Yeah, it's the one you gave me. From the house. Remember how you said you couldn't stand it because of the notes your mom put on it? Well, here it is. Ready for you!"

Connie didn't get it. She was missing something terribly important. She looked to Ariel. Both of the girl's legs were jumping now, only her boot tips making contact with the hard soil.

Then it hit her.

"Oh," she whispered. "Oh."

They were going to box her.

They were going to lock her in the refrigerator and fire their guns at it. The bullets might miss, or they might hit her in the chest. It was a kind of Russian roulette.

She shook her head, in time with the frenetic rhythm of Ariel's legs. "No, no, no, no. This wasn't the deal."

"We didn't have a deal," Trevor said. "If you assumed we did, that's your fault."

No getting through to Trevor. He was nearly frothing at the mouth for someone to hurt her. She had actually been in a relationship with a guy who now wanted her dead. Had planned her death.

"Trevor," she said. "You are an embarrassment to yourself and your brother."

Even as Trevor reddened and his fist rose against her, she turned to the thin boy-man who fancied himself a leader. "You do this and you will be hunted. You kill me in this town—my town—and you won't get away with it. I have people, too."

I have people. The few hundred Lakers-on-the-Go. Seth and Mel. McCready. Even Dizzy. The people who'd applauded her at the Polar Dip.

She inserted her left thumb between her fingers and pressed on the diamond. Ben.

Boy-Man jutted out his chin belligerently. "I *want* word to get out. I want everyone to know that those under me stay in line or there's consequences."

"There'll be consequences for you, too. There always are."

"You can't prove a thing. Especially if there's a bullet in your brain."

"My dead body will be proof enough."

Ariel cried out, "Pick me. Pick me! Auntie, don't do it. It was my fault, my fault. I can do this. I'm smaller. They'll have less chance of hitting me."

Ariel was never illogical.

"That's not happening," Trevor said. "It's her. We agreed."

Boy-Man cut him a cold look. "Shut up." He switched back to Connie. "This is the way it's going to be. You will be tied up and put in the fridge. There will be nine bullets, one from each of us. We untie her—" he jerked his head toward Ariel "—and leave. You two take it from there."

"How do I know there'll only be nine bullets?"

"You have my word," he said. Which meant she had nothing at all.

He motioned to his people, Trevor gripped

her arm and suddenly they were upon her. She hadn't meant to struggle. She didn't stand a chance against them, but instinct kicked in and she thrashed and flailed, punched and screamed.

In the end, it was no use. She was bound and wadded, like a bag of garbage, into the fridge.

It was dark inside, except for a sliver of grayness around the edge. Then even that line of dim light was snapped away as the door was tightened and the whole fridge rocked. From the noises, she gathered they were tying it shut. It stunk of metal and plastic, and… baking soda?

Her head. She had to protect her head from the bullets. And her spine. Her head and spine. How?

She squirmed and twisted like a baby in a womb—in a hard, unyielding womb—until her back was against the rear of the fridge. Her spine was now as protected as she'd ever make it. Now what to do about her head?

The end where the freezer was located would have more insulation. It was also the end where they'd shoved her in, so that's where they'd expect her head to be. Trevor would shoot there.

But if she moved, would they guess what

she was doing, sense her movements? She needed to decide fast. The last thing she wanted was to be in the middle of a maneuver when they started shooting.

She tried to move. She was stuck. Maybe she could do it bit by tiny bit, but it would leave her spine exposed. She curled her neck so her head was tucked against her chest.

If she survived, she would get this fridge crushed until it could fit in her purse.

She had one final trick open to her.

She rocked her body back and forth in the claustrophobic confines, and then, with all the power vested in her, she threw herself against the front of the fridge.

It teetered forward and she pressed into the door.

Do it. Do it.

It toppled forward and Connie's cheek bumped against the curved mold of the upper door rack.

Perfect.

Now all they had to fire at were the coils and the insulated sides. In fact, one of the bullets might ricochet and hit Trevor or one of them.

Or, just as logically, Ariel.

Connie strained to hear what was happening. She thought she could pick out Trevor's voice and, once, Ariel's, but it was hard to hear anything above the humming of the fridge. For a wild moment she wondered if it was plugged in, and then she realized that the sound was the blood pounding in her ears. She raised her hands to try to cover her ears. Her face was wet with sweat; her whole body soaked. Except for her mouth. It was so dry. She was so thirsty.

She waited. There was only silence. Unbearable silence.

It stretched on. Had they left? Had they decided to leave her in the fridge to suffocate to death? And what of Ariel? Were they doing something to her while she was locked inside here? No, she would hear Ariel screaming.

Unless she no longer could.

Connie lifted her head to scream Ariel's name when there was a sudden bump and explosion.

The shooting had begun.

AT THE GUN BLAST, Ben, already in a crouching half run across the field, broke into a full run, McCready matching him stride for stride.

Six more shots rang out, and Ben stumbled on the rough ground, praying. They slid to a stop at the back of the shed, where Mc-

Cready grabbed his shoulder and Ben forced himself to stay put. If one gun had gone off there could be others. And neither he nor McCready was armed.

McCready reached inside his jacket and pulled out a piece. Okay, one of them was armed.

Ben exhaled slowly. He crouched beside McCready to look through a hole at the base of the shed wall. It was a sizable opening, large enough for both McCready and him to rest on their elbows side by side and see into the open space beyond. Two lights were on. A young male held a halogen light on Ariel, who was sitting in a chair with her ankles and wrists tied. She didn't look blindfolded but it was hard to tell. She was hunched, her head on her knees, her hands curved around her face so her fingertips were pressed against her ears. Probably in reaction to the gunshots. The other light was a second halogen lamp set atop a fridge lying on its front. Eight guys and Trevor were in a loose line in front of it.

Where was Connie?

A gun was passed from one of the guys to another. He aimed at the fridge and fired.

A bunch of jeers went up, the kid apparently having missed the object entirely. Ben mouthed to McCready, *Connie?*

McCready aimed his gun at Ben and mouthed back, *Fridge.*

The noiseless word exploded in Ben's mind, and he understood why McCready saw fit to hold him in place with the pointed gun.

The freaks were shooting at Connie.

Inside, the gun was handed to Trevor.

"Stand the fridge up," he said.

A round of grumbling ensued.

"It looks heavy."

"Why?"

"Just shoot it."

"Then we can check inside."

"Why do you think she pushed it forward?" Trevor said. "All your shots have been wasted. No way is it going through the sides or the back. She's sitting in there all pretty. But not for long."

He passed the .22 to one of the other guys. "I brought my own."

From inside his jacket, he pulled out a revolver.

Beside him, McCready hissed. He raised his gun into the air and fired. Instantly the kids in the shed froze or spun in place.

"Police!" McCready yelled. "Put down your weapons."

Instead, all of them ran to the side door of

the shed. They poured out, and into the night air rose the slamming of car doors, revving motors and the beat of wheels and chassis over fields riddled with molehills and hollows.

They wouldn't get far. A bike trailer was pitched a quarter mile down the road. The stage for another old-fashioned disciplinary session. Any compunction Ben might've felt for that was swept aside knowing what they'd subjected Ariel and Connie to.

Trevor hadn't moved. As the roar of the cars faded away, he swiveled to face the back of the barn. "Show yourself, brother."

"Let Connie out," McCready called. "Let her and the girl go."

"I will. I get my shot and then it's done."

"You know that shot could kill her. You do that and you go to prison."

"I won't aim to kill her," Trevor said. "I've figured out where she is in there. But I want to wreck her pretty face. Besides, you won't turn me in, brother. Not with all the stuff I have on you."

"Yeah, but *I* will," Ben called.

Trevor laughed. "Ben Carruthers. Didn't I warn you Connie would bring you grief?"

"You don't give it up now, Trevor, and *I* will bring *you* grief."

Trevor aimed his revolver at the fridge. "I'll take my chances."

Two guns went off. McCready's shot dropped Trevor, whose own bullet blasted into the fridge.

Ben broke into a run, rounding the side of the shed, and tore through the already open side door.

"Ben!" Ariel screamed. "Get her!"

He ran past the downed body of Trevor and reached for the ropes around the fridge.

"Connie!" he yelled. "Can you hear me?"

A thud from inside assured him something was happening. Then again, a dead body—

He sawed on the ropes with his pocket-knife, McCready working the other side. Why wasn't he with Trevor? Then again, Ben wasn't about to question McCready's priorities. When the ropes fell away, the two men heaved and righted the fridge. Ben heard the distinct bump and thump of a body inside.

"Connie!"

Ben pulled on the door and out she fell, head between her knees, bound by her wrists and ankles. He dropped beside her. "You okay?"

She was quivering all over and he pulled her balled-up body into his own shaking arms, all the while patting her down for injuries. She flinched when he touched her right side and again when his hands grazed her shoulder but other than that—

Unless her head—

"Connie," he said softly, "I'm going to lift your head, okay? Just to see your face. Okay?"

He slowly pried up her head until he could check her face. A bruise reddened her right cheek and a cut sliced open her lip.

Both lips trembled and she whispered, "Ariel?"

"Auntie Connie! I'm okay. Are you?"

Connie sagged against him. "Yes," she whispered. "Yes."

Because Ariel couldn't possibly have heard, Ben turned to her. "She's good. We're all good."

Except for Trevor.

McCready squatted over his brother, who moaned and twisted on the dirt floor of the shed. Blood gushed from his side.

"McCready?" Ben called softly.

Trevor's brother held up a hand. "You three clear out. I'll clean up here." His voice was low and Ben didn't question him. He cut Ariel free and, with an arm around each of his girls, took them away from their nightmare. And his.

MIDNIGHT. ARIEL WAS tucked in her bed downstairs under a thick pile of quilts and books. Connie had offered her a spot in bed with her, but Ariel claimed that no way was she bunking with that much pink. Besides, and here she looked at Ben, the bed would likely be full, anyway.

Ariel was partly right. Ben was in bed with Connie. Not doing what Ariel assumed they'd do. He lay on his back on top of the covers. Connie, dressed in his old flannel shirt and sweat shorts, snuggled against him, her head on his shoulder.

"This is nice," she murmured, and wiggled closer. "Ben?"

"Yeah?"

"There's a steno pad and a pen in the drawer beside you. Could you get them for me?"

It took a bit of shifting and rolling but he got them. She drew two lines, tossed aside the pad and snuggled back down.

"Don't you want to frame it or something?"

"I'd rather not have a daily reminder of what I had to go through to strike off those names. Time for a fresh start."

He thought of the wood box high on his shelf where he'd stored the ring. "I have just the place for all of them."

"Later," she murmured. "You're not going anywhere."

He wrapped his arms around hers and squeezed her harder than he ever had before. She emitted a muffled squeak. What was he thinking? Holding her tight when she'd just been forcefully bound.

He relaxed his arms. "Sorry."

She molded her body to his again, her hand warm on his chest.

"Ben. After I've had bullets fired at me while I'm in a fridge, you are allowed to hold me as hard as you want. In fact, I insist on it."

"Okay. How about after a hard day's work?"

"Lots of people have those. That only deserves a quick hug of sympathy."

"Then I get to drive you home?"

"Sure. But every third trip, you should ask me if I've done anything about getting my own wheels. No. Never mind. A car will be on my new list."

"And home renovations?"

"Why would that involve hugs?"

"It could be a hard day for *me*."

She snorted. "Fine."

"And if you puke because you drank too much?"

"I've learned my lesson. If I'm puking it

won't be because of that. Roll over and go back to sleep."

Roll over and go back to sleep. Him with her, together. He tapped her abdomen. "If it was because of a growing bump here," he said, "I would." He drifted his hand to cover for her hand on his chest, and encountered a small hardness. His ring. On her finger. Huh.

"When?"

"You finally noticed?"

"Let's just say that after tonight's events I wasn't expecting this."

"I put it on in Trevor's car. I discovered you'd sneaked it into the box in my purse."

"I meant to tell you."

"It stopped a bullet."

"I don't think—"

"My story and I'm sticking to it."

"Okay…does it mean what I want it to mean?"

"Ben. What about a fresh start don't you understand?"

He hugged her tight and she let him. Finally, finally, they were ready.

* * * * *